SUDDEN DEATH

With thanks to the best team of beta readers any writer could
ever wish for:

Rob Ballon
John Ashmore
Manie Kilian
Dawn Lynn Cline
Scott Walker
Marti Panikkar
Steve DeBacker
Charles Obert

A BIOGENESIS WAR FILES NOVEL

SUDDEN DEATH

LL RICHMAN

Published by Delta V Press
Cover Copyright © 2021 L.L. Richman

ISBN-13: 978-1-7373636-3-7

0 9 8 7 6 5 4 3 2 1

Produced in the United States of America

ALSO BY LL RICHMAN

You can always find the most up to date listing of book titles on LL Richman's website, www.llrichman.com.

THE BIOGENESIS WAR SERIES
The Chiral Agent
The Chiral Protocol
Chiral Justice

THE BIOGENESIS WAR FILES: THE EARLY YEARS
Operation Cobalt
Ambush in the Sargon Straits
The Chiral Conspiracy
Sudden Death

THE VISION RISING SERIES
Vision Rising
Vision's Gambit
Vision's Pawn

THE BATTLEFIELD DIPLOMACY SERIES
Battlefield Diplomacy
Lost Colony
Insurrection

THE ENFIELD GENESIS SERIES
Alpha Centauri
Proxima Centauri
Tau Ceti
Epsilon Eridani
Sirius

THE SOL DISSOLUTION SERIES
Venusian Uprising

Assault on Sedna
The Hyperion War
The Fall of Terra

CONTENTS

For Rob, the original Archangel.
Sine Pari

In any moment of decision, the best thing you can do is the right thing, the next best thing is the wrong thing, and the worst thing you can do is nothing.

– Theodore Roosevelt

PROLOGUE

Humanity has reached the stars.

With colonies established throughout the Sol System, explorers hungry for new ventures traveled beyond its borders to colonize nearby Alpha Centauri.

At the same time, a brave pair of ships set their sights a bit farther afield—on the binary stars Procyon and Sirius. Those who settled there called themselves the Geminate Alliance.

Such distances made interaction prohibitive. Even with the Scharnhorst drive's ability to triple the speed of light, travel between the colonies was measured in months, if not years.

In the mid-twenty-fifth century, that all changed. The Geminate Alliance stunned the known worlds with the invention of the Calabi-Yau Gate. The gates folded space, enabling instantaneous travel between star systems. True interstellar commerce became a reality.

Humanity as a whole prospered, but it wasn't perfect. In certain pockets within the settled worlds, dictators flourished. In others, organized crime had carved out a foothold. Free speech allowed dissenters a voice, yet some weren't content with the results that came from such a platform.

In a word, humanity was still... broken. As a result, it still needed the service and sacrifice of rough warriors, willing to stand in the breach between the innocent and the profane...

1: PIRATE NEST

GNS Callaghan
The Atliekas

Nine Geminate Navy Marines shot silently through the black, catapulted from a destroyer's missile tubes with a force no unaugmented human could withstand. Despite the one-hundred-*g* shove, the catapult added very little to the warriors' velocity. The ship they'd emerged from was traveling more than nine times that speed. By default, that meant the Marines were, too.

Cocooned safely inside a viscous bath that dampened the catapult's effects, Boone Brady mentally gritted his teeth and held on during two interminable seconds of agony. The lattice of carbyne nanofloss woven throughout his body might have kept him from turning into a slurry of organic goo, but it didn't mean the push the GNS *Callaghan* had imparted was a fun experience.

The filaments of SmartCarbyne embedded throughout his soft tissue and critical organs were tied to an accelerometer inside his head. These automatically hardened when excessive forces were detected, but the material could also be triggered manually—which is what Boone and his team had done prior to launch. The feeling they engendered as they transitioned was maddening; his organs *itched*, and there was no way he could reach them to scratch.

Behind them, *Callaghan* continued its deceleration, coming about to keep pace with the Atliekas belt. Rigged for quiet running, the destroyer was a giant shadow, a silent sentinel guarding their six.

Their target was a derelict mining platform, located seventy-five thousand kilometers inside the Atliekas. Currently, it harbored a small band of pirates. If Boone and his teammates had anything to say about it, the station wouldn't be their home for much longer.

Boone wasn't worried about detection; the clamshell encasing each squad member was covered in the same material as the stealth drakeskin suit he wore. The carbyne-reinforced suit was made of metamaterials that used transformation optics to guide incident waves around the wearer. The nanoweave was tunable, providing full-spectrum stealth.

Total flight time would be a little over an hour. Boone used that to cycle through his head-up display, keeping one eye on telemetry while reviewing the team's playbook for the upcoming mission. He felt the clamshell sway as the onboard Synthetic Intelligence rocked him gently to one side to avoid a chunk of ice that had broken free from a nearby rock.

Despite conventional wisdom, asteroid belts weren't densely packed. Space was vast, even deep inside the Atliekas. The rocks in orbit around Procyon's main sequence star didn't require much navigation; the suit's SI negotiated the path with ease.

As they neared their destination, the squad's sergeant called out, *{Two-minute warning.}* The comm channel's EM burst was localized and low-powered, designed to reach only those flying in tight formation.

The clamshell's thrusters engaged, delivering a surprisingly gentle deceleration compared to the kick in the pants Boone had experienced at the beginning of the journey. The thrusters were encased in a unique 'meringue' spun from aerogels and metal foams. These concealed the bloom that came from heating the propellant gases. The material absorbed all emissions, effectively masking them from detection. As far as the SI running the platform's automated defenses was concerned, the suits were little more than micrometeorite dust.

Boone's position in the formation was toward the rear, but that would soon change. For today's action, he'd be filling the role of overwatch, the rest dividing into fireteams to scour the structure and clean house. The Geminate Navy had a zero-tolerance policy for those who preyed upon honest merchants.

The platform enlarged on Boone's HUD as the squad neared. They came to a stop relative to one of its maintenance hatches, the location provided by the manufacturer and confirmed by stealth drone the day before.

{Grant. Breach.} At the sergeant's command, a figure moved forward, breaching canister in one hand.

{Boone.} That single word had Boone slipping behind Grant.

The breaching canister, commonly known as a Bravo Charlie, flashed green as the unit successfully hijacked the control plate governing the airlock. Grant flashed the all-clear hand signal and the hatch opened.

Boone followed him inside, the rest of the squad floating in behind. He snagged one of the built-in handholds at the same time he disengaged thrusters. The platform's rotation did the rest, orienting him in the 'down' direction as centripetal force asserted the equivalent of one-third of a *g* of artificial gravity on his body. He heard a hiss over his suit's speakers, the hatch sealing and repressurizing under Grant's command.

{Power down,} the sergeant ordered.

Despite the fact they were once more in atmosphere, communication would remain nonverbal throughout the mission, the team using the combat network established before leaving *Callaghan.* The network was courtesy of an evanescent wire embedded in each Marine's brain. They'd explained to Boone how it worked when it was implanted, but it might have been an alien language for all that he understood it. If it wasn't a weapon, it was pretty much a black box to him.

Boone pushed his helmet's visor up, unsealed his clamshell, and slid out of it. The armor landed with a soft *clunk* against the bulkhead as he laid it alongside the others. From the corner of his eye, he caught the glitter of audio chaff, tiny motes of light flickering in and out of view. The cloud of noise-cancelling nanostructures would attenuate the sound of nine Marines divesting themselves of their outer suits. Too cumbersome for direct action, they would remain in the airlock until the mission was complete.

{Boone, Grant: Recon.}

At the sergeant's command, Grant stepped forward and applied the Bravo Charlie to the inner hatch. While it worked, both he and Boone donned their balaclavas. The hood was made of the same material as their drakeskin suits, shielding the wearer from view.

Once the inner hatch was bypassed, Grant slid it open a fraction of a centimeter and launched a surveillance microdrone. The two Marines watched the feed as the drone scanned the area.

{Clear,} Grant said, palming the door open.

Boone's P-SCAR—the Navy's pulsed, special combat assault rifle—had been secured against his chest during the flight. He brought it around into high-ready and nodded once to Grant. They slipped through, weapons inscribing slow arcs as they swept the corridor. Grant motioned he would go left and for Boone to go right. Boone nodded and turned, disappearing into the shadows of the dimly lit corridor.

The place was a dive. Ransacked, with anything of value long removed. Access plates hung open where wires had been stripped. He ducked beneath broken conduit that hung limply from breaks in the corridor's ceiling, sidestepped around debris littering the floor.

About all that could be said of its enviro plant was that it had a breathable atmosphere and could generate enough spin to simulate a modicum of gravity. Boone had to modulate his steps to keep from bouncing and hitting the ceiling.

Boone launched a surveillance drone of his own, the tiny machine an advance scout, searching for traps—and warm bodies. He was pretty sure he'd be able to see his breath if he removed his balaclava. His suit's thermostat was turned up as high as it could go while still remaining stealthed, but that wasn't saying much. He clenched and unclenched his hand to work more warmth in them and to keep them flexible.

Grant must have thought the same thing. *{Let's bag these assholes and get back home where we can thaw out.}*

{Hooahh, brother.}

Half an hour later, he and Grant completed their sweep and reported in.

{Tangos scattered in two main sectors,} Boone said, dropping pins on top of a map he pushed to the combat net. *{Five are in this room here, looks like a dining facility. The rest appear to be asleep in their quarters.}*

Grant supplied the locations for those.

The sergeant nodded and speared Boone with a look. *{Catwalk in place like the specs showed?}*

Boone nodded. *{Can confirm.}*

{All right then. We proceed as planned. Fireteam Bravo will take the D-FAC. Charlie and Delta, round up our sleepers. Boone, you're Archangel.}

That meant Boone would go high, operating as the squad's overwatch. Heads nodded and the fireteams formed up. Then nine stealthed figures slipped through the hatch.

The predictive systems of Boone's drakeskin suit tied into the combat net and pulled the Navy's IFF transponder code from each of his fellow Marines. The code squawked an 'identify friend/foe' signal that outlined each soldier in green on his overlay. Those who'd taken up residence on the platform didn't have such an advantage; until the moment the fireteams struck, the pirates would remain oblivious to the Marines in their midst.

Boone slowed as he approached the catwalk, eyes tracking up the support beam to the framework above his head. The walkway encircled the platform, suspended from a support truss. Since the platform was built like a donut without the hole, it was the most unobstructed view he'd get of the space. Though Boone's vision inside the buildings was limited to his optics' infrared heat maps, he'd easily spot movement anywhere else.

He climbed to the top and settled in, deploying additional surveillance drones—one per fireteam. The small airborne devices jetted ahead of the Marines, advanced scouts that used active sensors to ping the area ahead of the men and women, with blips that cycled on and off too quickly to trigger the platform's warning system.

Above their heads, Boone did much the same, using his P-SCAR's reticle to methodically scan each area, in search of IR signatures indicating hidden tangos or unusual structures that might hide traps.

Bravo was closing in on the dining facility when the cluster of pirates split up, two of the five heading straight toward the fireteam.

{Bravo, two tangos coming your way, spinward, first cross corridor on your left.} Boone's words were measured and calm as he pushed the mental warning to the fireteam. From his position, he could just see the spot where the two groups would intersect.

{Copy.} The sergeant's voice was curt. *{Charlie, Delta: you're about to lose your element of surprise.}*

Boone realized he was right; the moment Bravo engaged the pirates, the rest would be alerted.

His hand tightened around his P-SCAR, the rifle's barrel braced against the railing of the crosswalk high above their heads. The three Marines he'd just pinged sent back a round of two-clicks for reply. The sergeant was in the lead. Through his reticle, Boone saw the man send a flurry of hand signals to the two Marines with him. They broke apart, heading for the sparse cover a pair of exposed steel trusses would provide, while the sergeant took a knee behind a broken piece of equipment.

{Five seconds… three…two…} Boone's mental voice was soft as he counted down the time to intercept.

{Eyes!} The sergeant leading the team called out the warning, his P-SCAR tucked into the pocket of his shoulder, the muzzle of his rifle aimed head-high.

The moment the two pirates rounded the corner, the sergeant fired. The P-SCAR's 'P'—its pulsed plasma burst—ripped electrons from the air in a laser pulse that lasted a mere quadrillionth of a second, creating an invisible ball of plasma. Another slightly longer pulse followed at its heels, detonating the ball of plasma in a combined flash-bang/flash-blind.

Dazed, and with both vision and hearing temporarily impaired, the pirates stumbled back. Reaching for their weapons, they blindly sprayed the hallway with fire. Return fire from the Marines cut the pirates down in seconds.

{Damn idiots,} the sergeant grumbled as he rose. Motioning his team forward, he said, *{So much for bringing them in alive. All right kids, bag 'em and tag 'em.}*

Heat maps from Boone's advance scout drones showed the sleepers were stirring in their quarters. The warning had been sounded. Highlighting the feeds, he pushed them to the two corporals leading each fireteam. *{Getting movement on scan, expect resistance.}*

Two-clicks sounded in his ear.

He returned his attention to the third scouting drone, the one preceding the fireteam to the D-FAC. Bravo had rounded the corner, moving out of his direct line of sight. Suddenly, the feed's heat map lit up like a Christmas tree.

{Bravo! I've got blooms, two and ten o'clock!} Boone's own muscles coiled, a visceral fight or flight response to the explosive devices he saw coming online as he willed the Marines to safety.

{Cover!} the sergeant barked. Through the feed, Boone saw all three launch themselves back toward the intersection.

The drone disappeared in a flash of blinding light just as three forms flew around the corner, partially assisted by the overpressure wave from the detonation.

He flinched sympathetically as a wall of fire rushed over them.

The drakeskin suits were well-equipped to handle incendiary burn-overs, but no one would call it a pleasant experience. Telemetry from their suits flashed briefly yellow, then returned to green as the three rolled to their feet.

{*That's it. I'm done playing nice,*} the sergeant growled. He motioned his team forward and they disappeared down the corridor.

With no drone left to scout ahead for Bravo, Boone switched his attention to the drones above Charlie and Delta, only to discover they'd already routed the sleepers and had them well in hand.

While Bravo mopped up, Boone positioned his P-SCAR for one last visual sweep of the platform. That movement saved his life.

The high-pitched sound of a projectile sang in his ear. He expected to hear the *thwack* of a slow-moving bullet smashing into the bulkhead behind him; what he heard instead was the fast ping of a ricochet.

Shit! That's not a station-approved weapon!

Boone threw himself into a roll, momentum carrying him up to one knee. He pushed off, feet pounding against the brushed steel walkway as another shot *whinged* past.

His drakeskin suit hid him from view and the cloud of audio chaff that encased him partially masked his steps as he ran, but it could do nothing to mask the sound that traveled through the steel structure itself each time his feet struck the walkway's surface. That meant whoever was shooting at him had a damn good idea where he might be.

{*Archangel taking fire,*} he called out, as he reached mentally to recall his scout drones. If he could get a lock on this joker's position—

A shot hammered into his left side, hitting him in the floating ribs just above the kidney. The drakeskin's synthsilk did its job, diffusing the bullet and turning what would otherwise have been a through and through into a massive bruise. He stumbled but caught himself, his attention split between his destination up ahead and the feed pouring in from the two scout drones.

Pain shot through him as he dragged air into his lungs, the action causing his ribcage to expand. The triage app stored in the data partition of his wire flashed an alert, indicating medical nano was being routed to the injury.

{Sitrep!} Bravo's sergeant snapped.

His scout drones had located the asshole. Boone pushed the feed to the sergeant. *{One tango, tucked between a wall and a charging station, anti-spinward, quarter-klick.}*

{I see that, private.} The sergeant's words were dry. *{What's **your** situation?}*

Every breath Boone took was painful. *Dammit, how long does it take medical nano to—* His thoughts fragmented as his side fell blissfully numb.

A shot hit the railing just in front of him and he dug deeper, pouring on additional speed to close the last few meters. Without slowing, he caught the edge of a support beam in one hand and let momentum swing him around until he was snug against its back side.

{I've taken cover behind one of the beams,} he reported, breath sawing in and out in great gasps. *{Going to try to get off a shot.}*

{Negative,} the sergeant replied. *{That's your only cover up there, and he knows it.}*

As if on cue, the pirate began concentrating his shots on Boone's location.

{Copy. Taking steady fire now.}

There was a pause, and then a female voice cut in, clear and crisp. *{Delta has eyes on.}*

A map appeared over the combat net, limning the tango in red. A firing solution appeared, its engagement cone also in red, a warning to the others to remain clear of the area.

{Taking the shot,} she said calmly.

The hail of bullets ceased at the same time Boone heard, *{Tango down.}*

Boone pushed away from the bulkhead, his bruised side awash in numbness. His mouth twisted when he thought about what awaited him back on the ship. Once his suit synched with the armory and ratted him out, he'd be ordered to report to the infirmary, no doubt.

For now, he'd return to his duty as overwatch. *{Archangel back in position.}*

By his count, the asshole who'd shot at him was the last of the resistance, but after that recent bit of excitement, Boone wasn't leaving anything to chance. It never hurt to perform an 'idiot check,' to make sure he hadn't missed someone.

The scouting drones came back null.

{Archangel, idiot check complete,} he reported over the combat net.

{Bravo team, idiot check complete.}

{Charlie, same.}

{Delta, same.}

When a voice from *Callaghan* cut in, Boone knew the sergeant had reported the mission's success. Though the destroyer was ninety thousand kilometers away, latency was hardly noticeable.

{Prisoner head count?} The icon tagged to the voice indicated it was the platoon's lieutenant who had spoken.

{Charlie has four,} Grant reported.

{Delta, three live, one bagged.}

There was a pause. *{Bravo. Three live, two bagged.}*

{Daaaay-um,} a second voice from the destroyer, the corporal running comms, drawled. *{Looks like Bravo's buying tonight.}*

{Can the chatter, corporal,} Bravo's sergeant growled.

{Copy.} The voice on the other end sounded crisply in Boone's head. *{Shuttle's inbound, ten mikes.}*

An hour later, they were back on board the *Callaghan*. After Boone checked his P-SCAR back into the armory, he and the rest of the Marines involved in the skirmish had time to hit the showers before reporting in for an after-action report.

Boone winced as he stripped out of his drakeskin suit and pulled his base layer shirt over his head—or tried to, at any rate. Getting the damn thing off took a bit longer than it should have.

He heard a long whistle and then hands grabbed the material, clearing it over his head.

Payne, the corporal who'd led Delta, held his shirt in her hands. Her eyes were on his left side.

"That's going to be one colorful bruise," she said with a shake of her head. Dropping the shirt into his hands, she sidled past and into the showers.

"Colorful's right, bro." Ramirez came to a stop beside him and stared critically at Boone's bruised ribcage. "You do know the overwatch is called Archangel because you call down death on the enemy, not because you have a desire to *become* an angel, right?"

"Ha-ha. Funny." Boone scowled at the other man as he tossed the shirt into the laundry.

"Has it reported the strike yet?" Ramirez jerked his chin in the direction of Boone's drakeskin as he began stripping out of his own.

Boone stifled a resigned sigh and bent to retrieve the suit. "No, but it's just a matter of time." He folded the armored camouflage and then slipped it inside its protective case to be auto cleaned.

Ramirez watched, his head cocked. "In three… two…" His countdown accompanied Boone's hand as he sealed the lid. An alert popped up, ordering him to report to medical.

Boone's mouth twisted in a resigned smile. "Yep. There it is."

Ramirez clapped him on the shoulder, causing Boone to wince.

"Only incident in the entire action." The other man pointed a finger at Boone. "Maybe *you* should be buying the drinks tonight."

Boone turned for the showers. "Figures you'd say that. You were on Bravo." He paused at the entrance to shoot Ramirez a long, narrow stare. "If I hear that you tried selling the others on that idea, I'm coming for you."

Ramirez's laughter followed him inside.

Ten minutes later, Boone reported to the infirmary. The medic looked up when he appeared and waved him in.

"I received a notification that you'd been hit. Let's take a look."

The medic shoved his hand into a medical bracer, the unit

extending up to his elbow. He palpated the area, earning him a flinch and a scowl.

The medic ignored Boone's reaction, his face distant, eyes trained on the results the unit fed to his overlay. "Two cracked ribs, localized tissue insult," he said as his bracer-clad palm tracked over the wound.

Straightening, he reached for an ampoule and held it up for Boone to see. "These are tissue nanotransfection agents. They'll promote in situ regeneration through cellular reprogramming."

Boone blinked at the explanation. He had no clue what the medic had just said, but it sounded impressive. He'd be down with anything that programmed the pain and bruising away.

The medic snapped the vial into the bracer and then centered his palm over the spot where the bullet impacted. Boone felt a slight pressure and then a tingling sensation. Injection complete, the man stepped back.

"You might feel a bit itchy inside while the nano accelerates the healing," he told Boone as he pulled the bracer off. "I'll issue you an extra meal rat ticket for tonight."

"Thanks." Boone nodded his appreciation. He'd been injured enough to know how fast the body burned through calories when rapid therapy was used. He'd likely awaken in the middle of his sleep shift, ravenous.

Pulling his shirt down, he stood. "Am I good to go?"

The medic had already turned away. He lifted a hand in a silent wave goodbye. That was all Boone needed. He was out the door in a flash.

The debrief was in full swing when he slipped into the room and took a seat beside Ramirez at the table. The lieutenant leading the briefing gave him a subtle nod, letting Boone know she'd been informed of his whereabouts.

As the sergeant wrapped up his summary, the lieutenant switched off the holoprojector and leaned forward, her gaze sweeping the table.

"Good job out there today. Initial reports from the engineering team indicate these are the folks who've been hitting the Mercer-Merki space lanes. Taking them out of the equation will put a big dent in pirate activities in this area. And now…"

She lifted the sheet in front of her, the security nanofiber embedded in the plas decrypting the document when it registered her biosignature. She held it up for them to see.

"Orders," Ramirez whispered.

Boone nodded.

"The XO informed me earlier that *Callaghan* has been recalled. This was our last sortie in the Atliekas," she told them. "I'll be sharing this with the platoon shortly, but since you're here, you might as well know."

Murmurs spread through the group at her words. They'd been patrolling this sector of Procyon's asteroid belt for the past six months. Everyone knew they were due for a billeting change, but no one realized it was coming up this quickly.

Looking down at the sheet, she read, "The *Benfold* is on its way here to take over patrol of this sector. When she arrives, we're heading for the heliopause. Once we're back on Beryl, *Callaghan* goes into spacedock for a refit." She looked up at them and added, "at that time, promotions will be handed out, and you'll be given new duty assignments."

Lowering the document, she straightened. Her action elicited the same from everyone seated.

Nodding, she said, "That'll be all. Dismissed."

2: AT LOOSE ENDS

PORT DEFIANCE, BERYL

GEMINATE ALLIANCE

(SIRIUS B)

It took six weeks for *Callaghan* to arrive at Procyon's Calabi-Yau gate and transition to Sirius's heliopause. It was another six weeks before the destroyer berthed at the orbital base above the planet Beryl.

Those aboard the ship had been in the black for more than a year. Most put in for leave before reporting to their next post. Boone and a few others remained on base.

Orders were slowly trickling through the pipeline, as were promotions. Boone was now a lance corporal; in his inbox sat invitations to two advanced training 'A' schools. He hadn't had much chance to think about it before Ramirez strong-armed him into joining the rest for dinner in town.

Boone's eyes followed the coastline as the transport neared Port Defiance's South Bay Harbor, but his mind was on those two invitations, and the decision he knew he must soon make.

He tried to focus on the sights, how the city glittered like a jewel as the white dwarf sank low on the horizon. Lights popped up everywhere, businesses preparing for the throngs that would soon descend when the bay area transitioned from day to night. Some came from Port Defiance, while others like him were from Ouray, the military base where he and his platoon were temporarily housed.

But his mind kept drifting back to those two invitations. The 'A' school he chose would determine his career path. It would have a profound effect on his life in the coming years.

The back of his seat dipped, bringing Boone out of his reverie as Ramirez leaned a forearm across it, gaze riveted to something up ahead. He pointed. "Now, that's what I call a good time, right there. The three 't's."

The Marine seated in front of Boone turned to see what Ramirez was looking at. Boone followed his gaze. A cluster of young women stood outside a restaurant, all long legs, tight clothes, and lithe figures.

Davila laughed. "Lemme guess, tacos, tequila, and—"

A hard smack landed on the back of his head before he could finish.

It was Payne. Leaning across the aisle, the corporal sent him an arch look. "You sure you want to finish that statement?" Her finger helicoptered around, indicating the passengers inside the transport. "Not everyone here's into that third 't' of yours, you know."

"Gotcha covered, Corporal." Davila's eyes danced with mischief as he shifted to slap at his butt. "You be sure to let me know if you want a piece of this action right here."

Payne smacked him on the head once more, then sat back in her seat, rolling her eyes. "The only action you'll be seeing is on the mat, when I *hand* you your ass… you ass."

The PFC in front of Davila laughed. Reaching back, Edmundson punched Davila on the shoulder. "She's got you there, bro."

Davila didn't bother to turn; he just lifted a hand and flipped the man a one-fingered salute in reply.

Boone choked back a laugh. "Yeah, well. I'd be fine with anything, just so long as it's not 3-D printed from formation material."

A hungry expression crossed Davila's face as Boone steered the conversation back to food. "You have any idea how long it's been since I had a real bluesteer burger? The kind hot off the coals and dripping with cheese?"

Boone's stomach took that opportunity to growl.

Ramirez barked a laugh and shoved at his shoulder. "You're on the *coast*, my man. Go for something fresh-caught, like conch, straight out of the diver's hands. No, wait." He sat back, palms spreading wide. "A sea bass this big, taken right off the ship. So rare it's still wiggling."

Boone shook his head. The bluesteer he could handle. He still hadn't acquired a taste for fresh fish.

Ramirez caught his expression. "I know that look. The seafood they served on the mess deck do *not* count."

"Yeah, you can't count stuff printed from DBCs." Davila's lip curled as he mentioned the digital-to-biological converters. "You can't call that food. It's fuel, plain and simple."

"Could've been worse. Think of what they had for meal rats a couple of hundred years ago," Boone said with a grimace. "You can't blame the Navy. Formation bricks take up a lot less room, especially when they can use them for temp partitions and other things."

Ramirez coughed. "Yeah, right." His hands inscribed the air as he drew the mental picture. "Tonight's dinner is from sector four, deck Bravo-Yellow. It has a lovely bouquet, aged for months beside Combat Support 3-2's sweaty boots…"

His platoon mate's humor pulled a reluctant smile from Boone. "Well, unless you're on one of the ships of the wall—"

"—and the *Callaghan* was only a destroyer, not a battleship or cruiser," Ramirez interjected.

Boone plowed past the unnecessary reminder. He'd been stationed aboard the ship for the past year; he knew her type rating as well as Ramirez did.

"—even then, you'd have to be in officer country to get invited to the captain's table."

Davila had tired of the conversation, his gaze returning to the wharf as the transport pulled into a passenger loading zone and slowed. "Well, I'm just glad to get off base. It's not like I could have made it home for a visit before I was due back."

Boone heard the poorly disguised curiosity in Davila's voice. He knew the PFC still didn't understand why Boone hadn't put in for leave during their two-week break between deployments.

Davila's family lived light years away, in the Geminate Embassy at An Yang, the star nation that had colonized the Proxima Centauri system. Boone's home must seem ridiculously close in comparison. The family ranch was right here on Beryl, a quick, three-thousand-kilometer jaunt north and west of their present location.

It would take too much effort to explain the complexities of ranch life, so Boone didn't bother. Plus, there was the matter of the choices the Navy had just offered him. He had a lot of thinking to do and the ranch—well, he was better off doing his thinking at Ouray.

It's what he'd be doing right now, if promotions hadn't just been handed out. Since he and Ramirez had been in the same class, as expected, they both got Lance Corporal's pips. Edmondson and Davila had joined mid-tour; both had been bumped from private to private first-class. Payne had been kicked up to corporal.

The others felt this was worth celebrating. Boone might have required a bit of persuasion to join them, but now he was glad he had.

The transport came to a stop, handily deflecting Davila's unspoken questions. Ramirez pushed to his feet, his palm lightly cuffing the top of Boone's head. "C'mon Archangel. Let's go get some chow, some *real* chow."

As they piled out of the transport, Boone's gaze was drawn to the coastline like a magnet, and he stopped to stare. It had been over a year since he'd set foot on the beaches of his homeworld. The city of Port Defiance was a sprawling mass of humanity, built up along the curving shore as far as the eye could see.

Buildings ringed the far side of Bay Harbor, clustered together along the beach. A massive pier stretched far out into the bay. At its other end sat the planet's main spaceport.

From there, Beryl's primary space elevator rose into the air. Its upper half glistened like a silky strand of spiderweb in the setting rays of Little Blue, the white dwarf about which the planet orbited.

He wondered again why he'd let Ramirez and Davila talk him into an evening at the Thirsty Whale when he could be quietly walking the strand. He'd much prefer that to an evening standing around in a crowded bar, shouting to be heard.

He took a few steps toward a stone pathway that led down to the beach. "You go ahead. I'll catch up to you."

Beside him, Davila hooked an arm around his neck in a loose choke hold. "C'mon man, no ghosting on us."

Boone ducked, breaking free of the hold. "No worries. I'll be there, just give me a few."

Ramirez cocked a finger at him, firing an imaginary gun. "Okay, amigo, but if you don't show up soon, we're coming for you, *comprende?*"

Boone lifted his chin in silent acceptance of Ramirez's well-intentioned but misplaced plan to force him to 'mingle' and clapped Davila on the shoulder before heading down the stone path that led to the beach.

He'd always been more isolated than most of the people in his platoon. He just needed a minute alone, and the sound of the waves was calling to him.

He kicked off his shoes and let his feet sink into the still warm sand of South Bay Beach. The cry of seagulls sounded above him, circling hopefully, seeking morsels of food he might have brought. When they realized nothing was forthcoming, they broke off to land on a nearby sandbar before taking off again when they spied another human in the distance.

The slight breeze tickled his nose with the briny smell of the ocean as he transitioned from dry sand to wet. He stood, eyes closed, and let the warm waters lap against his ankles.

Boone had spent the past year crammed into a destroyer with the forty-three men and women that made up his Marine platoon, along with thirty officers and more than two hundred enlisted Navy sailors. This was a welcome change.

To say space was at a premium—in *space*—had always struck him as ironic. Yet it was true. Nearly four hundred souls would comfortably fit into an Alliance destroyer; they hadn't been anywhere near max capacity, and yet somehow it had still felt crowded. For the first month or two, things weren't so bad. But as time passed, such proximity could begin to weigh on a person.

It helped that the barriers made of formation material slowly disappeared as they were harvested for the destroyer's cooks to use. This had been a deliberate tactic employed by the Geminate Navy; they knew that slowly opening up space within a vessel would help ward off claustrophobia.

Still, nothing compared to being beneath open skies, on a planet with the wind kissing your face. This moment was the first in a long while where Boone felt he could truly breathe.

His gaze swept the shoreline, where historical landmarks still dotted the area, left by the original settlers centuries ago. In the distance, he could see shuttles taking off and landing at the spaceport and, farther off into the distance, container ships headed south toward the Tanzanian Atoll, and beyond into the shipping lanes that led to Beryl's southern continent.

He took his time, waiting until the sun fully set before he turned his back on the open sea, brushed the sand from his feet, and made the trek back to the Thirsty Whale.

Boone could feel the energy that emanated from the bar before he even stepped inside. Despite excellent sound mitigation, the deep thrum of bass notes and the muted strains of a stringed instrument wafted on the air as he approached the entrance.

He spotted Ramirez, Edmundson, and Davila immediately. The three were hanging out next to a stage where a small band played.

They held drinks and were scoping out a small crowd of female bodies crammed onto the dance floor, moving to the beat.

Boone lifted a hand in response when Edmundson spotted him and raised his beer in salute. Boone envied the seeming ease with which they slipped back into civilian life, even though he had no real desire to join them. For Boone, mingling felt about as comfortable as an ill-fitting pair of combat boots.

He sought the shadows, his back to the wall as his gaze swept the darkened interior. A few meters away, a bartender eyed him with a knowing look. Pulling a glass off the top of a stack, he filled it from the tap. Rounding the bar, he headed Boone's way.

"Just off a tour?"

Boone accepted the proffered drink with a brief smile. "You profile all your patrons?"

The man chuckled. "Only the ones who look like they've forgotten what civilian life is like. You getting out, or are you between deployments?"

"The second," Boone admitted.

"Well, there are plenty of those here tonight, too."

The bartender inclined his head toward the far wall. Boone turned to look at the table the man indicated, studying it for a long moment. The people grouped around it were a bit older than he, but not by much. They also had the seasoned look of the quiet professional.

Boone coughed a short laugh, his gaze fixed upon the people who sat there. They looked... exhausted. Wrung out. And yet they had an indefinable quality, an alertness Boone had only seen twice before. In both instances, *Callaghan* had stopped to pick up a small team of elite warfighters. "Yeah, well, I wouldn't group myself in with them. Those folks are way above my pay grade."

An enigmatic expression crossed the bartender's face. "We each walk our own paths. There's no shame in that, brother." He slapped his hand lightly upon the top of the bar and then pushed away, leaving Boone to his thoughts.

Boone studied the special operators at the table, for he was certain that's what they were. Three men and a woman, one slightly older than the rest. They carried themselves with an assuredness he envied and hoped one day to attain.

And that had his mind returning right back to the decision he had ahead of him. One look and he knew his friends wouldn't notice if he slipped away. He set the glass down, nodded his thanks to the owner, and stepped outside.

3: HELL WALK

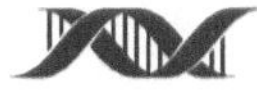

THE THIRSTY WHALE
PORT DEFIANCE, BERYL
(SIRIUS B)

The muscular, dark-skinned man at the table Boone had just been studying sat contemplating the beer in his hands. He'd been doing that a while, actually; it was just too much damn effort to bring it to his lips for a drink.

Despite the fact the bottle in his hands was his first of the night, Thad Severance already felt hung over. It wasn't the kind that came from too much alcohol, though. This hangover was courtesy of Hell Walk.

The grueling, aptly named experience came at the end of a six-month, invitation-only Qualification Course. Successful completion earned warriors the right to wear the tab of the Special Reconnaissance Unit.

Thad let his gaze drop to where the image of a coiled viper readying itself to strike sat on his sleeve. He'd been set on attaining it, of moving from the Marines into the special forces group ever since he'd enlisted four years earlier.

Around the patch's border was inscribed the Unit's motto:

Fortitudo, Furtim, Celeritate.
Strength, Stealth, Speed.

He glanced down at the beer cradled between his hands and then around at the people in the bar, blinking hard to shake his lethargy. A mix of civilians and military personnel populated the Thirsty Whale. Some crowded into the darkened area surrounding the bar proper; others spilled out into the wide expanse of the Whale's back deck.

Two large, hangar-like doors were suspended high in the air. They allowed the briny scent of the ocean breeze to waft in, along with the sight of a brilliant sunset over crystal blue waves. Real tiki torches speared the amethyst sand that fronted the outdoor eating area, with cheerful lights strung between. They twinkled in the gathering dusk.

Everywhere he looked, Thad saw a civilian life that felt nearly alien to him, now. With a strange feeling of dissociation, his eyes dropped to the beer in his hands, his fingers tracing the logo of the local microbrew etched into the bottle's side.

A hand came into his field of view, knuckles rapping smartly on the table in front of him. "You're thinking too hard, butterbar."

Thad glanced up, his gaze colliding with that of Shadow Recon pilot Captain Rafael Zander.

Since Shadow Recon was a different branch of the service, in casual settings like this, the formalities of rank could be ignored. Because Rafe was an elite pilot who flew special forces teams into dangerous places and then pulled their asses back out again, Thad usually greeted Zander with a respectful 'sir,' anyway.

Not tonight.

This Shadow Recon pilot had inserted himself into Thad's Hell Walk and purposely suckered him into lowering his guard. Thad figured he still owed the man some grief for that.

Zander chuckled as if he knew what was going through Thad's

mind and gestured to the chair across from him. Thad waved a hand in silent invitation, and Rafe pulled out the seat and deposited himself into it.

No one who took the Q-Course knew precisely when Hell Walk would begin. It was rumored that it started with each candidate being taken captive. Like so many others who'd come before him, Thad had been convinced he had the skills to outwit his trainers. He'd been wrong.

Rafe had been instrumental in taking Thad down, and he'd done so when Thad least expected it.

Thirty-two out of the two hundred fifty-three men and women who had begun the Q-course made it to Hell Walk. All thirty-two had been ambushed during a tradecraft exercise, where they'd each been sent out to different locations to either conduct surveillance on a target or execute a pick-up from a staffer posing as a human intelligence source.

When Rafe showed up as Thad's HumInt source, Thad had been mildly surprised, but he'd rolled with it… and walked right into Rafe's trap.

Thad narrowed his eyes at Rafe in mock anger. "You owe me, you know."

The pilot spread his hands, a look of innocence on his face. "Hey, don't blame me. *I* didn't take you out."

He dipped his head, looking pointedly at Thad from under lowered brows, and then jerked a chin in the direction of a nearby table. Thad didn't need to look to know the identity of the woman who sat there. He'd spotted her right away when he'd first come in.

Captain Lane Reid, Special Recon Unit Team Four, had been one of the people called upon to assist during Hell Walk. In particular, she had been lurking nearby while Rafe played decoy, drawing Thad out with the promise of an intel exchange.

Thad's eyes slid over to Reid and back again. He grunted and took a swig from the bottle in his hand. Rafe mistook that for annoyance. It wasn't. Thad knew very well that the attack had been orchestrated as part of the Unit's strategy to test his mettle in every possible way. He was simply too damn tired to respond.

"You were supposed to be blindsided," Rafe reminded him. "And you knew they take volunteers from active-duty personnel in the area."

Thad shot him a sardonic look, a tired smile playing on his face. "Let me guess. You were in the area, and they figured out we knew each other."

Rafe laughed. "Yep, you got played. That was the general idea, to see how well you handle the situation when the unexpected comes at you and the enemy has the upper hand. Start with nothing and work from there."

The goal of Hell Walk was to push already skilled warriors to the limit, to see how they performed when faced with a challenge of unknown difficulty and undetermined length. It wasn't the intent of the instructors to break the trainees but to hone them to the finest edge—and to instill in them the understanding that no man or woman was an island.

The Geminate Navy neither wanted nor needed supermen, hot-doggers, or heroes. They worked to develop strong, intelligent, and capable individuals who knew their strengths and their limitations, and who knew that collectively the team was going to be far more successful than any individual.

Rafe waved his beer bottle in the direction of Thad's sleeve, breaking into his thoughts. "Doesn't matter. You're patched now. You're Unit."

Thad blinked and glanced down once more at his patch, feeling a sense of unreality as he stared at the symbol that embodied everything he'd been striving for these past years. He looked away, striving to appear nonchalant. The knowing gleam in Rafe's eye told him he hadn't quite pulled it off.

"You look like you just woke up." Rafe squinted into the distance. "That'd be about… nineteen hours straight of rack time. More'n you've had in one stretch in sixteen weeks, am I right?" He paused for Thad's response.

The Shadow Recon pilot was correct; Thad felt all kinds of fuzzy right now.

"Yeah," he said, shaking his head hard to try and clear it.

Rafe drained his beer, set the bottle down, and then leaned back in his chair, waving a hand around.

"I remember it well. Makes things a bit hazy at first, especially with all the extra medical nano they pump into you at the end, to help your body recover from the shit they put you through. That alone is enough to wipe you out." He nodded and his expression turned distant. "They did something similar to us when we went through Shadow Recon."

Thad cocked his head, straining to recall a detail he knew well. After a moment, it came to him. "Green Platoon, right?"

"Yep. And let me tell you, that underwater part really messes with your head." Rafe lifted his bottle, frowned, and then pulled up the menu to order another. His gaze floated over the crowd as he settled back in his seat. The pilot's relaxed demeanor was deceptive. Even here, surrounded by Navy personnel, the pilot was ever vigilant.

Thad could relate.

"This chair force smartass bothering you?" The words, spoken in a jovial tone, came from a dark-haired man wearing the insignia of the Navy's Criminal Investigation Command. With him was a woman, whipcord lean and with short, dark hair. She sported the same patch Thad wore on his sleeve.

Gabe and Asha had completed the Q-Course, just like Thad. A swift, assessing glance told him they, too, were still recovering from it. Both took seats, Gabe sliding in beside him while Asha pulled out the chair next to Rafe.

"Chair force. Please." Rafe shot Asha an easy grin and pointed to Thad. "I'll have you know, this *Shadow Recon* pilot had no problem distracting that butterbar right there long enough for a certain SRU badass to get the drop on him." Rafe sat back and crossed his arms with a grin.

"Cocky *fils-putain*," muttered Thad, narrowing a one-eyed glare Rafe's way.

"*Fils*—? Ahhh," Gabe broke off as his wire helpfully translated the unfamiliar phrase from its Cajun patois into the standard 'sonofabitch.' He looked from Rafe to Thad. "Well, you probably got the 'cocky' part right. I can't comment on the other."

Rafe saluted Gabe. "Smart man. And that's *fils-putain* 'Sir,' to you, jarhead," he told Thad, pointing at Thad with the neck of his beer bottle.

Thad barked a short laugh and raised his up to meet Rafe's. "Sir, yes, sir," he said as he clinked the bottles together.

With a shake of his head, Gabe dismissed the byplay and turned to face Thad. Bracing his forearms on the table, he murmured under his breath, "Told you you'd make it through."

Thad looked the other man over. "Want the truth, *mon ami?* I wondered if *you'd* make it through."

Gabriel Alvarez wasn't like all the other candidates who'd gone through this final test before being pronounced members of the Geminate Navy's elite SRU Teams. He was a good ten years older than any of the warriors who'd gone through the course.

Alvarez chuckled and shook his head before pulling up the bar's menu on the small holoprojector embedded in the center of the table. "You and everyone else, Lieutenant. You and everyone else."

Rafe leaned forward, peering through the menu at Gabe. "What made you decide to subject yourself to that kind of torture, anyway? You're NCIC. Technically you're not even a soldier, you're a cop."

"We prefer the term Special Agent." Alvarez's tone was dry. He selected a brew, swiping his finger through the image, before dismissing it. He scrubbed a hand through his hair, a thoughtful look crossing his features.

"It was a special kind of torture, though, you got that right. As to why…" Gabe blew out a breath. "The deputy director thought it might give us some training tips we could implement with our own people."

Thad nearly choked on the beer he just swallowed. "You're shitting me, *ami.*"

Alvarez shrugged. "Seemed like a good idea at the time."

Thad stared at the man. "Well, you did okay… for an old guy."

He grinned when Alvarez lowered his chin and stared back at him.

"This old guy came in ahead of you more than once on that course."

"A guy as big as Thad? Yeah, it's pretty easy to slip past, especially during the recon and surveillance sections," Asha agreed.

Thad mimed a shot through the heart. "I'm wounded, *cher*, that you'd side with these cretins."

A glimmer of amusement lit Gabe's eyes. "It's not always brute strength that wins the race. Sometimes cunning comes in smaller, more lethal packages."

Asha lifted her drink in silent agreement; Alvarez saluted the medic back with his own newly arrived brew.

Thad let the good-natured ribbing wash over him. He realized his lethargy had lifted. For the first time since completing the course, he could truly savor his success.

It had been his goal for years. He was exactly where he wanted to be, and that felt good, damn good. He looked around, spotting several classmates—unsurprising, really, as the Thirsty Whale was one of the places those from Ouray Base liked to frequent.

He was honestly glad Alvarez was among them. The two couldn't be more different, but they'd found an instant rapport during that first day of the final qualification heat, when circumstance had forced them together.

"So, when are you headed out?" Asha shot Gabe a questioning look, drawing Thad's attention back to the present.

The NCIC agent shrugged. "Since no one ever knows how long Hell Walk will take, the agency cleared my slate for two full weeks. I have to be back at headquarters on Ceriba in five days."

"Excellent. I see a trip to a sky park in your future."

"A— What? Come again?"

Rafe laughed. "Careful. Asha's been saddled with taking her niece up to the Searcy Sky Park tomorrow, and she's looking for any poor sucker who will go along with her."

"Do you blame me?" The medic shot him a black look. "*You* try to ride herd over four teenage girls. I'd rather face an Akkadian onslaught, head on."

"Aw, come on, *cher*, it can't be that bad."

The medic angled a jaundiced eye his way. "You just got volunteered to keep me company, LT."

Rafe plucked the swizzle stick out of his rum and coke. Pointing it at Thad, he said, "Know for a fact that you aren't due anywhere in the next couple of days, either." He clamped the stick between his teeth, and then grinned an evil grin. "Now who's laughing?"

Thad shot Rafe a narrow-eyed look and then turned it on Asha. "How come you're not wrangling this *couyon* into your posse for tomorrow's excursion?"

Asha sat back. "Because I know better than to piss off the Shadow Recon pilot and call him names. Something you forgot, maybe?"

He started to snap off a reply, but then he got a good look at Asha's face and saw behind her joking exterior to the barely concealed plea buried deep in her eyes. A quick glance over in Gabe's direction told him the other man had seen it, too.

"Ah, what the hell."

With the faintest of nods, the agent turned his attention back to Asha. "Okay, I'm in, too. We don't have sky parks in Ceriba; it'll be interesting to see what one of those things is like."

Thad saw tension flow from Asha's shoulders, though the medic kept up her sardonic facade. "Tomorrow morning it is, then. We'll hang out by the pool, drink fancy drinks, and keep my niece from doing anything stupid."

Thad couldn't help but needle her a bit. "Like platform diving, or bungee jumping?"

She gave him a baleful glare. "Don't even think that. My brother would *kill* me if he found out his daughter tried one of those rides."

"No worries, *cher*. After what we've been through? Shouldn't be too much of a problem to keep four girls in line," he said. "What kind of dangers could a sky platform offer? Biggest risk I see is we'll die of boredom."

4: CLANDESTINE MEET

PELICAN OCEAN
FIVE KILOMETERS OFFSHORE
PORT DEFIANCE, BERYL

Starlight glinted faintly off the small skiff as it pulled away from Port Defiance's spaceport pier. It gained speed, angling out toward the open ocean and veering away from the Tanzanian Atoll with its standard trade routes. Its bow skipped across the waves, the sound of its motor and the slap of saltwater against the boat's hull combining to make verbal conversation between the two onboard impractical. The wind alone was strong enough to snatch the very words from the air.

Petra Cooke waited until she was certain they'd passed beyond Port Defiance's surveillance ring before cutting the motor. The small speedboat settled into the water, swells gently lapping at its sides.

"Are you—" the man seated across from Petra cut his words off when she raised her hand.

With a mental command, Petra sent a puff of audio chaff into the air, providing an effective yet unobtrusive security screen. The colloids were held aloft by brownian motion; a magnetic field kept the chaff ensconced in a sphere around the boat's two occupants.

She let her hands drop when the app controlling the colloids indicated they were in place.

"We're clear," she told him. "Want to tell me why you asked for this meeting?"

The man leaned forward, bracing his elbows on his knees. "I was wondering if you had everything set for tomorrow," he said.

'Tomorrow' was shorthand for the heist Petra had been planning for the past three months. It was a heist her bosses in the Mastai Cartel knew nothing about, and she intended to keep it that way. Clandestine meets like this increased the chance of exposure. She knew it and so did he.

Petra glared at him in disbelief. "You asked for a secured meet so you could satisfy your *curiosity?*"

His brows drew together as if just realizing how inane his question had sounded. "No, of course not. I… had an idea, is all."

Petra's eyes narrowed at his words, and she took a moment to study the man. Jay Henson was small, with features more refined than the average man. What he lacked in brute strength, though, he made up for in intellect and cunning.

He'd only been with Mastai for six months, but he'd already proven himself to be far more than the average thug, so she'd let him say his piece. She motioned for him to continue.

"Do you have buyers already lined up for the weapons?" he asked.

Her expression must have telegraphed her annoyance. He lifted his hands in a placating gesture.

"The only reason I ask is because those are Navy weapons in those cases you're grabbing. They use a trapped-key biolock to prevent unauthorized use. It's going to take time to crack that, and to scrub their serial numbers."

Petra's voice dipped dangerously low. "You'd better have a reason other than this for dragging me out here, Henson."

"I do. Look, every minute that passes between the time you snatch those cases and the time they land in your buyer's hands, you risk getting caught. We all do. Think of all the places where things can go south." He lifted a finger as he enumerated each one. "When you illegally enter the spaceport's Military Operations Area. When you break open the cage where the cases are stored. Sneaking them out to the shuttle you've rented. Getting them up to the sky park."

"Enough! You've made your point. You said you had an idea. What is it?"

"The weakest point, or at least the point where you're the most vulnerable for the longest amount of time is while you're up at the sky park, laundering the merch. If you're found out, you may need a little something on your side."

"I thought that's what the swamper was for," she said, tone sharp with exasperation. "Are you telling me you're not up to the job?"

A swamper did exactly as the name implied; it could 'swamp' a local segment of the net, temporarily overloading it and causing a brief outage before the system rerouted itself. The net was too sophisticated for the overload to last very long; the error was corrected almost immediately. The swamper then attacked the newly segmented route, crashing it. This played out countless times each minute. It would continue to do so until someone shut down the malicious device.

"No, no," Jay said. "The swamper's good to go. I'm taking it up with me to Searcy in the morning."

"You anticipate any problems getting it installed?"

"No. It'll go in line with the network booster they have sitting on top of their tallest building. The thing's isolated. No one will see me while I work."

"Good." She studied the thin man. "So again, I'm forced to ask, *why* did you call this meeting?"

A speculative gleam lit his eyes. "You said you had a manifest for those cases?"

"I do."

Those cases were a gun merchant's wet dream. They were packed with P-SCAR rifles, CUSP pistols, flechettes, even sniper weapon systems. One case alone held frag and sticky grenades. Another was filled with explosive devices and all the det nano a pyro could want. The cases even contained less deadly but highly useful tools like LockPiks, Zipties, and body armor.

Something about the way Jay asked the question, though, had Petra's guard up. "Why? What are you thinking?"

"Just an idea." He shrugged. "Call it insurance, something a bit more substantial than the swamper, in case things go south during the op."

Petra stared at him. "Go on."

"Just hear me out, okay? I'd like to borrow some of it."

"Borrow. Now, there's an interesting turn of phrase." For some reason, his choice of words amused Petra. "I'm not sure I've ever heard anyone say they want to *borrow* ammo. That's not the kind of thing you usually return."

A grin crossed his lips. "Yeah, I'll bet that sounds a bit strange," he admitted. "But I mean it. I just want to borrow the stuff, nothing more."

Petra remained silent; she just continued to stare at him.

"I can get them back to you after the park closes tomorrow so you're not out anything if we don't need them."

"Them," she repeated, keeping her expression impassive.

Jay's deep intake of air warned Petra she might not like what the man was about to say. As he laid out his strategy, she realized he'd been right; she didn't like it.

Petra was used to working from the shadows. What Jay suggested would shine a very bright light on the location they'd chosen to launder the goods. But his reasoning was sound, and she found herself nodding in agreement, despite her misgivings.

In the end, she gave him the green light to proceed.

5: MEMORY LANE

Ouray Base, Beryl

Boone's feet had taken him kilometers down the coastline as he turned his decision over in his mind yet again. It wasn't until a familiar sign breached his consciousness that he realized he'd walked all the way back to Ouray.

He was on the recruit side of the camp, the same stretch of beach where he'd pounded out countless kilometers of drills during his three-month training. He moved forward, through the shadows of the darkened training camp, the area awash in memories.

He dropped into the sand pit, feet sinking deep into the soft amethyst grains. He reached down, fingers burrowing into its depths as he recalled the hours he'd spent sweating inside its confines.

Straightening, he dusted off the sand, still warm with residual heat from the sun long after it had set, and continued on. He paused at its edge to glance around before stepping onto the parade deck that spanned the area between barracks and pit.

Ouray Base was quiet now that the day's ceremonies had ended.

He kicked at a stray bit of litter, likely left over from some well-wisher who had come to see a friend or family member officially sworn in as a Marine.

Cleaning bots would make short work of the debris. Graduation was one of the few times they were brought out and used. Normally, it fell to the recruits to keep the grounds spit-polished, 'scuzzing' the deck with one hand while the other remained at parade rest, behind their backs.

His lip quirked in a half smile. *Who the hell thought I'd ever feel nostalgic about that kind of shit?*

He glanced around, hearing very little in the still night air, the next crop of Marines-in-training enjoying their lone hour of rest before hitting their racks. The half-smile stretched into a full grin at the memory of lying at attention until given permission to relax into the thin mattress. So many nights he'd fallen asleep in that rigid position, too worn out from the day's drills to do otherwise.

The scuff of a boot sounded behind him and he pivoted to face the man who materialized out of the darkness. Habit had him straightening to attention.

"At ease, Boone." The sergeant's eyes scanned the holopips that declared Boone's rank, and then dipped farther down. "You're tracking sand all over my deck."

Boone lifted his chin as he dropped into a modified parade rest. "Sorry, Sergeant."

Sergeant Salvatore Franco had been one of Boone's toughest instructors during his thirteen-week stay at Ouray, but he'd also become both mentor and guide.

His former drill instructor's eyes made another critical sweep. Boone knew for a fact the man had taken in a mountain of information in that quick perusal, from the shine of his shoes to the crease of his collar.

"What brings you back this way? One round through the Crucible not enough for you?"

A smile ghosted Boone's lips. "One round was plenty, thanks."

The sergeant crossed his arms. "Spit it out. What's bothering you, son?"

Boone shook his head and a soft laugh escaped. "Are all DIs mind readers?"

"Only the ones who care," drawled Franco. "Now, spill it. I don't have all night."

Boone drew in a breath, suddenly unsure about how much he wanted to share. "I've been offered my choice of two different 'A' schools."

Franco nodded sagely when it became evident Boone was done speaking. "You having trouble deciding?"

Boone jerked his head to the side, the action both nonverbal and noncommittal at the same time.

"Intelligence or Scout Sniper," he listed them off. "One gets me off Beryl. The other keeps me here."

"Ahhhhh, now we're getting somewhere. I take it you're leaning toward the course that'll get you off planet soonest."

"It's not that," Boone protested. He stopped when Franco gave him The Look.

"Don't feed me that bullshit."

Boone just shrugged.

Franco must have found the unspoken admission funny. His eyes crinkled in sudden amusement. "Well, it's good to know this Marine's Navy at least had the good sense not to offer you something in Medical."

Boone resisted the urge to wince. Weapons, marksmanship, tracking—these were all things he'd excelled at in boot. Triage, on the other hand, was a thing he'd never been able to wrap his head around. He could feel embarrassment heating his cheeks at the memory of his failed attempts to pass basic field triage, and the extra 'incentive training' he'd earned in the pit, as a result.

Franco waved a dismissive hand. "No shame in knowing your weaknesses, son. You've plenty going for you in other areas. It was just a matter of time before someone decided that raw ability you have with weapons should be honed."

He gave Boone a considering look. "Out of the two options,

what's your gut telling you?"

"Sniper," Boone admitted after a beat, and then closed his eyes as Franco began to laugh.

"Which won't get you off this rock. I understand your dilemma. But allow me to point out, that school doesn't last forever. I can assure you, the Geminate Navy won't let you cool your heels on Beryl for long after you finish."

Boone pressed his lips together to cut off an incipient protest, and then nodded. "Appreciate the advice."

Wise eyes drilled into him. "Son, we're going to keep your ass too busy for you to know or even care where you are. Go with your gut on this one. Now, get out of here, before I find myself a scuzz brush and order you to scrape all that sand you tracked back into the pit."

Boone braced. "Sergeant, yes, sergeant!"

He and Franco exchanged a smile, and the sergeant extended a hand.

"It was a pleasure having a role in your training, Boone. Just don't embarrass me out there, y'heah?"

"I hear."

Franco nodded. "Dismissed."

6: HEIST

PORT DEFIANCE SPACEPORT

Petra's job with the Mastai Cartel didn't usually require her to handle the merchandise. Mastai used cutouts for that, untraceable drones and the like that offered deniability should they be caught.

Her department handled reconnaissance. Her people were the advance scouts that secured the area prior to any cartel action. They never touched the goods, and she liked it that way.

As with most things, there were exceptions. Such had been the case earlier in the year when her job had brought her down to the spaceport to pick up an item for the Boss. The cartel's leader had made a particularly sensitive acquisition and decided he wanted a human to handle it. Petra had drawn the short straw twice in a row.

Interestingly, the task brought her somewhere she'd never been before: the spaceport's lowest level. Someone within the organization had deemed the sea-level tier the least likely to draw curious eyes.

They were sure right about that, Petra thought as she stepped from the lift. The carton-laden maglev hand truck that floated beside her hummed a dismal counterpoint to the dreary panorama that lay before her.

She studied the dimly lit area. Slips ran along the dock, framed by empty barnacle covered pilings that rose from the sea floor, slimy and green. Somewhere in the distance, a pipe dripped, the steady *plop-plop-plop* a counterpoint to the slapping of ocean waves.

For every ten slips, one was occupied. The vessels moored there hardly looked seaworthy—certainly nothing she'd trust to take her safely beyond Beryl's atmosphere.

She headed toward the distant wall that separated the commercial zone from the Military Operations Area. Beyond the security fence that separated the two sectors, she saw more of the same: open maws of empty slips as far as the eye could see. It appeared as if the Navy felt the same about this lowest tier as commercial industry did.

Petra stopped well short of the barrier. To her left stood a large shipping container, shoved up against the dock's rear wall. Sliding doors were inset into its side, and it was toward these that she turned.

She'd ordered the thing delivered two weeks ago. Its metal sides were dented, the lower half showing rust from years of neglect, but it would work just fine as a staging area for the team.

She glanced casually over at the MOA's barrier. The Navy had an electronic door inset into its fence, the latter ending at the waterline. From there, an ES field extended out into the bay, climbing high above her head as it spanned the four-level structure.

Petra had eyes only for the wire cage, filled with six rugged hardcases, sitting just inside the MOA.

She pulled the maglev hand truck up to the shipping container, the thing little more than a prop to assuage curious eyes that might be watching the feeds. Using an untraceable token to unlock the door, she slid it open and pushed the hand truck through.

"Boss," a voice greeted her from within. Petra looked up to see Ike rise from a crouch.

He tossed a rag into the air; she fielded it with a nod of thanks, wiping her hands with it. The door's handles were as grungy as the rest of the place.

"Military transport arrived, I see," she said once the doors slid shut.

"Yeah," another voice said from deeper in the shadows. Delia emerged, Kele by her side. "The merchandise is in place; won't be picked up until late tomorrow afternoon."

She nodded. "Is Bobby in position?"

Bobby was her cyber geek, the one person on her hand-picked team whose skills no one else could duplicate. He'd be the one to bypass the spaceport's security.

Delia nodded. "He'll be down in a bit. Said he had to backdoor in from a node on Tier Three."

Petra consulted her chrono. "How long has he been gone?"

"About half an hour, give or take," Delia said after a moment's thought. "He guessed it'd take about that long."

Petra nodded, "Good. Then he should be back soon."

She waved to the boxes loaded onto the hand truck. "Dinner. And a couple of camp mattresses. We sleep in shifts."

Ike tore into the top box. Pulling out one of the mattresses, he triggered it to auto inflate. He accepted the meal box Delia handed him, then settled onto the air cushion with a low grunt. "Guess there's nothing left to do but wait it out til the night shift's last round."

The hours passed slowly. Finally, it was time to move.

Petra's crew was in position well before shift change. Kele had left an hour earlier to board the shuttle that would be their getaway transport. Ike, wearing identity obscuring clothing, was lookout. Posing as spaceport janitorial crew, he was emptying recycling bins along the dock, a small sweeper-bot in tow. Petra and Delia remained inside the shipping container, waiting for their cue to move.

At exactly 0630, Ike sent them a heads-up. *{Two MPs, inbound.}*

Petra held her breath as the Navy's third shift security team made their scheduled stop at the cages.

{Okay, they're gone,} Ike reported.

Petra sprang to her feet. *{Bobby. Go.}*

There was a long pause, then *{Security feed's down,}* came the tech whiz's reply. His mental tone held a nervous waver to it.

{You're doing great, Bobby,} she assured him. *{How about the gate?}*

With the level considered low traffic, the only thing installed to guard the electronic gate was a military SI. Bobby had assured her he could easily circumvent it.

This time, the pause was a little longer, and when he replied, he sounded out of breath. *{Done. It's offline.}*

Delia shot Petra a worried look.

{Slow down, Bobby. You'll just draw people's attention if you start rushing around.}

There was a laugh on the other end, Bobby's words tinged with anxiety. *{I'm not running. I'm hyperventilating!}*

Petra gave Delia's shoulder a small shove. "Go. I'll talk him down."

"You'd better," she muttered. "There's no backing out now."

As the other woman strode toward the gate, crowbar cylinder in hand, Petra retrieved one of two maglev carts stored inside the shipping container and motioned Ike over.

{Breathe for me, Bobby. No need to panic.} She pitched her voice soothingly when what she really wanted to do was slap him upside the head and order him to grow a pair.

She heard a gulp. *A friggin,' honest-to-stars actual* **gulp**, she thought to herself with some irritation.

{I'm… okay.} He did sound steadier.

{Good. Kele's on the way with the shuttle. All you need to do is get down here, and get onboard. We'll do the rest.}

Petra reached back inside the dented, rusty container, retrieved the second maglev cart, and moved to join Ike at the gate. Delia made a pleased sound, pocketed the crowbar, and with a small flourish, swung the gate open.

Petra sent her a stern look. *{We have five minutes, folks! Move it,}* she ordered tersely, keeping to the private channel they'd set up between them.

They swarmed through the opening, Delia and Petra moving to the cage, while Ike ran ahead and stood forward guard. Petra maintained contact with Bobby while Delia applied the crowbar to the cage's lock.

{No indication anyone suspects,} came Bobby's report. His voice sounded increasingly steady the closer he came. *{And no one's remotely near your location. All clear.}*

"Hsssst!" Petra sent the sibilant call audibly to Ike. The man abandoned his post and trotted over to help unload the empty cases they'd swap for the legit ones. They'd acquired the cases from a Navy surplus store a week earlier, then given them a facelift, adding current Geminate Marines holo decals and fake seals.

As Ike began offloading, Petra upended the bag slung over her shoulder. Out slid six Faraday-weave sleeves. She and Delia each grabbed one and began working them over the armored Navy cases. As soon as each case was sealed inside the weave, it was hauled over to the empty cart. Five minutes later, six Navy surplus cases sat in place of the six Petra's team had stolen.

Bobby had arrived while they were making the exchange; he was currently pacing nervously on the commercial side of the dock, his attention split between watching their frenzied activity and monitoring the airspace for Kele's arrival.

His head jerked back toward them when he heard Petra's *{Go! Go! Go!}*

Petra and Ike rushed the gate while Delia paused to secure the lock on the cage. She caught a flicker of motion to her left as they passed through and let out a silent, relieved breath when the snub nose of a delivery shuttle floated down to the slip where Bobby stood.

{Get inside!} she barked to Bobby as the transport settled against the dock.

He jumped at her harsh words but wheeled, arrowing for the hatch, which Kele had just unsealed. Petra was pacing on one side of the maglev, Ike on the other. They skidded to a halt in front of the open maw of the shuttle's cargo space and reached for the top case, their actions perfectly in sync. Just as the last case was shoved inside, Delia came running up, flashing the 'okay' sign. Slapping the side of the shuttle, she ducked inside with a gruff, *{Move your ass}* to Bobby.

Petra and Ike rounded the passenger side, Ike taking shotgun, Petra sliding in, sandwiching Bobby between her and Delia. Doors sealed, the shuttle lifted off.

"Hang on!" Kele said from the pilot's seat.

Petra looked at her chrono. Fifteen minutes had passed from the time they'd left that dank, rusted-out metal box of a shipping container to the time they departed the spaceport, stolen cases securely loaded. They'd beat their best time estimate, and now they were bound for Searcy Sky Park.

Petra reached behind them, her hand coming to rest on the nearest armored case; with a smile, she traced the symbol of the Geminate Navy embossed into its tough hide.

Damn, but we did it!

"How're we looking on scan?" she called up to Ike, seated in the co-pilot's seat.

The man checked something on his holodisplay and then gave her a thumbs-up. "All clear, boss. Only traffic in sight's on final approach to the spaceport. Nothing unusual there."

"Good. Let's keep it that way." Petra dropped her hand and turned back around, her voice calm and confident for the benefit of the man seated to her left.

She'd always known Bobby was their weak link. The man could sometimes behave as if he was afraid of his own shadow, but his skills at accessing networks and bypassing security protocols were the best in the cartel. She knew there was a very good chance they'd need his skills up on Searcy as well.

Jay had been right about how much time they'd need to scrub the weapons of any identifying marks. The guns were keyed to activate only when presented with an ID from active service

Geminate Navy personnel. She'd acquired codes off the splinternet that should break past the weapons' military lockouts, but Petra wasn't willing to rely on 'should's. If they didn't work as promised, it would be Bobby's job to bypass them and make them serviceable for the buyers she'd lined up.

She understood Bobby's nervousness, to a degree. Mastai usually only trafficked in white collar crime, things like fine art, gemstones, and rare metals. Munitions was a major departure from the norm.

Despite his nervous habits, she knew Bobby was trustworthy. Everyone on the team was. Her cadre of five had practiced for weeks to prepare for this heist. They'd proven themselves today.

"What do you think is in there?" Delia's low voice sounded from the far left.

Petra let a thin, satisfied smile crease her face as she leaned around Bobby. "Oh, I don't *think*. I know."

When she didn't elaborate, Delia lowered her chin. "And?"

Petra's smile deepened. "You'll see soon enough."

"I still don't understand why we have to take them up to Searcy to launder the goods," Bobby said.

Delia elbowed Bobby in the side. "We've been over this. Jay laid out all the reasons with the boss." She hooked her thumb Petra's way. "If the boss is cool with it, you should be, too."

"Yeah, but… a *sky park,* for stars' sake."

Petra understood where Bobby was coming from, but she was getting tired of hearing it. Besides, his reaction was the very reason no one would think to look for them there. It was what had landed Petra in a shuttle altered to resemble a food and beverage supply company, on final approach to an aging amusement park in the sky.

Bobby opened his mouth to complain some more, but the look on her face must have convinced him not to push his luck. He cut off his words with a mumbled, "Just saying."

Searcy had not been her first choice, either. Jay had made a compelling case for it, though.

"More than fifteen thousand people pass through the damn park every single day," Jay had told her. "That's a goldilocks zone."

When she'd arched a brow at the odd phrase, he'd explained. "Plenty of people there, so it's easy to get lost in the crowd. Yet it's small enough, and *old* enough, to be considered a low value target."

"And that means?"

"That means there aren't going to be any eyes looking in our direction."

He'd been so taken with his plan that he hadn't complained about her stipulation that *he* be the one to infiltrate the park ahead of time, posing as an employee.

"Five minutes out, boss." Kele's voice came from the pilot seat, up front.

Petra nodded. "Ike, you heard from Jay yet?"

"Hang on a sec, I'll ping him," the man in the co-pilot's seat responded. A few moments passed, then Ike turned and gave her a thumbs-up. "Jay says we're green. Swamper's been installed. He's even disabled the cameras for us, down at the loading dock."

"Good." Petra peered at the forward holoscreens, the sky park growing larger as they neared. Kele's heading would bring them in at an oblique angle to the platform's main approach vector. It kept them beneath the stream of traffic that brought park-goers to Searcy.

The loading dock was located just beneath the topside shuttle pad where park visitors landed when they arrived. As the shuttle crossed beneath the lip of the upper deck, Petra could see the bay was wide but shallow, with enough room to comfortably fit no more than four transports at a time. Other than theirs, there was only one other vessel currently at the dock.

Four sets of landing rails connected to loading ramps, to facilitate the transfer of goods. Kele angled for the far side opposite the other craft, bringing the vessel to rest on the rails with a click and a soft thump.

As Kele powered down, Petra saw a figure detach itself from the shadows. The man lifted a hand in greeting as he strode toward the ship.

Petra left Kele and Ike to their post flight procedures. Opening the transport's side door, she jumped down to the landing bay's deck and turned to face the newcomer.

"Boss," Jay greeted with a brief nod. He stood casually, hands tucked into pockets, his head tilted slightly to one side.

She motioned to the aft hatch, and Jay obligingly ambled in that direction. As she opened the rear door, she shot him a questioning look. "Everything set?"

Jay leaned against the side of the shuttle, still in what Petra privately called his 'indolent' mode. One hand finally came out of the pocket to scratch at the side of his neck as he considered her question.

"I guess Ike told you the swamper's in place," he said finally. Nodding toward their bounty, he added, "All I need to do is borrow what we discussed, and I'll be on my way."

Petra pointed to the third crate. "They're in that case, there."

Her words prompted the normally laconic man to move with an energy he didn't usually demonstrate. He shoved the first two cases aside and pulled the third toward him. He stopped, eyeing the lock doubtfully.

"You have the key to unlock it?"

Petra reached into a pocket and brought out a crowbar cylinder. "This'll do the trick," she said, waggling it at him.

He looked skeptically at the piece of metal in her hand. "You sure it won't cause everything inside to go boom, and us with it?"

Petra blew out an annoyed breath. She wasn't used to being questioned, especially not by the cartel crew. "Sounds like someone's a bit nervous."

His expression hardened. Wordlessly, he grabbed the cylinder from her hand and bent to give the case his complete attention. "There's a difference between nervous and cautious." His words were curt.

Petra's eyes narrowed at his response. This kind of attitude wasn't what she was used to seeing from the man. His behavior had always been carefully polite and deferential—until now. Something had changed. Something wasn't adding up, and this job was too critical to her own future to let any suspicions slide.

"Bingo," he said softly, eyes riveted to the contents inside. His hand dove in and came back out with a handful of small devices.

"Don't think I've ever seen anyone quite as excited to be handling death in the palm of their hands before." She kept her words low so that none of the others would hear.

Jay laughed at her comment, his easygoing manner sliding back into place like a mask.

Delia's arrival with maglev carts distracted Petra momentarily as they offloaded the cases. That task complete, she turned back to Jay.

"It's your show; lead on."

Jay nodded and headed for the exit. The rest followed.

"I have you set up inside a laundry room on the lower level," he told her. "It's down a side hallway, just off the main corridor. The place isn't used much, only at night or after the park is closed. I recoded the lock to accept your ID tokens."

They passed silently through the park, Jay in the lead. When they entered the room procured for them, Jay crossed to the back where a portable toolbox was stashed. Petra slid the Navy case that contained the devices Jay would borrow down to the end of the long table that ran down the center of the room. With a subtle nod, she left Jay to the task while she turned to help the others offload the rest of the haul.

With her back turned, Petra couldn't see what exactly went into the toolbox. If she had, she might have questioned the addition of an item they'd not discussed. A few minutes later, toolbox in hand, Jay stopped beside the case she was helping Bobby unpack.

"You have everything you need?" he asked.

She paused to consider his question, taking a careful look around. "We're good. Monitor the team channel. If something comes up, or if we're drawing unwanted attention and feel we need the swamper, I'll ping you."

Jay nodded. "I guess I'll be on my way then." He turned for the door.

"Hold up." She closed the distance between them and motioned for him to walk with her.

"I want to talk to you about what's in that box you're carrying."

Jay froze at her words, a wary look crossing his features.

"Stealing military weapons is dangerous enough," she said in a low tone. "The last thing we need is to get some clueless kid killed, you hear me? If that happens, they'll slap the term terrorist on us so fast, our heads'll spin."

He nodded silent understanding.

Her voice was soft, but it held clear warning as she pointed to his toolbox. "Those things are a last resort. And only to be used as a distraction, you hear me? Theater, nothing more. A way to buy us time to get the hell out of here if we're found out."

Exasperation broke through the wariness at this last. "All right, all *right*, I get it. No killing any kids." Grabbing the toolbox by its handle, he straightened.

She held his gaze for a moment longer. Jay was the first to break it.

"I'll be in touch," he muttered, eyes downcast. Slipping through the door, he disappeared.

* * *

The devices in the bottom of the toolbox were the only thing occupying Jay's mind on the way back to the sky park's maintenance department.

"A distraction," Petra had said.

Oh, they'll be a distraction, all right. And some of these…

Jay looked down at the toolbox floating obediently along and smiled.

Some I'll put to a different use.

7: LIBERTY

Ouray Base, Beryl

Boone was still turning Sergeant Franco's words over in his head the next morning after PT as he headed back to the barracks. Edmondson lifted a hand in silent greeting as Boone passed by, headed for the showers.

There was a rucksack sitting atop Edmondson's bed when Boone came back out. The private was clearly packing.

Lifting his chin toward the ruck, Boone asked, "You shipping out?"

The PFC paused, his gaze lifting as he studied a readout only he could see. "Yeah. In about an hour, I guess."

Boone stopped next to the man and held out his hand. "Luck to you, brother. Been an honor serving our first tour together."

They shook, and Boone moved on to the corner, where his day's assignment lay. They still had a lot of gear to check in. The larger items—combat rifles, ammunition, CUSP batteries and the like—had all been left behind on the ship. What remained were the smaller items, like zipties, breaching canisters, LockPiks, and surveillance microdrones. He figured it'd take half a day to catalogue it all.

Boone stared at the messy pile of bags tossed against the front wall and then pulled up the inventory form the platoon's sergeant had sent him when they landed planetside. He'd use the DD-1149 to reconcile what had been checked out with what remained. It was busy work, but the Geminate Navy required that all its equipment be accounted for, always.

Pulling up a chair, he got to work. He'd just started to sort the sundry bits of equipment when Ramirez and Davila tumbled through the door.

"Woot! Yassss dawg." Ramirez pumped a fist into the air. "Orders just came in. I've been assigned to jump school. Got a whole week to burn between now and then. You know what that means. It's party time!"

"Not me," Edmundson grumbled from where he stood by his rack. He looked up from his packing with a mournful face. "New deployment is St. Clair Township, as part of the parliamentary detachment. I have to catch the first shuttle out to the heliopause tonight. Gotta be topside by four."

Davila looked over at Boone. "What about you, Archangel? You got your marching orders yet?"

Boone shrugged. "Not sure. I have two options. One will keep me here on Beryl."

"Which two?" Ramirez asked.

"Intel or sniper."

At Boone's words, Davila broke into a grin. "Nice! I knew you'd get sniper school, with your scores. Where and when?"

"Fort Weskah, two weeks."

Ramirez looked envious. "Damn. Wanna trade?"

Davila elbowed Ramirez in the ribs. "You have to know which end the bullets come out of first, dumbass. Right, bro?"

Boone began separating surveillance drone canisters into a separate pile. He shook his head. "Nope. Not touching that."

The two came to a stop in front of Boone's table and Davila

rapped on it with his knuckles. "Come on. We're getting out of here."

Edmondson looked up. "Where you headed?"

"Searcy Sky Park," said Davila.

"Aw, man." Edmundson's tone made it sound as if he'd just lost his dog. "I hear there's some killer wave boarding up there. The infinity pool makes it look like you're going to surf right out into the black."

"Isn't that the place with the freefall platform dive they call the Sudden Death?" Davila's hand arced and then plummeted, miming the action. "Boosh. Right into the Pelican Ocean."

"Yeah, that's the one." Ramirez looked bored. "Not interested. Nothing beats boots in the black, slamming and jamming a smuggling ring out in the Atliekas. Hell of a lot more exciting than anything they could cook up."

Edmundson made a scoffing noise. "No amusement park's gonna have that kind of EVA as a ride, asshole. Civilians have *safety* regs."

"We do too," protested Davila.

Edmundson threw a wadded-up shirt at him. "*We* take risks. What's acceptable for us and what's acceptable for Suzy Starshine ain't the same, bro."

Ignoring the exchange, Ramirez speared Boone with a look. "You skated on us last night, amigo. Not letting you get out of it again today."

Boone shook his head, reaching for the first surveillance drone cylinder. "Can't," he replied. "Too busy."

Ramirez slapped the canister out of his hands. "Do it tomorrow. I've already cleared it with the sergeant."

Mildly annoyed, Boone bent to pick up the cylinder that had rolled under the table. He felt a tug on his shorts as Ramirez wrapped a fist around the waistband and pulled. Irritated, Boone swiped up the canister and then hastily rose before Ramirez's efforts ripped the shorts right off him. Not that he was modest; he just had a limited number of PT clothes, and it would piss him off to have to buy another pair.

Shoving the cylinder absently in his shorts' pocket, he straightened to face the grinning man. "I'm not dressed for it."

"You're fine," assured Ramirez. "You just take those boots off once we get up there and stroll around barefoot. See?"

Davila planted his palms on the table and leaned forward. "Give me one good reason why not."

Boone hesitated. He *had* no reason, other than he wasn't much of a people person, and… Well, he wasn't a people person.

"You're not going back home to visit family, are you?"

Boone shook his head.

"Well, that's settled, then." Davila straightened. When he moved forward to strong-arm him, Boone gave in. Ramirez had been right; he *had* ghosted last night and felt a bit guilty about it.

As they exited the barracks, Edmondson's sardonic voice filtered out to them. "Hey, don't worry about me. I'll be fine."

"You can't come anyway," Davila hollered back. "You have a shuttle to catch."

As they settled into their seats, Boone felt the weight of the canister in his shorts and groaned.

"What?" Ramirez turned to face him.

"I gotta return this." Boone rose, canister in hand.

Davila pushed him back down. "No, you don't. Just hang onto it and add it to the pile when you get back," he said reasonably. "Besides… You're not the only one."

A cunning look crossed his face and he dug into his own pocket. Holding up a small disc, he shot Boone a sly grin.

Boone's eyes narrowed as Davila flipped it back and forth, making the disk dance across his knuckles. "Is that—?"

Davila's grin widened. "A LockPik? Sure is. Ought to gain us access to any of the rides, free. The girls love that kind of stuff."

Boone's hand whipped out, snatching the disk from the air. "That's government property. You can't go around using it for personal gain, asshole."

Davila's eyes narrowed as he shot back, "Who are you to judge?

You're carrying around a canister of surveillance drones."

"That was an accident," Boone ground out. "It's going back on the pile as soon as we return."

"Suuure it is," Davila chuckled and gave Boone a wink. "Come on, man, gimme back the LockPik."

"No." Boone stared hard at the man. "You wanted me to come along? Well, this is me. So get over it."

"Chill, bro. It's all good." Ramirez lifted his chin out the window. "Look. We're nearly there."

Davila subsided after one last look in Boone's direction that silently promised retribution.

Boone quirked a half-smile in return. *Bring it on, dude.* He'd served with Davila long enough to know the other man was mostly bluff.

The sky park looked better from a distance, Boone decided, as he got his first good look at the platform. The closer they got, the more wear and tear he saw on the aged structure.

Davila caught his eye, previous conflict forgotten. "Hey, no worries." He grinned. "It's not like this was built by the military or anything."

Boone lifted a brow. "Name me one single private corporation that doesn't go with the lowest bid, just like the Navy," he remarked. "Not much difference, from where I sit."

"Shit, man, you're way too serious," complained Ramirez. "Lighten up; we're about to score ourselves some fun."

"Yeah, don't you want to try the Wipeout?" Davila teased. He laughed aloud at Boone's scowl.

"Stupid name for a bungee jump," Boone said.

"A half-*kilometer* bungee jump," Davila added. "They reach terminal velocity at that distance."

Boone gave Davila a flat stare. "No, thanks. We do enough crazy stuff while we're deployed."

Davila inclined his head, silently acknowledging that. "Okay, well, this place is more than just the thrill rides. They have a saltwater pool with a decent beach. Imported green sand from An

Yang, the works."

Boone choked. "We're over the damn ocean. Why in hell would they put a beach up there?"

Davila shrugged as the shuttle came to a stop and he rose from his seat. "Why not?"

Boone followed his fellow Marines off the shuttle and into the sky park. The platform's twenty-five-kilometer elevation meant they were firmly in the troposphere, and the sky above was as black as space. It also meant the platform needed an ES field to maintain atmosphere. He was relieved to see Searcy's interior looked a lot more well-maintained than its exterior.

The park was crammed with visitors. Everywhere he looked, people were either waiting for rides, standing in line at concession stands, or hanging out in the water.

Staring out at the infinity pool where its edge met the darkened sky of the horizon, he had to admit Davila was right; it was a neat trick.

By mutual agreement, they ended up at the saltwater pool that did, indeed, have a real sand beach. Boone unsealed his boots, unable to resist, and waded in, beer in hand. He floated on the gently rocking waves and watched as Ramirez and Davila gravitated to a cluster of girls who were taking a day away from their studies.

One of the girls tossed her head back and laughed at something Davila whispered in her ear. He and Ramirez shared a look, then Davila rose, tugging on the girl's hand lead her out of the water. Ramirez did the same.

Boone jackknifed up. "Where are you guys going?"

"Don't worry, dad. We'll be back before curfew," Davila mocked.

Ramirez tossed Boone a sloppy salute, hooking an arm around the brunette beside him. "S'okay, man. We're leaving you in good hands," he said with a wink.

"Wait, I don't need any—" Boone protested, but his words quickly died when a hand pulled him deeper into the water.

"They said you were the strong, silent type," a voice purred into his ear.

"What?" He turned toward the voice but froze when a second hand wrapped around his biceps and squeezed.

"Ramirez said you have to have ice water in your veins in order to kill a man with a sniper rifle from six thousand meters," a second, breathy voice said. "What's it like?"

The urge to roll his eyes was strong. Boone couldn't believe the bullshit his platoon mates had fed these girls. It wasn't that he minded the female attention, but he much preferred to be the one who did the pursuing. And he sure as hell wasn't going to use a lie to gain someone's attention.

I'm going to kill those grav-suckers. "Look. I'm not a—"

The first girl stopped his words with a finger to his lips. "They said you'd deny it. They said no one is supposed to know you're an elite Marine sniper. That's… soooo… *sexy.*"

Boone stood. He'd had enough. "Either of you ladies want a drink? I'm buying." Not waiting for a response, he waded to shore, feet sinking deep into the wet green sand as he fast walked his way up the dune to the row of tiki huts that lined a boardwalk.

The farther along the beach he got, the more he congratulated himself on his plan. He'd do as he promised and buy them a round of drinks. He just wouldn't be the one to deliver them. He'd have one of the servers at the bar do it.

Boone completed the order and left the server with the information on where to deliver the drinks. He stepped away from the open-air bar, wondering what else he could do to kill time, when a group of people dressed in park employee's uniforms caught his attention.

Correction, it wasn't the people who'd caught his eye; it was the maglev cart they were escorting. The thing was laden with shipping crates that looked disturbingly familiar.

Boone had seen his share of the rugged, reinforced cases the Navy used to transport weapons and ordnance. One of his jobs aboard *Callaghan* had been to help restock the armory after each engagement.

In his experience, he'd never seen cases shaped quite like that outside the Alliance Navy. They were unique and distinctive. And to his practiced eye, someone had done a hasty coverup. They'd masked the Navy markings on the cases' sides but hadn't altered their profile.

I suppose they could be Navy surplus...

As if under their own volition, his feet turned to follow. He shadowed them, debating how to proceed. Pinging Ramirez and Davila did no good; both men had their wires set to Do Not Disturb. Just as he'd concluded he'd have to either reach out to park security or maybe even ping Sergeant Franco back at Ouray, they stopped before a door marked 'Employees Only'.

Boone cursed softly to himself. He couldn't lose them, not until he'd confirmed they either were or were not carrying illicit arms...

He sidestepped to a recycling receptacle and crouched behind it. As he did, the weight of the cylinder in his pocket caused his shorts to thump wetly against his thigh.

The surveillance drones.

He retrieved the canister, pressing the activation sequence on its side. It came online, handshaking with his wire. He selected one of the drones and the end of the canister sprang open, a tiny machine rising from its depths. Boone flew it forward, bringing it to a hover just behind the group.

He moved the drone around to see if he could determine what they were using to access the interior, but heads were blocking his view and it happened too quickly for him to be certain. If they had employee access, Boone might have been convinced to abandon his surveillance, reasoning that the cases had to be legit Navy surplus. If he'd spied a lock pick or crowbar in the hands of the person accessing the door, that would have confirmed their actions were suspect.

Without new input to go by, Boone had to go with his gut—which was still telling him something was off. When the door opened and the group with their load of Navy cases filed inside, he made his decision. He held the drone back until the last moment, then sent it darting forward. It slipped inside just before the door slid closed behind them.

Rising, Boone followed the pathway around, casing the area for another possible entrance point. If these people were up to no good, as he suspected, then he wanted a way in, and fast.

He kept one eye on the feed as he walked. Based on the visual the surveillance drone sent, the interior was as plain as the park's public area was colorful. The group pushed the cart past closed office doors, coming to a stop in front of a lift. Employees, cart, and drone entered, descending to the platform's lower level.

By the time they drew to a stop in front of a door labeled 'Laundry,' Boone had identified three possible entry points, and had a vague plan to try and duck through the open door after an employee exited.

His attention snapped fully to the feed as they began offloading the cases. When the first one opened, the sight that greeted the drone's feed had Boone's jaw tightening. His gut had been spot-on.

Now, what are you going to do about it? he asked himself…

8: AMUSEMENT PARK

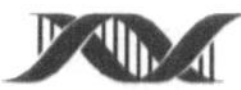

ENTRANCE

SEARCY SKY PARK

Gabe could hear the calypso music playing all the way out at the ticket booth. While they waited their turn in line, he looked around. From where they stood, he could see the tips of two tall arches rising on either side of the platform beyond the outer edge of its ES field. When he spied a figure floating up and then back down again, he realized these were the park's bungee rides.

The diving attraction was easy to spot; it was housed in a long, squat building just to the left of the entrance, the holodisplays splashed across its surface declaring Searcy 'the home of the Sudden Death'.

He noticed it had caught Thad's gaze. The newly minted SRU operator was studying it with a frown, one brow lifted.

"It does grab your attention," Gabe murmured as Asha handed out tickets to the bright-eyed young teens.

"So does a kick in the balls, *ami*. Can't say I'm fond of either one."

He smothered a smile at Thad's response. That was quickly forgotten when screams erupted from the crowd up ahead. Gabe tensed and Thad took a step forward, both turning toward the sound. Asha's head jerked up, eyes alert as she inserted herself between the girls and the direction the screams had originated.

After a beat, Thad relaxed and let out a low chuckle. "I think that was for the poor brave soul who just leapt to his 'death.'"

Gabe could hear the quotes Thad wrapped around that last word. The former Marine lifted a chin in the direction of the dive building.

"Wait for it. If I'm right, we'll hear it again any minute."

Sure enough, another roar erupted from the crowd as they trooped through the holographic turnstile and the SI running it matched their ID tokens with their tickets.

Gabe shook his head.

"What? No bungee in your future, hoss?"

Gabe shot him a jaundiced look. "I think I filled my adventure quota for the year this past week, thanks."

Thad barked a laugh. "You and me both, *ami*. C'mon, let's get ourselves one of them fancy umbrella drinks and pretend we're enjoying ourselves while keeping four teens out of trouble. Shouldn't be hard."

It was Gabe's turn to laugh. "You don't have any nieces or nephews, do you? Teens are trouble magnets. Just ask my sister."

Throwing Gabe a look that said she hoped he hadn't just jinxed their day, Asha turned to the girls and pointed in the direction of the water attractions. "What's first on the agenda? Lazy river or infinity pool? Or would you rather hang out by the beach?"

Thad appeared to give the question great weight, but it was clear to Gabe who held the real decision-making power.

"Beach!" cried one of the teens.

"It's where all the cool guys hang out," explained another.

"Well, there you go," said Thad, shooting an amused look Gabe's direction. "Lead on, *mes cheries*."

9: SPOTTED

EMPLOYEE ENTRANCE
SEARCY SKY PARK

Boone decided to confirm what he saw before he contacted anyone back on Ouray. The last thing he wanted to do was blow the lid off a legitimate operation. He imagined the odds of that were pretty low on the probability scale, but he was also well aware of the fact that he was a mere lance corporal. If such an operation *did* exist, he wouldn't be privy to it.

He also felt a bit foolish loitering beside the employees-only entrance but figured anyone who saw him there would assume he was waiting for a friend to get off work. The door finally opened and a woman in a park uniform carrying a load of towels stepped out. She gave him a friendly nod as she passed.

He waited until he was clear of her field of vision before launching himself toward the slowly closing door. He jammed his fingers into the opening just before it sealed, forcing the door back until the space was wide enough for him to slip through.

Luck was with him. The corridor inside was empty of any

onlookers, though he could hear voices sounding behind closed doors. Striding toward the lift with a confidence he didn't altogether feel, Boone passed by a line of offices, windows inset into their doors providing him with fast glimpses of the people inside.

Most were seated behind desks. Some were working with holodisplays. A few were gathered around tables, discussing stars knew what. Not a single person looked up as he crossed their field of view.

Boone left the quiet buzz of office chatter behind, eschewing the lift for a stairwell just beyond it, the entrance lit by the glowing red of a holographic exit sign. Treading softly, he descended the single flight to the door that led to the platform's lowest level. Pausing at the bottom of the stairs, he considered his options.

He had two remaining drones. Now might be a good time to launch another one. He let it loose, the drone handshaking with his wire in the same way the previous one had.

An ear pressed to the door revealed nothing; he couldn't hear a thing through the thick, fire-resistant metal. On a deep breath, Boone took the plunge, palming the door open and sending the drone through.

Boone split his attention between the two feeds, watching as the smugglers lifted the stolen ordnance and applied some sort of code to it that cracked their biolocks. That last became evident when they cycled each weapon on and off before transferring it to a new container.

The boxes were smaller than the Navy's ruggedized cases, with a far less distinctive profile. The logo for an adventure sports company was emblazoned on their sides, making them far less likely to catch anyone's eye, especially inside a theme park such as Searcy.

Boone scrubbed back through the feed from the first drone, paying close attention to the path the group had taken, reconciling it with the imagery from his second drone. Comparing the feeds told him they should be a few doors down an adjacent corridor. He could always have the first drone send its location, but he'd purposely ordered the thing to its lowest power setting. The feed it was trickling to Boone was low resolution and unobtrusive. A location ping could draw attention he'd rather not have.

He sent the second drone drifting down the empty hallway, bringing it to a halt right before the intersection. Slowly, it crept forward until its tiny sensor array just breached the cross corridor.

Boone considered what he was seeing. There *seemed* to be nothing there, and yet Boone couldn't accept that this was the case. Surely those reinforced containers held a supply of these same surveillance microdrones. They were ubiquitous within the Navy.

He straightened as a horrible thought occurred to him. Quickly routing his way through the drone's app, he came to the command menu that controlled its 'Identify Friend/Foe' protocol and shut it off. He only hoped he'd been fast enough…

* * *

Inside the laundry room, Petra's attention was drawn from the weapons she was transferring to a sudden movement at the door. Looking up, she saw a frown cross Delia's face.

"What is it?" she asked.

Delia tilted her head in a listening motion, eyes slitting almost shut as she considered what she'd just seen.

"There was a blip," she said, then stopped and shook her head. She began again. "I thought I saw a blip, but then it disappeared. The drone out in the hall isn't showing anything, so it must have been some sort of a glitch."

"What did it look like to you?"

"Well, for a second there, I could have sworn our surveillance drone intercepted a ping from another one. Did any of you turn one of those things on?" She looked sharply around at the three men who were loading the crates.

Kele lifted his hands in silent denial. Bobby glared. "We *had* to cycle the canisters to make sure the interlock and serial numbers were removed," the hacker retorted, "or did you forget the reason we're hanging out inside a laundry room with a bunch of dirty towels that smell like sweaty kids?"

Petra raised a calming hand and turned to Delia. "Could that have been what you saw?" she asked the other woman.

Delia scowled thoughtfully. "As fast as it came and went, I suppose it *could* have come from that. But I could've sworn the ping came from outside the room, not inside."

Petra considered the other woman's words. She motioned to Ike. "Go back out. Make your way up to the surface. Be very sure no one followed us here, got it?"

Ike nodded, grabbed a weapon, and headed for the door.

"And Ike…"

He turned at her words.

"If someone did, you know what to do."

* * *

Enough time had passed that Boone felt confident the drone had evaded detection. Moreover, he'd not seen any evidence the thieves were using their own drone for reconnaissance.

Sucking in a breath, Boone braced, and then stepped out of the stairwell. He tried to ignore the wet chafing of his PT shorts between his thighs and focused instead on approaching the intersection on silent feet.

He instructed the drone to do one last sweep of the corridor that led to the laundry room, and when it returned null, he stepped out into the hallway. He hadn't gone three steps before the laundry room doors snapped open.

Boone froze, but the sight of the weapon in the hand of the man who stepped through the door quickly galvanized him. He pivoted and went racing back the way he'd come.

The pounding of feet behind him told him the man was in pursuit. The sizzling sound of a pulsed laser strike just above his left shoulder indicated the man had reached the intersection.

He ducked into the stairwell, pulse hammering as he took the steps two at a time and burst into the upper-level hallway. The ringing of footsteps on metal treads had him pouring on the speed, his eyes riveted to his goal, the exit now mere meters away.

He reached the door and slapped at its controls, willing it to open. A round of gunfire smacked into the wall beside him, trashing the door's control panel and freezing it halfway open. A quick glance behind him showed the man had resumed running. Boone jammed his shoulder into the opening, forcing his way through— just as the man fired once more.

10: SHOTS FIRED

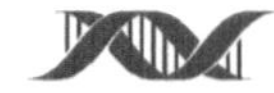

Saltwater Wave Pool

Gabe suppressed a smile as Asha tried once more to get her niece to join a water volleyball game.

"Why not give it a try?" The medic pointed to the net, hovering just above the waterline, and injected a cheerful tone into her words. "Just think how much fun you'd have."

Tatiana wrinkled her nose in distaste. "It's too hot."

Thad made a choking sound. Asha shot him a warning glare, which she then turned on her niece. "You're in the water. You won't get hot."

"But it's, like, *exercise*, Aunt Asha. And I need to relax and destress."

Thad had just brought his water to his lips. That last comment sent him into a fit of coughing, which had the teens turning to stare at him in alarm.

"You okay, Mister Severance?" one girl asked.

"Jus' … great… " he wheezed before another round of coughing hit.

Asha, on the other hand, knew exactly what had caused this. Her narrow-eyed look held no sympathy. Hand on hips, she pivoted back to the girls and expelled a slow breath through pursed lips like a balloon leaking air.

"Fine," she said, giving in. "We'll be over here if you need us for anything."

Marching past Gabe, she whacked Thad on the head as she collapsed into her deck chair.

"Nice recovery there, soldier," Gabe murmured as Thad straightened.

"*Destress,* she said." Thad's words were low and came out raspy from the water that had gone down the wrong way. He hid a grin behind his hand.

Gabe's lips twitched. "I'm thinking your definition of the word might be a bit different from theirs." He nodded in the direction of the wave pool, where four girls were pushing a mammoth float out toward the edge.

Thad sat back, eyeing the girls as they scrambled aboard, the inflatable lounger rocking gently on the waves. He looked up past the sky park's ES field and the cables that attached it to its tether. The sky above was dark and glittering with faint specks of light from ships coming and going from Beryl's orbital spaceport.

"Can't think of anything much more boring than just sitting around, doing nothing," he admitted. "Only time I've done that has been when I've been laid up after taking a hit on an op."

Asha snorted. "Even then, I had to strap you into the surgical suite so it could do its job."

Thad shifted and looked around as if the mere mention of inaction made him restless. Gabe knew the former Marine well enough by now to understand that idleness didn't suit him well.

Thinking now might be a good time for a distraction, Gabe stood and looked over at Asha. "I think I'll go stretch my legs. Want me to grab some snacks from the concession stand for the girls while I'm up?

Thad jumped to his feet. "I'll help."

Gabe managed to keep his face impassive. Lifting a brow, he asked, "Think I can't manage a few trays of food?"

Thad took his time pretending to size Gabe up. "Dunno 'bout that, with you bein' NCIC and all. Better to err on the side of caution."

Asha groaned and rolled her eyes. The exaggerated movement pulled a deep chuckle out of Thad. White teeth flashed in a dark face, and the deep brown eyes that met Asha's danced with amusement. "You know it's true, *cher*. Plus, who knows what hungry hordes this *special agent* might have to fight off to get to the front of the line."

Gabe fielded the jab good-naturedly. Slapping Thad on the shoulder—which he actually had to reach up to do, the man was so much larger—he said, "Come on, jarhead. We can't abandon the medic to the tender mercies of these teens for too long. That's considered hazardous duty."

Despite his words, Gabe had no issues with spending some time just wandering the sky park. By unspoken agreement, he and Thad strolled through the crowd, familiarizing themselves with Searcy's layout. Reconnaissance was second nature to both men, yet it was something they'd been unable to do with the girls around. Gabe found himself unwinding a bit now that he had a solid mental map of the structure in his mind.

He pointed to a concession stand that had a shorter line than most. "What do you think?"

"Looks as good as any," Thad replied, angling for the back of the line.

Fifteen minutes later, they'd shelled out an insane amount for two trays of sad-looking food. Thad looked doubtfully at the tray he carried and then over to the identical one in Gabe's hands.

"Looks like something printed from a cut-rate fabricator."

Gabe winced. He didn't disagree. "Think they got their hands on the formation bricks the Navy uses to print meal rats?" he half-joked.

"Dunno, *ami*. We can always hope the girls have never eaten meal rats—"

He broke off, head whipping around at the hard slap of shoes against ceramacrete. It was the kind of sound someone made when they were running flat out. Both men went on alert, bodies tensing and eyes scanning the crowd.

"There." Gabe pointed to a figure, moving fast through the mass of people. Where the crowd thinned, they could see a young man, dodging and jinking in a way that made it obvious he was being pursued.

"Shit just got real, hoss," Thad said in an undertone when they spotted the man chasing him. The glint of a weapon had Thad grabbing Gabe's tray and thrusting both at the nearest person in line. He took off, Gabe at his heels.

Gabe nodded to the man in front. "I'll take that one. You take the—"

He broke off as the man fired. The man in the lead either had the instincts of a wild animal fleeing a predator, or he was the luckiest bastard on the planet. He threw himself flat just as a round of flechettes tore through the air, shredding a display of floats behind him. Rolling to his feet with an adrenaline-fueled agility, he used the shredded air mattresses for cover. Colorful streamers fluttered to the ground behind the man as he disappeared into the brush that bordered the lazy river.

{That's no civilian, ami.} Thad's voice sounded in Gabe's head as he launched himself after the shooter. *{You see his dress? That's standard-issue Marine PT dress; don't ask me why he's wearing that in a sky park.}*

{Yeah, I saw.} Gabe chanced a look over his shoulder and saw that the man with the flechette had come to the realization that the hunter had just become the hunted. With a large and angry special operator bearing down on him, the man had wisely chosen to switch his target.

Thad casually reached up and ripped a metal sign advertising cold drinks off its hinges, wielding the makeshift shield like a Spartan at Thermopalye. The next time Gabe caught a glimpse of the man, Thad had already acquired a small collection of the tiny, vaned projectiles.

Gabe focused on his own quarry, pinging Asha with an update as he stalked the kid. If the guy had as much of a tactical head on his shoulders as he did pure gut instinct, Gabe figured he knew where the Marine was headed. Breaking into a run, Gabe wove through pedestrians, racing toward a foot bridge up ahead that crossed over the meandering water ride. He ignored the irritated shouts of people as he brushed past, intent on reaching the bridge before the other man.

He skidded down the short ceramacrete embankment on the bridge's far side and stilled, listening.

There. When he heard the slight rustling to his left, he knew he'd guessed correctly. He crouched beside the bridge's support beam and waited for the man to appear.

The guy was good. Gabe saw him before he heard him, and he was fairly certain the man wasn't using a cloud of audio chaff to disguise his movements. Gabe eased forward just as the man crossed in front of him.

With an almost preternatural sense of awareness—and absolutely no warning—the stranger pivoted, a metal pipe in his hands slicing through the air with deadly accuracy, right at Gabe's head.

11: SANDY BEACH

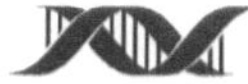

SALTWATER WAVE POOL

After the guys bailed on her—*as if anyone really comes to a sky park to eat the crap they serve*, she thought with some derision—Asha settled back in her deck chair, her eyes on the silhouettes of her niece and her friends.

She loved Tatiana, but that didn't mean she understood her. Asha's childhood had been very different from that of her niece. She'd loved sports and was competitive both on the field and in the classroom. Tatiana was more interested in the latest tri-D games.

Asha shook her head, still unable to believe none of the girls could be talked into playing water volleyball. All four preferred to lie on the float instead, immersing themselves in one of the hyperrealistic VR simulations the sky park offered.

She could hear the girls' reactions all the way across the sand-lined pool. The waves rocked them gently as they alternately squealed, shrieked, and giggled in reaction to whatever it was they were experiencing.

"Let me guess; you must be the 'fun aunt.'"

The voice came from Asha's left. She turned to face a man, seated in a deck chair identical to hers, parked beneath a beach umbrella. His legs were extended, ankles crossed, feet buried in the soft green sand.

He grinned over at her, and when she didn't immediately respond, his smile fell away, and he lifted a brow questioningly. Something about his expression looked familiar to Asha, though she could swear she'd never seen the man before. Belatedly, she realized she hadn't answered him.

"Well, I thought I was." She injected irony into her tone as she lifted a hand in the girls' direction. "But I guess my idea of fun and theirs are a bit different."

A twinkle appeared in his eyes. "Couldn't help but overhear that." He inclined his head toward the part of the pool where another group of teens were tossing the volleyball back and forth over the net. "My son wouldn't have turned down the extra numbers. Hard to get a decent game going if you can't recruit enough players."

Asha's lips twisted into a wry grin. "Can't say I didn't try." She shrugged. "I guess teens are different now. Or maybe it's just the way I was raised. Seems we were always outdoors, or at the range."

The man's other brow lifted to meet the first one. "Range," he mused. "You sound like my cousin."

His stare turned appraising, as if he was trying to figure out who she was and what place she held in the world. The look was one Asha had encountered often.

"Let me guess; career military?"

Asha knew it wasn't necessarily her body's build, although she was fit and had a whipcord lean frame that was so common with the Unit operators. In the era in which they lived, body modifications were the norm and easily accessible to all, which meant one could look as fit or as voluptuous as one wished. Asha was rather proud of the fact that hers had been achieved through sweat and hard work, though she had to admit the augments she received from the Navy hadn't hurt.

She realized that once more, she'd waited a beat too long to respond, and shook her head with a smile. "Yes. Sorry, guess I'm just a bit distracted today," she said, vowing silently to pay a bit more attention to the conversation.

The man sat back, a satisfied look on his face. "Thought so. You remind me of my cousin."

"Oh? She served?"

"Yep. Still does. She's a captain in Special Recon. You might've heard of her. Lane Reid?"

Asha had just taken a sip from her water bottle. The name of the woman who had been involved in the Q-Course, and more specifically, the Hell Walk she'd just completed, had her almost spitting the water out. She choked as she swallowed, mimicking Thad's earlier action.

The man shot her a concerned look. "You okay?"

She waved away his concern. Clearing her throat of the water that had gone down wrong, she rasped, "It's not that, it's just—" A wry smile settled over her face. It widened as she envisioned Thad's reaction when she told him. "Oh yeah, we know Captain Reid. Pretty well after last week, I'd say."

The man barked a laugh. "I should have guessed. I've seen some of my cousin's victims afterward. Hell Walk, right?"

She saluted him with her water bottle. "Got it in one."

He shook his head as he continued to laugh. His amusement caused Asha to narrow one eye at him.

"You seem awfully entertained by that thought," she accused with mock seriousness.

He grinned back at her, unrepentant. "Lane may have told me a thing or two about her tactics. She claims the process helps her accurately assess each candidate's skills. Personally, I think she just likes torturing people."

It was Asha's turn to laugh. "Thad would agree with you on that. She was the one who—" She broke off. "Sorry, OPSEC."

He nodded, seeming to understand that she couldn't say more, due to the need to maintain operational security. His chin jerked in the direction of the boardwalk behind them. "Is he one of the guys who just left?"

She nodded. "Uh-huh. The younger one." She spread her hands. "Tall, dark, massive shoulders?"

He chortled, eyes dancing in merriment, likely comparing the size of his petite dynamo of a cousin to the mountain of a man Asha had shown up with.

"Not asking for any details, but can you tell me if she messed him up good?"

"Oh, yeah. Thoroughly." She held out a hand. "Names Thacker, by the way. Asha Thacker. "

The man took it and shook. "Chris Reid." He dropped her hand and waved at someone over Asha's shoulder. She turned to see a woman walking their way.

"My wife, Amy," he explained.

Asha nodded a cordial greeting at the woman. As she settled in next to her husband, he turned to his wife and explained, "I just met another one of Lane's victims."

The woman turned and favored Asha with a sympathetic grimace. Asha waved it away.

"It's nothing we can't handle. Honestly, it's nice to know they're so rigorous during their assessment. I look forward to serving with her."

"You're tabbed?"

His smile widened at her nod.

"I am. So's Thad. He grumbles a lot, but it's all good-natured." Her eyes glinted mischievously. "And I can't wait to tell him who's here. He'll probably think Lane has him on surveillance. "

Amy snorted in amusement, the sound far more ladylike than it would have been if Asha had made it.

"I've heard special operators can be a bit paranoid." Reid's words faded into the background as Gabe's voice claimed Asha's full attention. She held up a hand and looked down as she concentrated on his words.

She could tell the special agent was running. Even though his words were mentally projected, Gabe's words sounded slightly rushed. He brought her up to speed on all that was going on.

{Be right there,} she responded. Looking back up, she caught a knowing look in Chris's eye.

"You need to go?" He jerked his chin in the direction of the float, where the girls lay. "We can watch over them for you if you like."

Asha considered that. Ordinarily, she'd never leave her niece in the care of strangers, but was a relative of an SRU leader, a storied SRU leader, really someone who fell into that category? When Gabe broke in again, this time telling her there had been shots fired, Asha shot to her feet, her decision made.

"Thanks." She pointed to the girls. "Two pinks, a tangerine, and a teal." Her words came out rapid and staccato-like as she named off the colors of the bathing suits the girls wore. "Teal is Tatiana; she belongs to me."

The man nodded. "Copy that," he said. All humor was gone, and there was a seriousness to his voice she hadn't heard before.

Something of her surprise must have shown on her face.

Amy smiled wryly. "I see Chris left a few details out, as usual. *Lieutenant Colonel* Reid is one of the commanders of Beryl's orbital base. I promise, you can trust him, and me, with your niece. We'll take good care of them. "

Asha blinked at that, spine straightening as the colonel added in a tone of sharp command, "Go. Do what you need to do. They'll be fine here." An invitation appeared on her overlay, the icon tagged with his ident. "If you need anything, ping me."

Asha nodded crisply. "Yes, sir." She paused and then used the ident to initiate a private connection.

{Shots have been fired. But it seems to be a lone incident and they feel confident they have a lid on things.}

He nodded his understanding, his eyes watchful as they swept the beach. *{Be sure to let me know if that changes.}*

Asha wheeled, bent to scoop up her shoes from where they lay in the sand beside her blanket, and then jogged up the hill to where the beach met the boardwalk.

12: TRACK AND ASSESS

Lazy River Area

Gabe caught the flash of metal slicing through the air and ducked, forearm coming up to deflect the blow. The pipe clanged hard against the bridge as Gabe reached for the Marine's wrist.

The younger man's eyes widened in recognition, though Gabe swore he'd never seen the kid before. Sucking in a deep, ragged breath, the young man released the pipe and stepped back, his eyes tracking nervously about, seeking his pursuer.

"My friend is hunting down the guy who shot at you," Gabe said. "Want to tell me what that was all about?"

Relief flickered in the kid's eyes. "Sir," he spoke rapidly and in a low undertone. "There's a smuggling ring on this platform. They have a shipment of Navy weapons they're moving. I accidentally stumbled upon it, and that guy caught me as I was headed out to find help."

Gabe eyed the man thoughtfully. The Marine seemed earnest enough... "You have proof of this?"

"Yes sir. Name's Brady, sir. Lance Corporal Boone Brady, with the 407th."

He thrust out his hand. Gabe took it, and the instant his fingers wrapped around the corporal's, a peer-to-peer request popped up on his overlay. Shunting it to a sandboxed partition he used when receiving case material from suspects, Gabe carefully accessed it.

Both eyebrows climbed into his hairline as he dropped the man's hand and looked him dead in the eye. "Seems like I owe you an apology, Corporal."

"From what I've overheard, they've infiltrated the park," Boone said. "I'm not sure who we can trust and have no idea how many of them are here. I counted five. There's a sixth they pinged over the wire… but there could be more."

As reports went, this one was succinct and organized. "Understood." Gabe thought for a minute, then nodded. "Good call, son. If I were them, I'd be tempted to try to plant someone inside park security, too."

When the corporal looked at him expectantly, Gabe realized he was waiting for instructions. He motioned toward the embankment. "Come on. Let's go see how my friend's doing."

Reaching out to Thad, he asked, *{You done yet?}*

* * *

Gabe's query pissed Thad off. Not at the NCIC agent, but at the shitbag Thad was chasing. Apparently, Gabe had no trouble bagging *his* target, while the *couyon* Thad hunted still evaded him.

It didn't take long for the man to realize his weapon was ineffective against Thad's shield. He switched tactics, upending every item in his path that wasn't anchored down. The impromptu obstacle course was fast becoming a pain in Thad's ass, extending a chase that should have lasted seconds. That was more time than he'd intended to invest in the *fils-putain*.

The man careened around a pile of fake boulders, and something—an innate sixth sense—stopped Thad from doing the same. He crouched low before launching himself forward into a roll, shield held over his head.

Sure enough, his quarry had been waiting, his finger on the trigger of his flechette. Also as expected, the man's aim had been higher than Thad's current position. Thad swept the man's legs out from under him with a quick twist of his hips. As he landed atop the guy, pinning him in place, his hand closed around the man's wrist, turning both hand and pistol back on itself. The flechette clattered to the floor, the odd angle snapping his wrist and wringing a cry of pain from the man. Not having anything to secure him with, Thad resorted to brute force. He brought his elbow down against the gunman's temple in a hard strike. He slumped, unconscious.

* * *

Gabe was just about to ping Thad again when a disgruntled mental voice came back on the line. *{Yeah, he's down. Had to bust out the elbow to get him to comply, though.}*

{You need ol' Asha to kiss it and make it better?} The medic asked sardonically. Then her voice turned crisp and businesslike. *{I grabbed some cable off that float display he shot all to hell. We can use those to restrain him. Old-fashioned, but it'll do the job.}*

{What about the other guy?} Thad asked. *{We need to restrain him, too?}*

{Negative,} said Gabe, and with a mental flip, brought the corporal in on the net. *{Corporal Boone Brady, meet Specialist/Medic Asha Thacker and Lieutenant Thad Severance, SRU. I'm Special Agent Alvarez. Folks, check his feed. He has a story you'll want to hear. We're headed your way.}*

13: SWAMPER

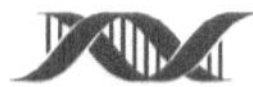

Park interior
Maintenance area

Jay was setting the final package when Petra's mental voice came across the connection.

{Ike's drawn some unwanted attention. Turn on the swamper.} Petra's voice was calm, but there was an underlying tension in her tone.

Jay sat back, package in one hand. *{Park security?}*

{No. Ike says it looks to him like some overeager Marine on his day off.}

With a low curse, Jay reached mentally for the app to activate the swamper. An icon popped into existence blinking its 'ready' status message. With a single command, the device would feed an overload signal into the platform's network.

After brief consideration, Jay dismissed the app, opting instead for an encrypted program that had cost a considerable amount of credits to acquire. The program routed the fake ID token of one Jay Henson through an identity-obscuring scrambler. Entering the code that would connect to the Mastai cartel, Jay waited for the person on the other end to answer.

Words were exchanged, swift and succinct, delivering the information the cartel's boss was waiting to hear. Disconnecting, Jay flipped on the swamper and looked down.

The package in Jay's hands was the last explosive device Petra knew about. There were four more held in reserve, plus one additional piece of equipment also liberated from the Navy case, waiting back at the hide.

With a swift look to ensure there was no one around to see, Jay set about executing a very different plan.

14: RECON

EXITING LAZY RIVER AREA

Footsteps fast approaching caught Gabe's attention. He ducked behind a nearby kiosk, signaling Boone to circle around the other side for an intercept. But the figure that came around the bend at a fast trot was a friendly.

"It's okay, she's one of ours," Gabe said. He stepped out onto the pathway and waved Boone over.

Asha spared Boone a curious look. "Planetary net's down." She hooked a thumb in Boone's direction. "This young pup you picked up know anything about that?"

Boone's reaction to her mention of the pubnet said that he did, indeed, know something.

"Spill it, Corporal," Gabe ordered.

Boone looked uneasy, as if somehow the communications blackout was his fault. "I overheard them saying they installed a swamper as insurance, in case they're discovered."

That would explain it. "Good thing our combat net's localized then, huh?" Gabe said. "Come on. Thad's waiting."

Thad was leaning against a palm tree, somehow making the tree look small by comparison. The big Cajun's arms were folded across his barrel chest to hide the weapon he held. It was aimed at a shadowed lump Gabe could barely see, tucked behind a nearby bush. Gabe suspected the Marine was trying to look casual, but with his size and build that was a near impossibility.

Thad straightened when they drew to a stop beside him. "I see you brought me a new recruit, *ami*." He turned to Boone. "What's your name, hoss?"

"Corporal Boone Brady, sir. Here on an afternoon of liberty."

Thad looked down at the younger man's PT shorts and shoes, his wet hair and t-shirt. "I can see that, son. You want to tell us why you were runnin' from my good friend here?"

Boone paused to let a small group of park patrons pass, then repeated what he'd told Gabe, his voice low. He told about the men and women who were dressed like park employees but whose movements had felt off. How he'd followed them, found the cache of weapons they were smuggling. How he hadn't been as stealthy as he'd thought.

"So someone caught you and you ran," Gabe said. "And that was when we saw you tearing through the park."

"Yes sir."

"You don't have to call me 'sir,' I'm with the NCIC. Them, on the other hand…" Gabe pointed to Thad and Asha, leaving it up to Boone to figure out who the two spec ops soldiers were.

Thad scowled down at his prisoner. "So this asshole had the presence of mind to send out a warning."

"Their inside man must have installed it," Gabe said. "I figured they would have planted someone in park security, but now it sounds like our ringer's in maintenance."

A considering look flashed across Asha's face. "Makes sense. Workers like that carry equipment around all the time. No one would question it."

That guilty look was on Boone's face again. "They weren't planning on using it unless they were caught," he said. "I… guess that means I'm to blame."

Thad's brows rose. "Didn't see you putting no gun to their heads and telling them to steal from the Geminate Navy, hoss."

Boone acknowledged Thad's comment with a nod, yet his expression remained uneasy.

Gabe looked over at the unconscious man Thad had tucked under the bush. "The question is, what message did he send before you clocked him, and do they realize they're dealing with more than just the person he was chasing?"

Thad stroked his chin thoughtfully. "I hear what you're saying, *ami*. Guess there's no way to know." He looked down, using his foot to roll the guy onto his back. "None of us came here expecting a fight. None of us is carrying, either. I'm not counting my knife, or this pansy-ass thing." He looked down with some disdain at the flechette in his hands.

Asha reached for it. "If it offends you that much, I'll take it off your hands."

Thad pulled back. "I didn't say it was useless, *cher*. The bad guys have good guns. This here'll work just fine as my gun-gettin' gun."

Asha hid a smile. "Mm-hmm. That's what I thought." She turned to assist Boone, who had liberated one of the cables from her hand to secure the prisoner. She stopped, a surprised look on her face. "Well, now. That's a nice surprise."

Gabe followed her gaze, to see that the man was already bound, Boone tying off the cables with a practiced ease.

Thad had noticed, too. "Not bad, hoss. Where'd you learn that?"

Boone sat back on his heels. "My family owns a ranch up north, sir, where the headwaters and the Swan Mountains meet. We all took turns riding the herd." He shrugged as he stood. "Fences go down, predators break through. Sometimes the things you have close at hand aren't high tech. You learn to adapt."

Thad grunted, but Gabe could tell he was impressed. "I'm assuming by the way you were runnin', you're not carrying, either?"

Boone shook his head. "No, sir. Only things I have are these." He dipped into the still-damp pocket of his PT shorts and pulled out a cylinder and a small disk. The look Asha shot him caused the young man to redden with embarrassment.

"What did you intend to do with a LockPik and a canister of surveillance drones on a civilian platform, Corporal?" she asked sternly.

"It's not what you think, ma'am," he said, back straightening in response to her tone. "I was inventorying gear when my platoon mates lassoed me into coming up here. I must've shoved it into my pocket instead of setting it down without realizing it."

That caught Gabe's attention. "Platoon mates. How many? Can we count on them to help?" he asked.

Boone's expression turned wry. "Ramirez, yes. Davila, probably. If we can reach them. I tried earlier. Both their comms are set to do not disturb."

"Okay, then." Thad blew out a breath and looked around. "This *couyon* drew a lot of attention with the mess he made while I ran him down. I'm surprised security's not all up in our chili, wanting to know what's going on."

Asha's lips twitched at her teammate's colorful phrase. "Well, since we don't know if they've been infiltrated, I vote we move out."

"Agreed," Gabe said. "Let's split up, see if we can run these guys down." He looked at Boone. "You know where they are?"

"Last I saw, they were sorting their shipment down in the lower level of the Employees Only section. There's a shuttle that's supposed to pick them up, but they never said when it's scheduled to arrive. They could be on the move."

Asha turned to Thad. "How do you want to handle this once we locate them? Since the pubnet's down, we can't call for reinforcements."

"We could send a shuttle far enough downrange to get past the swamper's influence," Gabe suggested. "We're not armed for a takedown. Plus, there are civilians to consider."

Thad turned to Boone. "What are we up against? You see the kind of weapons they have? P-SCARs?"

The young man's jaw tightened. "Yessir. The crates have P-

SCARs, CUSPs, frag grenades, and stickies. Hell, I even saw a RAU-19 railgun in one of them."

Asha gave a low whistle. CUSPs weren't lethal, but the ultra-short pulses of plasma they fired could paralyze, flash-blind, or debilitate, depending on the weapons' setting. As for the grenades and railguns…

Thad's gaze landed on Gabe, his expression unreadable. He inclined his head a fraction in Boone's direction. *{He a liability or an asset?}* he sent privately over the combat net.

Gabe sent him a subtle nod. *{Kid's got good instincts. You should see him fight.}*

Thad lifted his chin. *{Good. I'll take him.}* He turned to Boone. "We break into teams. One scouts the park, the other tries to get inside. First one to spot these *couyon* sings out."

Gabe motioned to the medic. "How about Asha and I find a way inside and leave the public space to you two?"

Thad gave an easy shrug. "That's cool." He clapped Boone on the shoulder. "Boone Brady, looks like you're with me."

15: CONTACT

Gabe and Asha slowed as they came to the cluster of buildings at the platform's core that was arranged to look like a quaint, small-town square.

Asha turned to Gabe. "You go left, I'll go right?" she suggested, then nodded to the other side of the square. "We can meet up on the other side."

He gave her a quick nod, and the two parted to scout the area. He pushed his way into the crowd, eyes seeking the landscaped pockets between buildings for potential access points. It took a while and involved negotiating his way around various obstacles, like kiosks offering funnel cakes and kids licking dripping cones.

Twenty minutes later, they met up on the other side to compare notes. Gabe had counted six different entrance points. Asha's count matched his.

"So what's our best candidate?" he asked.

The medic tilted her head. "I think the one by the lavs offers the most cover, but with all the drinks being served on this platform, that's a busy place." Amusement lit her eyes at that last comment.

Gabe's mouth quirked and he nodded toward a mother swiping a napkin across her protesting child's face. "And kids with sticky fingers."

She laughed. "Copy that."

They timed their approach to the employee door during a brief lull in foot traffic. Asha was right; once they were in position, the faux boulders shielded them from being seen by passing pedestrians.

She studied the door's access panel and then shot him a questioning look. "You have anything that'll get us inside?"

He shrugged. "I could try my NCIC credentials. Some manufacturers include us in with other federal organizations in their law enforcement override codes."

Asha stepped aside. "It's all yours."

Gabe pressed a hand against the door's sensor. There was a momentary pause, followed by a click, and then the door slid open.

"Nice," Asha commented as they slipped through and began traversing the long hallway. "It never would have occurred to me to try my military ID on one of those things."

Gabe shot her a wry look. "When the NCIC is called in to investigate a crime, sometimes it's done on Navy premises but often, it's not." He shrugged. "Let's just say flashing a warrant doesn't always open doors for us. Sometimes, we need a little backup. You have your everyday carry; we have ours."

Asha nodded her understanding. Her head came up as somewhere down the hallway a lift chimed. Over the low murmur of voices inside closed offices, they could hear the tread of several feet coming toward them.

Gabe touched her elbow and motioned toward the nearest door. Asha reached it first. It slid open to reveal a storage closet, filled with plenty of things to block them from view. They ducked inside.

Grabbing the nearest object that would work as a wedge, Gabe used it to prop the door open while Asha shut off the lights. The medic crouched in the shadows behind a stack of boxes. Gabe joined her, and they waited to see who approached.

{*Could be employees,*} Asha murmured.

Gabe shook his head. {*Too many, and too quiet.*}

Four figures strode past, each one pushing a dolly piled high with boxes.

{*Dammit.*} Asha's voice held a frustration that matched his own. She, too, had spied the bulge of weapons in their clothes. The weapons were concealed, but all four were carrying.

{*Even with the element of surprise, there's no guarantee we can take all four in this narrow space without one of them getting off a shot,*} she said.

{*Agreed. It'll be easier to pick them off, one by one, out in the park,*} he responded. {*I'll update Thad.*}

16: ON THE MOVE

SKY PARK GROUNDS

After Gabe and Asha left, Thad turned and motioned for Boone to follow. Boone kept pace with the dark-skinned operator and tried to observe the man without being obvious about it.

After a moment, curiosity won out. "You're Special Recon, right?"

Thad slid a sidelong look his way. "Where'd you get that idea?"

Boone returned to his visual sweep of the park. "The bartender pointed you out last night at the Thirsty Whale. All three of you were there."

He looked back over at Thad when he heard a low chuckle. "That's Connor," the man explained. "Retired from the Unit a few years back. Owns the place. Let me guess; you'd just come off deployment and looked a bit lost. He has a soft spot for greenies."

Boone tried not to bristle at the man's tone, but some of his reaction must have telegraphed itself to the older man. "No shame in that, Corporal. Everyone starts out green. It's what you do from that point on that counts. Only person you're competing with is yourself." Abruptly, he changed the subject. "You said they'll head for where the shuttles land, out front?"

Boone blinked, and then his brain caught up. He began to nod, but then considered the question. "I… don't know. I don't recall seeing a loading dock anywhere topside when we arrived. There must be a belowdecks shuttle pad we should be looking for instead."

The big man tapped the side of his head and gave him an approving look. "Now you're thinking."

They spent the next fifteen minutes striding quietly through the park, navigating through thatched kiosks that sold everything from stick candy to hats bearing the Searcy Sky Park logo to a bungee-jumping stuffed bear, wearing its own tiny, replica high-altitude suit.

Up ahead, there were more of the same—various service kiosks, some renting canoes and floats, others renting time with remote-controlled drones. These last, visitors could use to capture vids of friends and family as they rode the Sudden Death, plunging toward the ocean, twenty-five kilometers below.

They'd just come to an open area at the center that offered seating for the evening light show when the special agent's voice sounded on the combat net.

{Four traffickers just exited the employee area, pushing maglev dollies. Looks like they've got the goods parceled out and they're transporting them. We're following at a distance.} What came next were succinct descriptions of the four, plus what Gabe had seen of their payload.

{Copy. We'll be on the lookout.}

* * *

Petra pulled her three compatriots over to the side where the walkway widened to accommodate a park bench that sat unused. They came to a stop in the shadow of a tall, spreading tree. She glanced around; they were alone.

"Okay, then," she said in a low voice. "You know the drill. Nice and easy does it. No one working for a sky park vendor's going to be on fire to get his delivery back to his ship. Blend in. Smile at the brats in the stupid hats with cotton candy smeared all over their faces. Got it?"

"What about Ike?" There was a slight tremor to Bobby's voice, and fear lurked in the back of his eyes as he asked the question.

Bobby had done a hell of a job during the past hour, breaking past the trapped key interlocks so the team could launder the weapons. Now, they were operating outside Bobby's wheelhouse. Worse, this next leg of the journey required he step out on his own.

"He'll be fine," Petra said, ignoring the dark look Delia shot her way. "He won't ping us until he's taken care of the guy who was sniffing around."

Behind Bobby, Delia's brows rose disbelievingly. Petra ignored the woman. Now was not the time to get into what might have happened to Ike.

"You did a great job on all the stuff in these boxes." She patted him on the shoulder. "This last part is a breeze. Just a nice stroll through an amusement park. Act like you belong here and no one's going to stop you. Okay?"

The man jerked his head in a nervous nod. Petra smothered her frustration. It was obvious that no amount of encouragement would assuage his fear, so she reverted to her brisk, no-nonsense tone.

"All right, then. Bobby, you take the most direct route back to the shuttle. Head on out; we'll be a few minutes behind you."

She waited, looking at him expectantly. With a start, the man moved, his pace a bit too quick to be called leisurely

Beggars can't be choosers, she reminded herself. *This is the best he can give. Deal with it.*

She swallowed a sigh and waited until he was far enough away so he couldn't overhear.

"Yes, we have to assume someone got the best of Ike." She addressed the comment to Delia. "Look, whoever he is, he can't call for help with the swamper in place. Plus, we have Jay on the inside. He'd warn us if anything went south."

"So, we're just going to let Ike hang?" Delia's arms were crossed.

Petra shot her a quelling look. "It won't do Ike any good for us to be caught with the merchandise. Let's get this to the dock and then we'll look for Ike. Okay?"

Both Kele and Delia nodded in reluctant agreement.

"Okay, then. We split up in case security is looking for us. Sing out if you think you've been spotted. Kele, take the lazy river path. Delia, head for the town center shops. I'll take the walkway that swings around back, by the beach and the saltwater pool. Questions?"

They shook their heads. Without another word, the three broke apart.

None of the three noticed the two figures crouching behind the dense row of shrubbery behind a park bench, a few meters away.

* * *

{Be advised; they've split up. Repeat, targets have split up.}

When Gabe's report came through, Thad shot Boone a questioning look. The Marine gave a slight nod.

{Copy,} Thad responded.

He and Boone stepped out of the flow of traffic when the sidewalk widened up ahead, spilling out into the large town square. Thad did a slow visual sweep, stopping at the tall building that sat in the center of the square. It was made to look like an Old Earth tower, from a continent named Europa…

Or was that Europe? The thought flitted idly through the back of his mind as he studied it.

Boone must have followed his eyeline. *{That might come in handy if we need an overwatch,}* the young man offered.

{If it's not one hundred percent façade, it might,} Thad allowed.

Dismissing the building, he focused on the throngs of people passing by. Everywhere he looked there were kids. Some had balloons bouncing along in their wakes, others wore whimsical hats, crafted by ActiveFiber carnival artists.

Maglev strollers floated past, with toddlers in various stages of activity or exhaustion; some chatted animatedly while others cried for treats their haggard parents refused to give them.

And then a man in a black shirt, walking slightly faster than was strictly warranted for his occupation strode into view, pushing a dolly stacked high with boxes labeled 'Adventure Sports.'

Half a dozen meters behind, and on a parallel path, another man followed in his wake.

17: CONTACT

Boone saw them at the same time Thad's hand snaked out and snagged his arm. The special operator gave a discreet jerk of his head, indicating Boone should follow, and then ghosted behind a cluster of people.

{Two in park shirts, one pushing a maglev dolly, three o'clock.}

{Yeah, I saw.} Boone followed behind, risking a fast glance over his shoulder right before Thad ducked around the corner of a tiki hut.

{Looks like they're headed toward the front entrance,} Boone sent. *{Wherever that loading dock is, there must be access somewhere nearby.}*

The two men they tracked were on separate but parallel foot paths, though the one who trailed the man with the dolly kept pace at a distance. It was almost as if the one was shadowing the other. Why, Boone couldn't begin to guess.

Thad motioned to the one on the left. *{That one's mine. You get the other one. Swift and silent if possible, but do **not** let him leave this* *platform with those boxes. Copy?}*

The operator slipped away without waiting for a reply.

Boone turned to follow his mark, keeping as many people as he could between himself and his target. It wasn't too difficult. Park entertainers were everywhere.

He dodged a woman selling holographic pets. The area around her booth exploded with butterflies and faeries, miniature unicorns and griffins, all cavorting in the air and scattering ephemeral pixie dust as they went.

A caricature artist crafting instant holos of park-goers appeared in front of him, offering to craft his portrait. Boone sidestepped without comment, his eyes not leaving the box-laden dolly.

The only time he broke eye contact was to spare an occasional look around him for something, anything, he could use as a weapon. Passing a canoe rental stand at the entrance to the lazy river, he paused when he caught sight of the sturdy paddles that were tucked inside.

That'll do. He paused to lift one from the canoe on the end. His action caused the SI monitoring the stand to squawk a warning at him. Impatiently, he pushed his ID at the rental token that popped up on his overlay, quickly paying for half an hour's rental.

A glance over at the thief told Boone that the SI's protests had caught the man's attention. They made brief eye contact before Boone's gaze swept on past. He turned sideways and let his hand rest on the canoe he'd just rented, a bland expression on his face. He bent his head, tossing a quick look at his target. Though the man was no longer looking at him, he'd sped up and was now glancing nervously around.

Boone let out a soft *dammit*, pushed away from the canoe, and then sent a quick, *{I think I might have been made}* to Thad.

{Best make your move, then, hoss.}

Boone's gaze landed on his target once more and then tracked ahead of him, plotting the man's most likely path to the sky park's entrance. He noticed almost absently that the mental line he'd drawn mimicked a cable that flew overhead.

A crazy idea began to form. He continued to follow the man at a distance, but now he split his attention between the man with the dolly and the cable above him. Far away, he could see the cable affixed to the crenellated wall fronting the sky park. Closer in, it was attached to a support beam. It was this that held his interest.

That could work, he mused as he thought it through. He jogged over to where the support beam thrust skyward from the platform's base, artfully hidden behind a patch of landscaping. His eyes tracked up the beam, stopping where a small platform jutted out, a dozen meters in the air.

The average person habitually defaulted to the two horizontal axes of motion they were used to navigating, and often forgot to look up. From what he'd seen of this crew, they weren't especially well-trained; he'd be willing to bet this guy wouldn't be looking for trouble from above, either.

Before Boone began his ascent, he ran his hands over the beam until they landed on what he'd been hoping to find: a pair of carabiners, conveniently clipped around one of the beam's handholds, left behind by the park's maintenance crews. Helping himself to the small metal loops, Boone hoisted himself aloft, using hand- and footholds molded into its sides. Climbing with the canoe paddle was a bit of a challenge, but Boone had plans for the thing, so he powered through.

Stepping out onto the small metal-grated surface, Boone crouched to test the cable, where it looped through a sturdy ring just level with his knees. Then his gaze swept the park, fixing on his target once more.

By hooking one of the carabiners around the cable and the other around the center of the paddle, Boone figured he could turn it into a makeshift zipline. The only issue he saw with his plan was the stop at the other end.

Boone looked down at the man once more. He'd guessed right; the smuggler kept looking over his shoulder, but not once did he look up. Boone sat on the platform's edge, connected the carabiners, and readied himself to take the dizzying plunge.

He froze when movement caught his eye.

18: TAKEDOWN

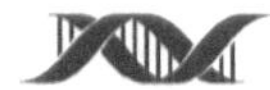

SKY PARK GROUNDS

Had the person atop the clock tower been looking in Boone's direction, the young Marine's intent would have been intuited and the man pushing the dolly warned. As things stood, it was the sky park's entrance that held Jay's undivided attention instead.

Wow, that was fast!

A quick look at the timestamp had Jay blinking in shock. For the Mastai cartel enforcers to have arrived this quickly, they must have been very close, indeed. That suggested Jay's preliminary heads-up had been taken seriously.

The imposter took two steps to the left to get a better view, anticipation bringing a smile.

I love it when a plan comes together.

Jay followed the enforcers' progress, waiting until they had progressed deep into the park and had begun canvassing the area before contacting Petra on a private channel. There was now zero possibility that the woman's small gang of thieves could avoid contact with the newcomers.

{Hey boss,} Jay infused urgency into the words *{We got company.}*

{Who?} Petra's voice was sharp.

{Enforcers. They're Mastai.}

Jay had to give the woman credit for inventive swearing.

{How many?} she demanded.

{Only three.} The lie came easily, cutting the numbers by half.

{Are they carrying?}

Jay leaned forward, carefully studying the newcomers. From the bulges in their clothing, the answer to that question was a resounding yes.

But how best should I respond? Surely, she'd realize I was lying if I said they weren't armed...

For Petra to continue accepting the information being fed to her, Jay knew the lies had to be seasoned with bits of truth.

{I can see bulges in their clothing, so yes, I'd say they're carrying concealed. Looks to me like you're more than a match for them.}

The silence from the other side made Jay wonder if that last bit was oversold.

Then Petra's voice returned. *{Understood.}* A map of the park appeared over the channel. *{Drop pins on their locations. And keep us apprised where they're headed.}* She cut the connection.

Jay chewed on the inside of a cheek and thought about which enforcer locations to add. Finally, with a mental shrug, three dots appeared on the map. That part of the plan firmly in place, Jay dismissed the enforcers, bending to scoop up the four explosives that had been held in reserve.

Casting a last, wistful look around, the thought sprang to mind, *Damn, but I wish I could stay and watch it all unfold...*

Vowing to return as soon as this final task was complete, Jay hastily headed for the tower roof exit.

* * *

Thad had a difficult time staying out of his target's visual range.

Taller than most adults, the former Marine towered over the kids who made up more than fifty percent of the park-goers.

It helped that the man was more focused on the smuggler pushing the dolly than he was anything else. When Thad's target tensed and ducked behind a display of balloons, Thad followed the man's eye-line to see what had elicited the action.

The thief carting the stolen weapons had paused to look behind him, as if to ensure he wasn't being followed.

Interesting… Now, why would you hide from your own team?

The obvious answer was that he wouldn't.

*Who **are** you, ami?*

One thing was now crystal clear: neither man was a legitimate park vendor.

When Boone's *{I've been made}* came a beat later, Thad knew he had to make his move. He was under no illusions that he looked anything other than what he was: a deadly Unit operator. If his target saw Thad coming, he'd respond viscerally to the threat. Whether the response would be fight or flight remained to be seen.

Thad knew there would be witnesses; the sky park was simply too crowded for the situation to dictate otherwise. But he couldn't let the opportunity pass to apprehend the man. Grabbing a water pod from a nearby concession kiosk, Thad fired it directly at the man's head.

He didn't wait for it to connect. Legs pumping, he raced to relocate so he'd be outside the man's field of view when he turned. He heard the slap as the drink landed. The fact that no startled exclamation issued from his target as he took the hit told Thad his opponent understood the need to maintain operational silence. Only professionals would react in such a way.

Coming to a stop behind a kiosk that sold colorful lanyards, Thad turned in time to see the man's head snap around, seeking the source of the attack. There would never be a better opportunity.

Thad pulled his Blackout from his shorts. When the foldable blade met his hand, it synced with his wire. A mental command unlocked the knife; the flick of a wrist snapped it open. He moved quickly, closing the distance in three long strides. Snaking an arm around the man's neck, Thad put the man in a rear choke hold.

His opponent reached up a hand, fingers digging into Thad's forearm, while his elbow rammed repeatedly into Thad's gut, seeking to break his hold. Thad brought his blade up and pressed it against his neck. The man stilled.

"Careful there, hoss, or I rearrange your carotid for you," Thad growled into the man's ear.

As predicted, their scuffle caught the attention of others. With a knife now in play, Thad heard a man's angry shout. A woman gasped in alarm. Ignoring them all, he dragged his opponent around one of the park's many faux stone walls. The man began to struggle again. Thad let the carbyne blade's sharp edge bite into his flesh.

He dropped to his knees behind the ceramacrete wall, pulling the man down with him. He increased pressure to the choke, and within seconds, the man was out.

The shouts swelled in volume, and Thad heard a man's voice call out, "Over there!"

He rolled to a crouch, quickly sheathing his blade when he saw the park visitor had flagged down a security guard. The man was closing on his position, weapon drawn. Thad carefully raised his hands, palms spread to show he was unarmed.

He knew there was a possibility this guy might be an accomplice. He sincerely hoped this one was legit, and then gave himself a swift mental kick in the pants for the stray thought.

Riiiight, idiot. Hope is not a plan, he reminded himself.

When the man motioned to him with his CUSP and ordered him to his feet, Thad let out a silent breath and rose.

"Lieutenant Severance, Special Reconnaissance Unit." His words came out staccato and fast. He ignored the growing crowd of onlookers. "I need your assistance."

The guard stared back at him for a beat, surprise written on his face. It was apparent this was the last thing the man had expected to hear, and Thad wondered briefly what kind of drunken altercations he was used to defusing.

When he hesitated, Thad took a step that placed the man inside his reach. When the man didn't react, Thad's suspicion crystallized into certainty. This man was legit park security. Bonus: he had no formal military training. With a quick motion, he disarmed the guard.

The man's reaction told Thad he was seconds away from wetting his pants. Thad lifted a cautionary hand. "Easy, there. I'm one of the good guys."

He looked down at the weapon. A fast assessment confirmed it was nonlethal, the civilian equivalent of the CUSPs the Geminate Navy used. It would do the job. Thad dialed it to its strongest setting, and then fired the CUSP at the downed man, who had just begun to stir.

There were murmurs and gasps from the crowd as the weapon discharged, but Thad ignored those, too. He turned back to the guard and handed the weapon back to the man, butt-first.

The look of consternation on the guard's face would have been comical under any other circumstances. "Why'd you do that?" he sputtered. "That'll—"

"—Knock him out for half an hour?" Thad interrupted. "I know. That's why I did it."

Silently, he waggled the CUSP at the guard, whose head jerked from the man Thad had just shot to stare down at the weapon. When he took it, Thad kept his hand extended, palm out. At the guard's questioning look, he said patiently, "My credentials."

Belated understanding crossed the man's face. Holstering the weapon, he shook Thad's hand, the physical contact initiating a peer-to-peer connection across their wires.

An icon floated on Thad's overlay, identifying the man as Ronald Jones, Searcy Sky Park. "Thanks for the assist, Mister Jones." Stepping back, he motioned to the unconscious man. "The Navy could use your help…"

"I, uh, sure," the man stammered. "What is it you need?"

"What's your security protocol for station emergencies? Does Searcy have shelter-in-place spots set up for its visitors?"

The man blinked in confusion at the unexpected direction of Thad's question. "Well yes, but—"

"Good. I need you to contact your superiors and begin an orderly evacuation of the park to its safe zones."

"But… why? This is just—"

Thad jabbed a bladed hand in the direction of the unconscious man. "This man is one of six people who are using Searcy as an intermediate location to launder a cache of stolen weapons." He lowered his chin and stared the man square in the eye. "Do you hear what I'm saying?"

The guard swallowed hard once more and nodded, but it was clear to Thad that the man didn't get it. "While the Geminate Navy's going to be very concerned about the lives of civilians, I can't say the same for a bunch of gun runners. Can you?"

Finally, the man's eyes widened in comprehension. "But… if you're chasing the gun runners, then why are you dressed like that?" he stuttered.

Thad barely managed to keep the exasperation he felt off his face. "I'm not here in an official capacity," he explained with as much patience as he could muster. "I was here on a day off. I stumbled upon their operation. Since it's Navy munitions they're trafficking, and since I'm with the Navy, it's my duty to do something about it."

"Oh, of course. I see." The man blinked in rapid succession, still struggling to reconcile what he'd just seen.

He looked off into the distance, the slightly vacant expression that fell upon his face a visible cue that he'd initiated contact with his superiors. Thad hoped the man had enough clout to get sky park security to agree to what he'd requested.

He'd just leaned down to check the man he'd subdued one last time when a flash of movement caught his eye. Looking up, he saw Boone crouching on a platform high in the air, a canoe paddle in one hand.

Now, there's a sight you don't see very often…

Shoving to his feet, he ordered, "Do *not* let this man out of your sight. He begins to stir, you stun him again. You got me?"

He gave the man his best Marine glare when he didn't respond fast enough. After receiving the guard's hastily stammered agreement, Thad let his glare sweep over the crowd of onlookers. They quickly caught on they weren't welcome here any longer.

He didn't wait for them to fully disperse. He took off at a run in Boone's direction. He rounded a kiosk just in time to hear Boone's,

{LT? We have company.}

19: NEW THREAT

MAINTENANCE PLATFORM

Boone fervently wished for a scope that would magnify his view beyond what his augments allowed. It would be nice to have more clearly defined evidence to pass along to the lieutenant, rather than just a handful of suspicions and gut instinct.

Slitting his eyes nearly shut, he let his vision defocus to better take in overall patterns of movement. His lips tightened as he realized what had caught his eye. Two small groups of people were moving deliberately yet discreetly through the crowd in a manner that screamed 'predator.' The clothing they wore suggested they *could* be sky park employees… but something about their dress felt off.

The glimpses he caught through the crowd suggested they'd come to the sky park prepared for a fight. What he didn't know yet was the 'who' and the 'why.' Did the gun runners call in reinforcements, or was he witnessing some sort of internecine conflict brewing?

The newcomers scanned the throng, clearly looking for

someone. As they came closer, Boone could make out slight bulges in their clothing. As a woman dragging a child behind her tried to stop one of them to ask directions, he brushed her off.

That settled it. *Definitely **not** Searcy, then.*

It was time to contact the lieutenant and give him a heads up.

{LT, we have company. New contact, two groups.}

He'd seen Thad running toward him. At his words, the Unit operator stopped and looked up.

{Not sure I want to know why you went high, Corporal, but it sounds like it's a good thing you did. Who are they, how many, and any idea who they're after?}

Boone had been asking himself the same questions. *{Definitely not friendlies,}* he replied. *{Two groups of three each, all armed. One's at your eleven o'clock about half a klick away and closing on your position. Another's headed my way. The others have dispersed and are moving through the park.}*

Thad hummed thoughtfully. *{Those headings are pretty specific. Are they reinforcements?}*

{No, I don't think so.} Boone drew the words out as he thought it through. *{The only person these gun runners think is onto them is me. I doubt I rate this much firepower.}*

Thad snorted in amusement, and Boone saw him pivot and race back toward the man he'd taken down. *{Got an idea. If that security guard has a ziptie on him, I can use it to mask this couyon's signal.}*

Thad came to a stop in front of the guard and Boone saw the two men engaged in brief discussion. The guard rummaged around in a pocket and pulled out a thin piece of film, which he handed over to the lieutenant.

{Got it. Okay. Let me know if this gets their attention…} Thad slapped the ziptie on the man's neck.

The effect was immediate. The man approaching Thad's location came to an abrupt halt. He appeared to mentally confer with the others before breaking into a fast jog.

{Yessir, that got his attention. He stopped, but now he's sped up, and headed straight for you,} Boone reported. *{The others are*

moving faster, too.}

At Boone's words, the Unit operator bent and scooped the insensate man up into a fireman's carry. *{Something fishy's going on, if they noticed when he dropped off the grid. Going to relocate this fils-putain so they can't find him. Keep me apprised of their movements.}*

20: ENFORCERS

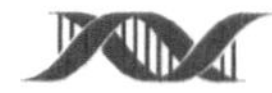

MAINTENANCE PLATFORM

Boone acknowledged Thad's last order, his attention split between the newcomers and the man Thad had told Boone to apprehend. It was quickly becoming apparent that one of the men from the second group was closing on Boone's man. He'd have to act soon or lose the opportunity altogether.

Gabe's voice cut into his observations. *{Corporal, can you share your optical feed with us, so I can get a better look at these guys?}*

{You think you might have an idea who we're up against?} Asha asked.

Boone could hear the speculation in the special agent's voice when he replied. *{Possibly. This whole setup's a bit unorthodox. I'd thought initially that these were just small-time thieves, but what if they're part of a larger organization, one that wouldn't ordinarily go after the Navy?}*

{You mean organized crime? And these new players represent some sort of internal police action?}

{Could be,} Gabe told her.

{But sir... that doesn't track,} Boone argued. *{None of the big, organized crime groups is dumb enough to hit a military shipment this close to a Navy outpost like Ouray. They must know we'd come down hard on them.}*

{If my guess is right, this wasn't sanctioned. Somehow the parent organization got wind of it and has sent a team to shut them down,} the agent replied. *{To be honest, if it weren't for the civilians, I'd be inclined to let them fight it out, and then come in and mop up afterward.}*

{You mean, let them thin the herd for us?} Asha's voice held a trace of sarcasm. Her tone quickly turned serious when she added, *{Seconding that part about the civilians, particularly the children. They open fire in here, someone could get real dead, real quick.}*

Boone dropped his feed to the combat net, and triggered it to play.

{Hold on,} Gabe interrupted. *{Roll that back. Stop. Right there. See that guy in the middle? Dark here, shades, taller than the rest. I think...}* His voice faded as he studied the feed. *{Okay, you can resume.}*

Boone reverted the feed to what he was now seeing, live. The figure turned and they got a clear view of the man's face.

{Oh, yeah. That's one of the enforcers for the Mastai cartel. Looks like we've got some rogues on our hands.}

{Mastai? Don't they usually deal with more high-end stuff, like rare metals and fine art?}

It was Asha who answered Boone's question.

{That's right,} she confirmed. *{They're into the white-collar crimes. I can see where they'd want to nip this in the bud before it gets out of hand. Bonus: disciplinary action not only stops them from branching into the kind of criminal activity the cartel doesn't want, but it'll serve as a warning to the rest.}*

Gabe voice was thoughtful when he replied. *{You know... A report crossed my desk recently that suggests Mastai might be going legit.}*

{You think this is evidence someone within his cartel thinks he's

gone soft?} Asha asked.

{I suppose it's as good a reason as any,} he replied. Gabe's tone turned brisk, and Boone could tell the man was in profiler mode. *{Okay none of these people will want to draw too much attention to themselves. That's the good news. Problem is, what their definition of drawing attention and ours is might be completely different —}*

Their voices faded into the background as Boone's attention swerved sharply back to the situation developing below. He tensed when he saw a gaggle of park visitors on a zero/zero intercept with the thief and his pursuer.

{I've got a cluster of kids headed right for my two targets,} he interrupted tersely.

Asha let out an expletive. *{I'm too far away. Won't make it there in time. You?}*

Boone could see the answer before Gabe spoke. *{Negative.}*

His hand reached up to wrap around the cable that swooped down to intercept their projected location.

{I can,} he said quietly.

There was no time for discussion. Before he had a chance to think too hard on his actions, Boone lifted the canoe paddle and hooked the carabiner over the cable. Gripping either end firmly in his hands, he mentally ticked the seconds off in his head as the man pursuing the thief neared the spot Boone had mentally identified. Before he had a chance to think too hard about what he was about to do, Boone launched himself from the platform and went careening downward.

21: ZIPLINE

SKY PARK GROUNDS

Boone might have underestimated how fast he'd be going when he hit the man. His target went down with satisfying speed—and stayed down. Problem was, once Boone's feet connected with the back of the man's shoulders, *he* kept right on going.

To put as much force as he could behind his initial blow, Boone had done exactly the opposite of what he'd been taught in close quarters combat. He kept his body stiff and his legs locked, allowing as much of the energy to transfer from him into the enforcer.

After striking the man, momentum carried Boone another three meters before he crashed into the platform. He tried to curl into a roll, but at the rate he was traveling through the air, there wasn't much time to adjust before landing.

The collision altered his trajectory enough to send him flying into a hedgerow, which lessened the impact somewhat. Though it probably saved him from broken bones, it still hurt like a sonofabitch.

Somewhere behind him, he heard a young boy's voice call out,

"Mama! Zip lines! I want a ride!"

"Hush," an adult voice scolded, the sound fading as the mother wisely pulled the child away from the scene of the collision.

* * *

Thad took off at a run the minute he saw Boone launch himself down the cable as if it were some sort of new park ride.

"Lord save us all from damn fool lance corporals who think they're supermen," he muttered under his breath.

He rounded the corner just in time to see Boone piston into the back of the enforcer. The thief, a scant three meters away wheeled. What he saw seemed to unnerve him. For a moment, Thad thought the guy was going to bolt. Instead, he shoved the dolly aside and reached for his weapon.

He fumbled the maneuver, his clumsiness telegraphing his obvious inexperience. This, combined with the clear panic writ on his face had Thad reaching for his reserves, urgency spurring him on. As the pistol cleared its holster, Thad launched himself into a flying tackle, one hand wrapped around the man's wrist and spoiling his aim.

They went down, the back of the man's head hitting the ceramacrete sidewalk with a loud *crack*. Thad came up on his hands and knees, ready to counter any move in case the thief was still conscious.

The man was out cold. Thad looked around until he spotted the pistol that had clattered to the ground when they'd impacted the sidewalk. He rolled to his feet and scooped it up.

* * *

The row of bushes that had broken his fall were obliterated where Boone had crashed into them, but they'd not gone quietly, and he had the bloody scratches to prove it. The small patch of grass was softer than ceramacrete, but still managed to give Boone one hell of a road rash.

He ended up on his back, staring up into the darkening sky. Taking a moment to run a quick mental assessment, he realized he held something in his right hand. Lifting his head was a mistake; it dropped back onto the grass, but not before he registered the fact that he'd somehow managed to hold onto the damn canoe paddle.

He chose not to think too hard about what that meant. The only way that could have happened was if one of the carabiners failed. He was lucky his jury-rigged system hadn't dropped him onto innocent bystanders from a much higher distance.

Sucking air into his lungs, he braced and he rolled up onto one elbow to look around. There was a man-sized hole in the hedgerow now, thanks to him. It provided an unrestricted view of his victim.

His target was knocked out cold, possibly worse. Boone knew the impact could have snapped the man's neck, unless he had a carbyne-reinforced lattice running through his skull like those in the Geminate Navy had.

A crowd had gathered, their attention drawn by the sight of his body flying through the air. Already a person crouched beside the unconscious man, and a few more were headed in that direction.

Boone scowled when the man stirred and emitted a groan.

You couldn't stay out for just a few seconds longer? he thought irritably.

With a groan of his own, he forced himself to his feet, using the canoe paddle as an assist.

"Geminate Navy," he called out to the civilian trying to render aid as he limped toward the downed man. "I'm going to need you to back away, sir."

The man scowled up at him. "You could have killed this—"

"And *he* could have killed you," Boone interrupted. He bent over the downed man and did a quick pat-down, pulling two weapons from their holsters.

The sight of the CUSP and the pistol drew gasps from onlookers. Tossing the canoe paddle aside, he stepped back, tucking the CUSP into his back waistband, and aiming the compact firearm at the man on the ground.

Pitching his voice so that the crowd could hear, he repeated, "Geminate Navy. This is a hot zone. Weapons fire has been exchanged. For your own safety, seek shelter, *now*." When he didn't sense movement from them, he risked a glance over his shoulder at the gathering crowd.

That was a mistake.

* * *

Thad hauled the unconscious thief to one side, out of the center of the walkway. The sound of fists hitting flesh had him pivoting. What he saw had him doing a mental double take. The younger Marine was engaged in a vicious hand-to-hand battle with the enforcer.

How the hell did that happen? The last time Thad had looked, the corporal had his weapon trained on the man.

It didn't matter what had happened to upset the balance of power. Boone's opponent was a brute of a guy who had several kilos on him. Even after the blow the man had sustained, the enforcer was a dangerous opponent.

Thad raced toward the two, assessing the fight as he went. He pushed past a growing crowd, people gawking at the spectacle as if it were some form of macabre entertainment, oblivious to the danger they were in.

"Get back! Get the hell away from there," he yelled as he shoved between two kids. When they pushed back, he swung his weapon toward them and added a growled, "*Now!*" to his order.

Eyes widening, they moved a few feet back. It wasn't nearly enough, but Thad had more pressing matters on his hands. He stopped just outside the reach of the two, gauging the best moment to intervene.

The enforcer had pulled a knife. He thrust toward Boone, and the corporal knocked his hand aside, countering by ramming his shoulder into the man's gut. At the same time, he grabbed the enforcer's wrist in both hands and gave it a sharp twist.

Thad heard bones snap, the enforcer roaring an invective. He wrapped Boone in a clinch, delivering several quick, hard blows to Boone's kidney with his functional hand. Boone drove his knee into the man's groin and when they broke apart, Thad saw the flash of gunmetal gray. The knife had changed owners.

Before Thad could take advantage of the separation, a figure dove into the fray, bending to scoop up Boone's discarded canoe paddle. It was Asha.

Wielding the object like a bat, she swung. It connected with the side of the enforcer's head with a satisfying crunch, and the man fell back to the sidewalk, out cold.

"Home run," Thad murmured as he pointed his weapon skyward.

22: NEW PLAN

SKY PARK GROUNDS

{Hey boss?} Bobby hadn't been gone ten minutes before his panicked voice sounded over the team's comm channel. In the distance, Petra saw Delia look skyward in exasperation. Her gaze snapped back down at Bobby's next words.

{Boss! They found me!}

Delia whipped her head around, seeking Petra, tension vibrating from her frame. Petra felt a matching tension coil in her gut, but she held up a cautionary hand, drawing to a stop beside one of the concession stands.

*{**Who** found you?}* she asked.

{Too late. They've already —} He fell suddenly silent.

Petra's hand fisted as anger crashed through her, along with a healthy helping of fear and frustration. Everything she had worked so carefully to achieve was crumbling to dust at her feet. She had to find a way to recover from this. She motioned Delia over. With a quick nod, the other woman reversed direction.

{Kele, get back here,} she ordered, sending him a mental picture

of the concession stand she'd parked behind.

{On my way,} he replied.

It would take a few minutes for the two to retrace their steps. Petra spent the time mentally flipping through their options. She could think of only one.

"New plan," she said when they both arrived. Motioning them closer, she flattened her palms against the topmost box. Looking down at it, she said in a low tone, "The items in these boxes will make us very, very wealthy. But only if we can get them off this platform and up to the orbital station in time to rendezvous with the buyers."

She looked over at Kele, and then shifted to meet Delia's eyes.

"We don't know what happened to Ike, and it sounds like they got Bobby, too. Based on Jay's description, they have to be Mastai."

Kele and Delia both nodded.

"One of us needs to get these boxes to the dock. The others—" she sucked in a breath, "—will go hunting."

Delia crossed her arms, a hard light glinting in her eyes. Kele made a rumbling noise that set Petra on edge until she realized it wasn't the sound of dissent but of agreement.

She held up a hand. In it was a case filled with zipties. "Each of you take a handful, just in case. If you manage to spot an enforcer before he spots you, use one of these on them. With luck, you'll be able to take him down without drawing unwanted attention to yourself."

She emptied the case and divvied up the thin sheets between them, each film containing one nano restraint package.

"Three against three," Delia began, but Petra shook her head.

"We can't leave the goods unprotected. Kele and I will fight; you take the boxes and get them to the shuttle."

Delia's expression turned briefly mutinous, but then it smoothed into resignation.

"Boss... are you sure?" she asked softly. "It's one thing to go behind Mastai's backs; it's another thing entirely to raise a hand against our own. You take this step, you sever ties with Mastai for good, you know." The other woman's face was creased with concern.

Petra shook her head. "That ship sailed the minute those enforcers arrived." She and Kele exchanged a grim look. Reluctantly, she added, "You both can move on, you know. Cut your losses. No hard feelings."

Delia coughed an incredulous laugh. "If they know this much about the operation, you think they're not aware that we're in it with you? She shook her head. "No, we've been made. For better or worse, our futures lie with you."

"Okay then. Let's do this."

Delia didn't bother with a reply, she just nodded and then departed.

Petra turned to find Kele press-checking his weapon, removing and then reseating the magazine. He grinned humorlessly at her upraised brow.

"I'd say the rules of engagement have changed, boss." There was a gleam in his eye that she hadn't been there before.

"Enforcers, yes. We still don't need the kind of heat killing a civilian would bring down on us," she warned.

Kele lifted his chin in silent agreement.

"Good hunting," he said, before he took off down the sidewalk and disappeared into the foliage that lined the waterway.

23: SAFETY MEASURES

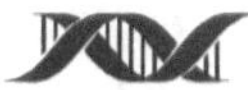

SKY PARK GROUNDS

Gabe winced sympathetically when Asha's swing connected with the side of the enforcer's head.

One thing's for certain, he thought. *That guy's going to know his bell's been rung when he awakens.*

His thoughts came to an abrupt halt when movement in the distance caught his eye. What he saw had him racing for the CUSP lying on the ground a few meters away. The thief Thad had tackled had regained consciousness and was about two seconds away from drilling a hole through Thad's head.

Gabe lunged for the weapon like a runner diving for home plate. Ignoring the burn as ceramacrete tore at his palms, he lifted the CUSP and fired. The shot lanced past Thad, close enough for the Unit operator to feel the sting of the beam, he was certain.

Thad pivoted on the balls of his feet, ready to engage whatever threat was lurking behind him. What he saw had him straightening and sending a nod of silent thanks Gabe's way. He walked over to where Gabe lay, massaging his thigh to alleviate the burn the beam's graze had imparted.

Thad held out a hand and Gabe grabbed it, rolling to his feet with a wince. Nodding to Thad's leg, he said, "Sorry about that."

Thad's face wore a matching grimace, but he waved off the apology.

"Better'n being holed, *ami*." He nodded toward the man Asha had felled. "Mind doing the honors? I know enforcers have hard heads, but I'd hate to have him wake a second time."

"With pleasure." Gabe stepped forward, thumbing the CUSP to narrow dispersal and shot the enforcer, point-blank. Grabbing the man by the collar and belt, he hauled him off the sidewalk, dropping him beside the unconscious thief.

"We're starting to collect bodies," he observed as he straightened. "Might have to do something about that soon."

Thad grunted noncommittally, his attention on the dolly. Gabe joined him, and together, the two men piled the strewn boxes back onto the maglev hand truck's flat shelf.

"Good thing these didn't break open when they spilled," Gabe murmured as he set the final box on top and lifted the lid to peer inside. "I'd hate to have to fight off a bunch of civvies wanting to get a closer look at a P-SCAR."

Thad grunted his agreement, steering the dolly back toward Asha, who was crouched beside Boone. As they neared, the young Marine tried to ease his head from her hand. Asha's sharp "stand down, corporal" had Gabe hiding a smile.

Boone turned when he saw them approach. "I had him, you know."

"I know you did. I was just helping things along." Asha's voice held the barest thread of humor. She forced Boone's head back around, fingers probing gently at his jaw. "You're lucky nothing's broken. Your medical nano should kick in soon. It'll help with that swelling."

Boone nodded his thanks, wincing as the movement tweaked his injury. Thad cocked a brow at him and then deliberately cast his eyes skyward.

"After that stunt you pulled, hoss, I'm sure those teeny little machines are already workin' overtime inside that body of yours. Best to cool it with the aerobatics for a bit, y'hear?"

"Yessir."

Asha pushed to her feet and strolled over to where Gabe stood, grabbing his palms and turning them over to examine their skinned surface. "Remember what it was like to feel young and invincible?" she murmured in a teasing tone, dropping his hands and slapping him lightly on the shoulder.

As roughed up as Gabe felt, Boone looked worse. The corporal was covered in scratches and had the beginnings of a shiner, courtesy of the enforcer. He rolled stiffly to his feet with an assist from Thad.

Gabe locked eyes with Thad. "What now?" he asked.

* * *

Boone was glad Gabe asked; he was wondering the same thing. Before the lieutenant could reply, Asha strode over to where the enforcer lay and squatted in front of him, examining the back of his head. Letting it drop back down to the pavement, she sat back on her heels, forearms resting on her knees.

"Hey corporal," she called out, tone thoughtful. Her eyes remained fixed on the enforcer. "Any chance there's a first aid kit in one of those boxes?"

Boone's brows drew together in confusion at the incongruous statement. He looked over at Gabe only to see the special agent glance over at him, mouth twitching in sudden humor.

Not sure what's so funny about her sudden concern for that grav-sucker, right after she told me to man up about my own injuries...

The whole thing was giving him mental whiplash.

But then the expression on Gabe's face altered. Boone caught the speculative look he and Thad exchanged before the dark-skinned man shot the medic a sharp look.

"Sad five bros?" he asked.

"Yup." Pushing to her feet, Asha turned to Boone with raised brows. "Well?"

"Uhh…" was all Boone could think to say as he scrambled to follow the conversation. The response wasn't exactly his finest moment, but damn, this was making no sense.

Oh yeah, right. The first aid kit.

He blinked, rehashing what he'd seen of the cases' contents. "No ma'am," he said after a beat. "There's nothing in there like that."

She slapped a hand against her thigh and blew out a breath. "Dammit. There goes the interrogation."

Boone wondered for a minute if he didn't have a mild concussion after all.

"The— What?" He looked from Asha to Thad and then over to Gabe. They all seemed to have no problem with her apparent non-sequitur.

Gabe seemed to take pity on him. He motioned Boone in closer. "Sad five bros is an acronym," he said in a low tone.

"Acronym?" Boone repeated.

Gabe and Thad exchanged a look. Thad gave a slight nod.

"What I'm about to tell you isn't classified exactly, but it's not knowledge anyone outside of the SRU knows…"

Thirty seconds into the explanation, Boone flipped on his wire's data recorder. If he'd learned one thing as a Marine, it was to pay close attention when those above him shared their knowledge…

* * *

While Gabe and Asha quietly finished recounting a technique known only to special operators, Thad's gaze swept the crowd, his mouth thinning in anger at the number of people still milling around. He was just about ready to have Gabe break out his NCIC credentials to encourage the park visitors to disperse when the voice of an SI broke in over the sky park's loudspeakers.

"Please proceed to the nearest shop." The voice repeated this instruction, adding, "A small breach in the sky park's ES field has been discovered. Do not panic; the situation is under control. But for your safety, please proceed to the nearest shop."

It was almost comical how fast the crowd of onlookers dispersed. Startled exclamations sounded, a sense of urgency permeating the air, as visitors suddenly rediscovered their missing sense of self-preservation. Kids began running in every direction, chased by frantic parents. People flooded the sidewalks, vacating pools and streaming from rides in their haste to get to the nearest building.

"*Now* they react," Asha muttered.

"Ain't got the good sense God gave a goose." Thad's words were thick with disgust.

"Anyone want to explain why a gunfight didn't register as dangerous, but an ES breach did?" Boone asked to no one in particular.

Gabe shook his head. "Bystander effect," he told the corporal. "It's not clear to them that the fight poses direct danger. An ES field breach on the other hand…"

A shout came from his left, and he turned to see two security officers bearing down on them. Beside him, Boone tensed.

"Easy there, hoss," said Thad, a large hand landing on the corporal's shoulder. "Sky park security. We'll handle them, too."

The two officials came to a stop, their eyes taking in the carnage. There was a lot to see, with two unconscious men, smashed bushes, Boone's scratches and Thad's scraped knuckles, and the canoe paddle draped casually over Asha's left shoulder. As if sensing that her stance might seem a bit aggressive, Asha lowered the paddle, letting it dangle loosely from one hand.

"Officers," Gabe greeted, activating his badge. The seal of the Navy's Criminal Investigation Command floated in the air between them. "I'm Special Agent Gabriel Alvarez, NCIC." He made a sweeping motion that included Thad, Asha, and Boone. "They're with me."

The older of the two Searcy employees shot Thad a sharp look. "We've been fielding reports all over the damn park. One of our security guards said a Navy lieutenant who matches your description called for the ES evac. That you?"

Thad nodded. "That's correct."

Before he had a chance to say anything more, the security officer turned narrowed eyes on Boone. "There are also reports of someone using our cabling as a zipline."

Thad's hand clamped down on Boone's shoulder as the corporal started to shift uncomfortably.

"You got that right, too," Thad said. His tone remained genial, but his expression had shuttered.

Gabe decided now would be a good time to intervene. "Gentlemen, you have a turf war brewing on your platform, between a rogue element of the Mastai cartel and its enforcers. Right now, the safest place for civilians to be is behind the protection of an ES field, which is why the lieutenant asked your office to issue the alert. I take it all your outbuildings have localized fields to keep patrons safe?"

The man blinked rapidly as he digested the information Gabe had just thrown at him. He swallowed hard at the word 'cartel,' darting a nervous look around. Shaking his head, he stuttered, "Ahh… we're not equipped to take on organized crime—"

"Well, you see," Thad drawled, "that's why you have us."

Gabe cut Thad a warning glance as the operator baited the man. He returned his attention to the guard in time to catch the skeptical look on his partner's face. It was apparent the man had his doubts. Given their attire, it was understandable; they were dressed like any other park visitor, in t-shirts and board shorts.

"We have all the equipment we'll need to bring them in," Gabe said. "There aren't that many of them, and now that the civilians are safe, we'll be able to do our jobs without concern one of them might be harmed in the process."

Asha stepped forward. "What we *don't* know, though, is how many of your own people are compromised."

Shock, revulsion, and denial played across their faces. Their reaction to her statement told Gabe that neither man had considered the possibility. The second man looked ready to argue the point.

Thad stepped in to head off any resistance. "We know for a fact that someone in maintenance is working with them." He inclined his head back down the ceramacrete path. "I've vetted one of your security guards; he's back by one of the kiosks, standing guard over one of the prisoners. He'll oversee them for us as we detain them."

The first guard looked from Thad to Gabe, wary acceptance settling on his face. "What should we do, then?"

Gabe chewed on the inside of his cheek as he thought it through. The man's response, whether or not he was aware of it, indicated he'd yielded to Gabe's authority. He stifled a laugh at that. *He* had no authority over a civilian facility, but if they hadn't noticed, Gabe sure as hell wasn't going to point it out.

"We'd appreciate it if you ran interference with the employees inside the buildings, the ones in direct communication with your park visitors. Do what you can to keep them calm and safely in place. We'll wrap this up as fast as possible."

24: EVACUATION

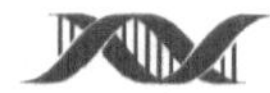

SALTWATER WAVE POOL

As the SI's announcement broadcast across the beach, Chris Reid rose from his deck chair and stepped out from under the umbrella's shadow.

"Chris?" His wife's voice sounded behind him, tense with worry.

He flashed her a reassuring smile before striding to the water's edge, his eyes on the water volleyball players who had stopped to hear what the SI had to say.

When the announcement repeated, Chris lifted his fingers to his lips, letting a shrill whistle pierce the air. The familiar sound had his son, Chase, spinning toward him. Chris pointed to the girls on the float and motioned for Chase to bring them in. The teen nodded and waded out to where the young girls lay, oblivious to the alert that had just sounded.

Amy stepped up beside him, her gaze on her son. "You'd think the park would have a way to interrupt that VR program and warn them," she murmured.

"I'm sure it violates some safety reg somewhere," he agreed

absently, his mind occupied by a fresh thought. A suspicion had begun to form that this 'minor breach' might have been sounded for another reason entirely. It hadn't escaped his notice that they'd suddenly lost their connection to the outside world when the public net went down.

An itch at the back of his neck, one he'd learned in his military career to pay close attention to, had him reaching out to the medic. When she answered, she sounded a bit distracted.

He cut right to it. *{Any truth to that announcement, or has your situation escalated?}*

{Escalated,} she said after a moment. *{He brought friends. And rivals.}*

{Rivals?} His mental tone sharpened. *{Want to clarify that for me, Specialist?}*

{The NCIC agent with me recognized one of the men as a Mastai cartel enforcer.} Quickly, she laid out everything that had happened thus far.

{And you're certain you have this well in hand? I could leave the kids with Amy, commandeer one of the shuttles, and fly it out of range of the swamper,} he suggested.

The medic hesitated. *{Let me run your offer by my lieutenant and the special agent. With civilians exiting the picture, they think the number of tangos is manageable.}*

Chris sent her a mental nod. *{I'm not going to second guess the boots on the ground. I'll get the kids into one of the concession huts. I'm here if you need me. Remind your team to take advantage of every resource they have.}*

Amusement pulsed his way. *{I can assure you, sir, Gabriel Alvarez is no grandstander. Neither is Thad Severance. If either one thinks we could use the help, they're not too proud to ask.}*

Chris nodded as Gabe's name registered. *{Alvarez. I've heard of him. It's nice to put a face to that name Man's got a good reputation; once we're out of this mess, I'd like to buy you three a drink, if you've the time.}*

{We'll take you up on that, sir. Sorry, sir. Gotta go.}

The connection cut out and Chris returned his attention to the kids pouring out of the saltwater pool.

"Tatiana," he called out as the girl in the teal bikini stood at the water's edge, looking around in confusion for an aunt who was no longer there.

She looked up at him as he stopped in front of her.

"I'm Colonel Reid. Your Aunt Asha had to step away for a minute, but my wife and I told her we'd look out for you. We need to move to shelter for a bit. Can you grab your things and follow us, please?"

He pointed toward the hut that sold concessions, situated alongside the boardwalk, at the edge of the beach. People from the pool were trudging up the small dune and streaming under its roof.

Tatiana looked from the crowd back to Chris and then shrugged. "Okay, sure."

* * *

Halfway across the platform, Petra sank down behind a row of bushes, contemplating the evacuation order. This was unexpected. She wasn't sure yet if it was a good or a bad thing. Either way, she needed to decide how the team was going to handle it.

{What the—} Kele broke in on their team channel.

Delia talked over him. *{Shit! How'd **that** happen?}*

Petra lifted a virtual hand to forestall their questions.

{Let me ping Jay,} she said. *{His employee access should be able to tell us something…}*

A minute later, the maintenance worker's presence popped up in the channel.

{Jay, is there any truth to this announcement about an ES field failure?}

Jay's mental voice was tinged with concern. *{No, it's bogus. I accessed the park's systems monitor the minute the warning began broadcasting. Everything checks out. The ES field's perfectly fine.}*

Kele sent a mental shrug. *{Well, with everyone rushing around,* *no one's going to pay much attention to a woman pushing three dollies.}*

{Yeah, but who ordered it, and why?} Delia sounded skeptical. *{Would the enforcers use it as a ruse to clear the area?}*

Petra shook her head. *{That makes no sense. Enforcers would want to blend in with the crowd, not call attention to themselves. No, this is someone else's work.}*

{Are you thinking it might be the guy Ike chased? The Marine, maybe?} Kele asked.

{He's just one guy,} Petra began, but then she tilted her head to one side as she gave his words serious consideration. *{You could be on to something, there. It would make sense, especially if he caught sight of an enforcer. Guys like that are hero types, always thinking about getting civilians to safety. He might have used that argument to convince security to get people out of the path of flying bullets.}*

{Does this change anything, Boss?} Kele asked.

Petra shook her head. *{No. The Marine is none of our concern. You see him, steer clear.}* She injected a bit of humor into her voice. *{Who knows; maybe he'll round up the enforcers and do our dirty work for us.}*

Delia's mental sigh was long and loud. *{If wishes were horses.}*

{Not gonna ask what horses have to do with that. Me, I prefer to have my wishes granted in cold, hard credits,} Kele said. *{Although today, I might settle for a couple of enforcers, gift-wrapped with a nice ziptie and a one-way ticket to the bottom of the Pelican Ocean.}*

{We're going to have to make that happen on our own,} Petra reminded him. *{Speaking of which… we need to get on with it.}*

Despite her counsel to the others, Petra didn't take her own advice just yet. She remained in a crouch, mulling over her next decision. After a moment, she reached out to Jay once more—but this time, it was on a private channel.

25: DISTRACTIONS

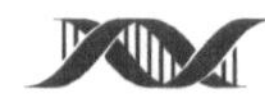

MAINTENANCE ACCESS HATCH

The third of the four reserve devices had just been placed into its cradle and the explosive sent on its way when the ping from Petra came across Jay's wire.

{I need a distraction,} the cartel boss ordered. *{Set off that charge you planted along the back of the infinity pool.}*

Jay glanced worriedly at the final device. Carefully placing it into its cradle, Jay activated the crawler and backed out of the access panel.

*{You **sure** you want me to set off one of the explosives? There's no going back from that once you begin.}* The question might not have been phrased as tactfully as possible, but Jay was running out of time.

{Yes, dammit. This whole backup plan was your idea. Don't tell me you're getting cold feet now.} The cartel woman's mental tone was acerbic enough to kick Jay into a fast jog.

{No, of course not. I'm only confirming.} The hide was just up ahead. Jay just needed to keep her talking for a bit longer. *{How*

about I set off the smallest one first, just enough to get the sky park's attention?}

{*Fine, set that one off. I don't care,}* Petra snarled. {*Just **do** it.}*

Jay sped up, hitting the stairs at a run. Stepping onto the roof, the maintenance worker took a deep breath and looked out over the sky park.

{*Copy that. Give me a minute. One distraction, coming right up…}*

26: REINFORCEMENTS

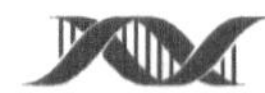

Sky Park Grounds

Visitors continued to stream into the park's outbuildings. Curious faces gawked at the tableau surrounding Boone as they rushed past. Acutely aware of time slowly ticking away, he chafed at the inactivity. He was relieved when Gabe made the executive call to hand their prisoners over to the two security guards.

Thad clapped a hand on Boone's shoulder. "Told you it'd all work out. They'll clean up after us and ride herd on the prisoners while we round up the rest."

The hand on his shoulder steered Boone away from the others, leaving Gabe to iron out the details. "Come on; let's get kitted up."

Thad stopped to check on their two prisoners, while Boone turned his attention to the topmost box stacked on the dolly. He flipped open the lid and began rummaging inside, pushing past frag grenades and CUSP batteries until he found what he was looking for—a way to secure their prisoners. He pulled out the small flat case and turned to the operator.

"LT!" he called out. When Thad looked up, Boone held out two sheets of thin, flexible material. With the flick of his wrist, he sent them spinning toward the man.

Thad caught the zipties midair, then bent and slapped one onto their prisoner's exposed neck. The nanopackage unpacked and the man, who had begun to stir, stilled once more. He crossed over to the thief and repeated the action.

Bending to scoop up the pistol the enforcer had dropped, Thad offered it to Boone with a questioning look, but Boone shook his head at the silent offer. He'd seen something else inside the box he'd rather use.

Boone had recognized the SWS case immediately. The Sniper Weapons System was one he was intimately familiar with, having used it to protect the herds on his family's sprawling ranch from predators for years. He pulled the case free of the box and applied his palm to it, expecting it to challenge him for his military ID. As he'd feared, the thieves had breached the case's security.

Opening the lid, he found exactly what he had expected to see: a Houghlin Kingsolver, pulsed tactical .308. The weapon could deliver both projectile and laser rounds, though the latter was reserved mainly for non-atmospheric combat. His hand closed around the frame's familiar lines. In minutes, he had the rifle assembled.

Tucked safely inside a spare sleeve was an optical scope that beat to hell any augments known to man. He hadn't had anything this sweet back home, though he'd used the precision tactical optic once on the range back at Ouray, when his instructor had brought it out to demo.

With this, he could easily dial in any location on the platform. He looked around at the sky park, recalling his earlier thought that most people—gun runners included—didn't often think to look up when fighting or trying to retreat. The clock tower caught his eye, and he studied it thoughtfully. He dragged his attention back to Thad when the Unit operator called out to him.

* * *

Thad watched with some bemusement as the young Marine deftly assembled the sniper rifle. The ease with which he did so had Thad exchanging a meaningful look with Gabe. Somewhere along the line, this young corporal had become exceedingly comfortable with one of the deadliest personal weapons in the Alliance Navy.

"You qualified to shoot that thing, *ami?*' he asked, with a dip of his chin toward the weapon in Boone's hand.

The corporal nodded. "I requalified a month ago, on the range aboard *Callaghan*."

"Score?" Thad shot back.

"Expert. Small bore and P-SCAR, too. Sharpshooter: flechette." He grimaced. "Marksman: RAU-19."

Gabe laughed softly. "You're not a fan of the big bastards, I take it."

A brief smile ghosted across Boone's face. "No, sir, I guess not."

Gabe gave him a pointed look. "Not a lot of call for a sniper weapons system on a platform this size."

Boone lifted the now-assembled rifle and attached a sling to its mount before placing it around his shoulder. Looking up at the special agent, he said, "No, sir, but I figure it's better to have it and not need it, than not have it around and wish you did."

Thad grunted out an *Ooh-rah* at the sentiment. It was one he fully understood and endorsed.

Boone moved aside, making room for Thad, Asha, and Gabe. Thad set the top box aside and opened the next one. He grunted in satisfaction as his eyes landed on a P-SCAR. Handing one over to Asha, he grabbed one for himself, along with a few extra magazines and a spare battery for the CUSP.

Asha had broken into a third box; this one had tactical vests and synthsilk shirts. The synthsilk was light armor at best, but he wasn't going to complain. He quickly pulled one of the shirts over his tee and grabbed a vest.

"Okay, *amis*." He glanced from Gabe to Asha and then over to Boone. "It's pretty obvious these guys aren't much concerned about collateral damage, so we go in weapons free and neutralize them before they have a chance to do any harm. Agreed?"

There were nods all around.

Pounding footsteps sounded, and the four wheeled, backs to each other as they prepared to meet the newcomers head-on. Thad lowered his P-SCAR a fraction when he saw two young men Boone's age rounding the bend at a fast jog.

He shot the corporal a quick look. "They with you, hoss?"

"Yeah." Boone pointed. "The one on the left is Lance Corporal Ramirez. PFC Davila's on the right."

Thad's hand snapped up, the P-SCAR's barrel pointing skyward. The two Marines stumbled to a halt, breathing heavily, their gazes bouncing from Gabe to Thad and then back again. One of them darted a glance toward Boone.

"What's going on?" Ramirez asked.

"Consider yourselves recalled to duty," Thad said shortly. "Know how to handle one of these?" He brandished the rifle.

"Yessir." At Thad's tone, both men had snapped to attention. Thad slapped the P-SCAR into Ramirez's palm. He was pleased to see the Marine handle the weapon proficiently, performing a quick magazine check before shouldering it and accepting a spare mag.

He saw Gabe had done the same for Davila. Boone was back at the boxes, pulling out more weapons. These were passed around as Thad filled them in on the situation.

"We have four down, but eight tangos are still at large," he told the two young men. "We're going to need to split up. It's not ideal, but we don't have much choice."

He turned to Boone, jerking his chin toward the sniper rifle and scope slung around the corporal's neck. "Need you to go high again, hoss. You're overwatch. And while you're at it, find me that sixth man, the one who installed the swamper."

Boone nodded, his eyes looking over Thad's shoulder. He pointed to the tallest building at the center of the sky park, the replica of an old-Earth clock tower. "I'll head there. That'll give a good view—and hopefully a bit more cover than my previous spot."

Gabe chuckled at that. "Good call."

Thad handed out assignments and the group split up... just as the deep rumble of an explosion sent the platform beneath their feet shivering.

27: DETONATION

"Go!" Thad barked, and the small band broke apart, each person racing to their assigned areas. They'd be able to cover all but the wide-open spaces around the three pools and the main entrance. These, Boone would cover on his own from his position high above their heads. They'd meet up beneath the clock tower once all threats had been neutralized.

{That explosion's not a good sign,} Gabe sent privately as Thad headed for the lazy river.

{Yeah, but think, ami. They scale this up from theft to murder, they'll never see starlight again and they know it,} he said. *{Plus, that didn't feel like a big boom to me. Felt more like a 'scare the shit out of them' boom, if you know what I mean.}*

{Still, we'd better wrap this up before they get desperate enough to escalate}, the agent warned.

{Ooh-rah.} Thad sent his agreement, cutting the connection as he hauled himself atop the thatched roof of a nearby hut that sold funnel cakes. The small standalone building didn't have nearly the height of the clock tower the corporal was headed for, but it gave

Thad a quick-and-dirty visual of his immediate surroundings.

It was enough. He caught sight of his next target, an enforcer. The man was bearing down on one of the smugglers, just outside the perimeter of the lazy river. The other man had holed up behind a half wall of fake rock that separated one of the park's lavatories from the public area.

Hopping back down to the ground, he set off at a quick jog, weaving around abandoned food trays and discarded pool paraphernalia—towels, floats and the like—as he pushed toward his objective.

* * *

Before transitioning to Beryl's space station, Chris Reid had spent decades commanding ships of war. He'd fired his share of missile salvos, and occasionally been on the receiving end when one impacted his own ship's hull. He instantly recognized the shiver of an explosion traveling through a superstructure, transmitted through the soles of his feet. The accompanying low rumble merely confirmed it.

"Was that—?" Amy bit off the rest of her words, in response to his grim expression, no doubt.

"It was," he confirmed, as panicked shouts sounded all around them. Where before there had been an orderly move from the pools into the concession huts, now there was a stampede.

People pushed against him in their haste to flee. Where they planned to go, he had no idea. He suspected they didn't, either.

Abruptly he realized that the group of youngsters they'd been shepherding had been rent asunder. Two of the girls were still with them, Asha's niece and one other. There was no sign of the other two.

"Stay together!" he shouted at Chase, motioning to his boy to lock arms with the kids on either side. "Get to the hut," he instructed Amy. "I'm going to go round up the rest."

Her worried gaze met his. "Be careful."

He smiled. "Always."

28: UNEXPECTED COMPANY

CLOCK TOWER

It took a few minutes for Boone to reach the base of the clock tower. When he did, he stood studying it for a moment before walking its perimeter.

Access must be from inside, he decided, seeing no obvious way to ascend. There was only one problem: the building's ES field was already activated. Turning the corner, he found his solution in another group of civilians nearing the entrance. He fell in at the back of the crowd, slipping inside along with them.

A small voice sounded about chest high and to his left. "Are those real guns? Cool!"

It was followed by a gasp and a shouted, *"Gun!"* from the mother.

Quickly swinging the HK around so that it hung from its strap behind his back, Boone raised both hands and said with as much reassurance he could pour into his voice, "Don't worry ma'am, I'm

Corporal Brady with the Geminate Marines." He pitched his voice to be heard over the murmurs of those assembled. "We have some intruders we're tracking down, but it's all under control. You're safe in here. I just need to get to the top of the clock tower."

People stared back at him, mouths agape. One man asked, "Wait. So, there really *isn't* any damage to the sky park's ES field?"

Boone shifted uncomfortably. "We can't say for certain," he hedged, "so for now, it's safest for you to remain inside. If you see someone dressed like a visitor, feel free to let them in. They're safe. The people we're after are dressed like park employees."

He turned to make eye contact with the lone park employee standing beside the store's register. The girl was young and looked half scared out of her mind. Her hand hovered, frozen, beside a holographic control board.

"Ma'am, I assume you know most of the employees here on sight?" he asked. When she didn't answer, he cleared his throat and looked pointedly at her. "Ma'am?"

With a start, she nodded.

"How long have you worked here?"

"This is my second summer." Her voice was barely above a whisper.

"Good. That's good. Then you'll recognize the regulars. Can you show me how I can access the clock tower?"

Her hand swung away from the controls, where he felt certain it had been hovering over a panic button, to point toward a display in the back.

"Wait, does the ES field cover the roof?"

Boone turned back to the crowd to see who had spoken. A young girl had stepped forward, concern on her young face. Concern for him.

Boone knelt so that he was at eye level with her. Smiling, he admitted, "Probably not. But that's what the Geminate Navy does. We go into dangerous situations, so you don't have to."

"But there's really no breach out there, is there?" The girl's father pushed forward, laying a hand on her shoulder. His expression was skeptical.

"Honestly, sir?" Boone kept his tone neutral as he rose to his feet. "I can't really say."

"Can't? Or won't?" The man's voice grew louder, more belligerent.

Boone locked his expression down as he turned to face the man. "We've secured four intruders already. *Armed* intruders. In every encounter, we had an audience. Onlookers, who behaved as if what they witnessed was some sort of entertainment." He let his gaze sweep those assembled, and he added, "Any one of you could have been hit by a stray round. Now, the Navy will go to great lengths to protect Alliance citizens, but *organized crime* doesn't much care."

Boone crossed his arms and waited. He'd placed as much emphasis as he could on the phrase 'organized crime.' He saw comprehension begin to dawn upon the faces around him as his words sank in.

With a chagrined expression on his face, the girl's father stepped back, raising a hand in apology. "Sorry," he told Boone. "We've traveled light years from Earth, colonized distant star systems, and figured out how to bend spacetime, but I guess we still haven't figured out how to cure stupid, have we?"

That pulled a wry grin from Boone.

"Ooh-rah," he agreed. He backed away, unslinging the Kingsolver as he headed for the display the woman had pointed out to him. Behind it, he saw a door with a discreet 'exit' sign projected above it. Nodding politely to the park employee, he opened it to find a set of narrow stairs. At the top was a second door, marked 'emergency exit only.' He pushed through it and stepped out onto the roof.

Boone spotted the man immediately. He was kneeling beside a block of equipment that looked like it had seen more than its share of repairs in its lifetime. He lowered the Kingsolver's barrel until it pointed straight at the man, who had turned startled eyes his way.

"Who are you, and what are you doing up here?" he demanded.

* * *

The sound of footsteps at the roof's door had Jay blanking the small, portable holofeed and spinning around to face the surprise visitor. The sight of a total stranger, one who obviously wasn't with Mastai's enforcers, was a shock and completely unexpected. And it wasn't something Jay had factored into the mix.

The man's bearing screamed military. Whoever this guy was, he wasn't someone to mess with; the business end of a very lethal-looking rifle made that very clear.

"Hands in the air and show me some ID," the man barked.

It wasn't too difficult to appear startled and a bit freaked out. "I work here." *Truth.* "I'm with Maintenance." *Also truth.* "Security reported there was some sort of jamming device in place on the platform somewhere. I was sent out to find it." *Lie.*

The man holding the rifle relaxed his hold slightly. "They're called swampers," the warrior said, stepping carefully forward.

His gaze was intense and unblinking, the effect more than a little unsettling. This man was clearly the predator, Jay his prey.

"Oh, really? I, ah, wouldn't know." *Yeah, very convincing there, Jay. Maybe it's time to change the subject.* "So, what are you doing up here?"

Annoyance flitted across the man's face at the question, and Jay realized another thing: this soldier hadn't expected to find anyone on the roof. This meant he was up here for some other reason, one Jay suddenly desperately wanted to know.

"It doesn't matter. You should get below with the others. Didn't you hear the SI's warning?"

Jay tried out a shaky laugh. "Yeah, well, I thought it might be more important to find this jammer-swamper thing and get it turned off so we could call in reinforcements, you know?"

The man blinked at that but said nothing. Jay tried to get a read on the warrior, but the man's expression had gone perfectly blank. Whoever the guy was, he was good.

He nodded toward the jumble of comm arrays and repeater

stations. "You find anything in there that doesn't belong?"

Jay swung around to stare at the messy rooftop collection. The park's aging network node had a bit of a Frankenstein look to it, thanks to the expansion bays the unit had acquired over the decades as upgrades were made. This, plus the snarl of cabling, both inside and out, made it the ideal place to stash the swamper. Tucked in behind one of the arrays, it looked as integral to the unit as anything else did.

"Everything here's supposed to be here," Jay evaded and then motioned to the rifle in the man's hand. "What's that? It looks a bit more official than anything I've seen. You with the Navy?"

"Marines," the man said dismissively, his gaze already focused outward. He walked over to the half wall that ran round the edge of the small rooftop and laid a hand upon its ledge. He peered over it and then straightened and looked around.

Jay stepped up beside the man. "How'd the Marines get notified so quickly? Did they send up an entire squadron of you folks or something?"

"No one sent us," he said. "We were up here on our day off."

"We?" Jay knew instantly that the single, sharp word had been the wrong thing to say.

The man's head turned, eyes narrowing in suspicion.

Backpedaling, Jay shrugged nervously. "Security said there was a shootout down there, that someone dressed to look like a park employee was walking around firing at people. They said he wasn't alone."

The man's expression turned hard. "He's not."

"Yeah, well…" Jay's throat cleared. "I'd feel a hell of a lot better if I knew there were more of you up here to take these folks out, is all."

The man said nothing to that, just walked over to where the comm node closest to the roof's edge butted up against its half wall. He pressed down on it, as if testing its steel housing.

Jay watched in frustration as the young Marine continued to examine his surroundings. It was sheer, rotten luck that some vacationing Navy guy would stumble upon Petra's operation today, tell his buddies about what he'd found, and then decide to put a stop to it. Apparently, he and his friends had already taken out Bobby and Ike. Who knew how many enforcers they'd already bagged?

Did they have to be so damned good at what they did? They're going to ruin everything!

Jay had worked too hard to orchestrate the conflict between these two groups to let this stand. What had started out as a nice, promising little war was now in serious jeopardy of fizzling completely out. Not even a skirmish, unless one counted the takedowns the military was enacting. It was all thanks in large part to the Marine standing mere meters away.

Jay sized the man up, coming to a fast conclusion that it would be impossible to go up against him; the disparity in their respective sizes and skill sets was far too great. Still, there had to be something that could be done to upend this balance of power…

Jay's eyes landed on the toolbox sitting unobtrusively beside a large metal enclosure, and abruptly recalled there *was* one other thing that might throw a wrench into the works for this man and his team.

"There are six of us. Don't worry; we've got this."

The voice was startlingly close. Jay whipped around and stared, shocked at how silently the man moved.

He lowered his chin, expression uncompromising. "You need to go. Now. Join the others downstairs."

"Yeah, umm, you're right. I'll just…" Feeling uncomfortably exposed, Jay sidled away from the man, hastened over to the toolbox, scooped it up and ran for the exit.

Letting out a breath when the Marine turned his attention elsewhere, Jay slipped through the door and then used the electronic master key to lock it. It probably wouldn't stop the man, but it might slow him down a bit.

With a new goal in mind, Jay wove through the people crammed into the store below, exited onto the sidewalk, and turned toward Maintenance, where a small yet powerful spherical device lay hidden, deep inside a locker.

* * *

Since arriving to discover the roof already occupied, Boone had maintained a careful but discreet watch over the maintenance worker. He'd known instantly that she was a woman masquerading as a man, but hadn't let on that he knew. He had some thinking to do about it first.

As a general rule, Boone tended to respect others' privacy, something he understood and even craved, himself. Given the circumstances, he couldn't help but wonder about the woman's motivation. Her actions had a certain furtiveness to them that raised his suspicions.

Clearly, she was an employee. She was able to access the door, she'd been working on the equipment, she had no trouble turning off the ES field to get back downstairs. What he hadn't figured out yet was if she was that elusive sixth person on the gun runner's team, the one the leader had referred to as Jay, their 'inside man.'

It concerned him enough to reach into his pocket for the cylinder that held his final surveillance drone. With a flick of his thumb, he opened the canister, and let the tiny machine handshake with his ID. It floated silently away. Using the drone's surveillance feed, he dropped an icon over the mysterious woman, instructing the drone to follow when she left.

As the door shut behind the woman, he decided he'd better let the others in on his suspicions.

{You in position?} Thad asked.

Walking around to the back of the comm node, Boone sent the lieutenant a mental headshake. *{Not quite. There was someone up here when I arrived.}*

{On the roof?} Asha cut in.

{Yes, ma'am.} He put his shoulder against the casing and shoved it closer to the ledge. *{She's dressed like a maintenance worker and is posing as a man. There's no law that says she can't do that, but...}*

{*But it feels wrong to you.*} Thad finished the thought.

{*Exactly.*} He straightened, unslinging the rifle from his shoulder. {*I sent my last drone after her.*}

{*Good. Keep an eye on it,*} the lieutenant ordered. {*She starts going roday around the park, you let us know.*}

29: NOT YOUR FIGHT

Thad left Boone with instructions to ping him once he was set up and then refocused his attention on the mental snapshot he'd taken earlier, atop the hut. Intensely aware that there were civilians still racing for cover, Thad held his P-SCAR at the low-ready as he crossed from building to building, coming to a stop behind a display stand.

He needed to put a stop to the brewing conflict between the smuggler and the enforcer bearing down on him before innocents got caught in the crossfire. If his mental calculations were correct, this location should put him about where the enforcer would emerge.

A scream rent the air. Thad risked a quick look around the display; what he saw had him pulling back with a harsh mental curse. A pair of familiar faces, friends of Asha's niece, stood frozen in fear, their eyes riveted to the gun in the enforcer's hand.

Dammit! His target was between Thad and the girls. It was impossible for Thad to take the shot without risk to the teens.

"Shut *up*," he heard the cartel man hiss, "or I'll *shut* you up."

Thad cursed silently once more. Reversing the P-SCAR so that it rested against his back, he pulled his knife. He knew the teens' eyes would automatically shift to him once he emerged from hiding. That meant slow and stealthy was out of the question.

Bracing, he launched himself around the display, rushing the target. As expected, the girls' reactions gave away his presence. The man turned but he was too slow; Thad was already on him, the impact sending them both slamming to the sidewalk.

Thad shouted at the girls, "Go! Get out of here!" One hand wrapped around the man's gun while the other plunged his blade toward the man's gut. The knife met resistance, skittering sideways across the man's base layer.

Thad didn't get a second chance to use the blade. The enforcer fisted the front of Thad's shirt, hauling him forward as he aimed his forehead at Thad's nose. Thad ducked, the man's head-butt crashing into the crook of his neck instead.

Thad slammed the enforcer's gun hand against the sidewalk once more and the gun went skittering away. He transferred his grip to the sling around the man's neck and tightened. The man's hands flailed wide as the pressure of the flat, reinforced lanyard cut off his air supply. They came back down in a brutal double-handed palm strike.

Thad rotated his head just enough to keep the blow from landing squarely against his ears. Still, the thunderclap hurt like a mother. The carbyne nanofloss lattice across his eardrums was the only thing that kept the blow from perforating them. Momentarily stunned, Thad's hold on the sling slackened.

The enforcer used the opportunity to press his advantage. Gripping Thad's knife hand, the man wrenched, twisting Thad's wrist in a direction it didn't want to go. Thad responded with another elbow strike to the throat before his adversary could snap his wrist—but not before the man forced him to drop the knife.

It clattered to the ground just as the enforcer's hold loosened. The two broke apart, Thad shaking his hand out to make sure it was still functional.

"This isn't your fight," his opponent rasped as he swung a quick jab Thad's way, "so quit playing hero and concentrate on staying alive instead."

"Nothing I'd like more, but not with civilians around."

The man feinted and then plowed into Thad, hooking a hand behind his knee. The two went down hard.

A sound to his right had Thad jerking his head around. The scuffle had caught the thief's attention, and the man had abandoned his hiding place and had raised his weapon, pointing it right at the two men.

Thad loosened his hold, allowing the enforcer to roll free. They broke apart just as the gun runner fired his flechette. Tiny, veined projectiles stitched their way across the sidewalk. Thad bit back a pained groan as the last flechette in the fusillade embedded itself into his upper thigh. He rolled and the enforcer did the same, which split the gunrunner's attention. His eyes tracked between Thad and the enforcer, the weapon in his hand wavering. It snapped to the enforcer when the man lunged for the pistol Thad had forced him to drop.

Thad reached for his P-SCAR, bringing the rifle around while the gunrunner's attention was fixed on the enforcer. Thad drilled the thief in the shoulder with a quick laser pulse, then dove for cover behind a nearby trash receptacle when he heard the enforcer's pistol discharge.

"Not your fight!" the enforcer called once more, and by the sound of his voice, Thad knew the man was retreating.

He lifted the P-SCAR until its barrel cleared the trash bin and he used its automatic sights to fire a final shot at the man's retreating back. The man stumbled, but then recovered, rounding a corner and disappearing from sight.

Both men temporarily out of the picture, Thad dropped the P-SCAR and bent to examine his thigh.

His last roll had driven the flechette deeper into the muscle until only the fletching remained. He wrapped his fingers around the small metal protruding from his leg, gritted his teeth, and yanked.

The projectile's barbed head ripped its way through his flesh on its way back out. The initial runnel of blood became a sluggish stream, dripping its way down his leg. He swiped at the wound, examining the entry point with a critical eye. He'd been injured enough to know that, as wounds went, this was on the superficial side; his medical nano would eventually repair it.

He used his knife to cut two long strips from the t-shirt he still wore beneath the synthsilk he'd donned. Balling one up, he stuffed it into the wound, biting back a mental yell. He wrapped the other around his thigh and tightened it, stanching the blood.

A sound from behind had him turning his rifle on the new threat. He sent the barrel skyward when he registered a pair of scared faces peering back at him.

"What part of 'run' did you not understand?" he growled at them. His hold on the P-SCAR was slippery, the grip slick with blood. He shifted it to his free hand, absently swiping his palm on the front of his shirt to clean off the blood.

His action caused the girls' eyes to widen. He ignored their response, cognizant of the dangers that still lurked in the sky park. He repeated the action with his other hand while bestowing his best Marine glower on the two girls.

"Rule number one," he bit out as he used the tail of his shirt to clean off the P-SCAR's grip. "Someone gives you an order, you obey immediately, no questions asked."

"We're not in the military," one girl said timidly.

"You think that matters right now? The shi— stuff," he rapidly self-edited to shield tender young ears, "going down right now has turned this place into a combat zone. That means you do what I say, no argument. Now, get your shiny little heinies to the nearest hut, *now*. Do I make myself clear?"

"But you're injured," the other was brave enough to protest.

"I'm a Marine," he countered, though the thought immediately popped inside his head, *Not any longer. You're SRU.* "I'm used to it. Now, go on. Scoot."

To Thad's great relief, the girls pivoted and ran. He rolled to his feet, groaning as his thigh throbbed. For good measure, and just for pissing him off, he shot the unconscious thief once more before following the enforcer into the forested landscape.

30: ARCHANGEL

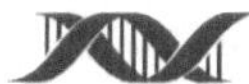

Clock Tower

Boone puzzled through Thad's parting words as he rolled up onto the steel casing of the comm node. Though he'd known the lieutenant less than a day, the man's turn of phrase had sent him reaching for the translator in his wire's database more than once. In this instance, context gave him a pretty good feel for what Thad's 'going roday' meant.

Problem is, she hasn't done anything concrete yet to prove she's 'gone roday.' The only thing I have right now is a gut feeling.

Dismissing that for now, he turned back to the task of setting up the Kingsolver. The Sniper Weapons System had come with a tripod. This, he wedged into the space between the comm node and the ledge. He brought the barrel to rest in the tripod's cradle, the rifle's butt tucked securely into the pocket of his shoulder. With a thought, he brought the optics' holographic reticle online.

Ordinarily, he'd have a spotter working alongside him, to guard his six while his focus narrowed to the world inside the reticle. Since that wasn't an option, he'd use the SI alternative the SWS offered. A biometric scanner at the base of the weapon's stock opened a hidden door. Boone touched it and out dropped a small 'spotter' microdrone. The smart program would act as his eyes and ears, monitoring his immediate surroundings while Boone concentrated entirely on what could be seen through his scope.

As overwatch, Boone kept the rifle armed and its SmartLock targeting system active. He didn't expect to use it, but like he'd told Thad earlier, it was better to have it and not need it.

None of them had come to the sky park today expecting battle. They were operating lean, thrown into this with zero mission prep. The way the day had gone so far, he preferred to be overprepared.

Boone settled into a routine, his sweep taking him from one edge of the sky park to the other. He began by scanning Ramirez's sector, the building they'd tagged as Bungee One.

As he located his platoon mate, the IFF app embedded in the scope briefly flashed green and an icon popped up, confirming the corporal's identity. The Kingsolver's barrel tracked the man as he slipped inside the building.

Boone panned the scope across the building's outer walls to see if he could spot any hot spots on infrared. Nothing showed but the uniform yellow, fading to green, as the building's metallic surface cooled under the waning sunlight. That didn't mean the building was clear; an enforcer wouldn't show up in his scope if they wore clothing made from EM-blocking metamaterials.

Ramirez was going to have to clear the building the old-fashioned way. So would Davila, who'd been tasked with clearing Bungee Two. This should pose no problem for either Marine. They'd conducted this same clearing exercise countless times while deployed, only this time, they didn't have to worry about zero-*g* or explosive decompression. It wasn't without its dangers, though.

Boone was glad to see Ramirez taking this seriously. Weapons didn't much care if they were wielded by a pirate in the Atliekas or a cartel enforcer at a carnival.

With nothing to report on Bungee One, Boone shifted to the next location, the rifle's barrel drifting down and to the left, inscribing a long, slow arc as he sought movement through his scope.

Twice he stopped. Both times, the scope revealed small clusters of civilians, people who'd opted to ignore the warning and remain outside. He shook his head and moved on.

The lazy river area was thick with foliage, ideal for cover. Boone cycled to IR once more and instantly found a heat signature, slowly advancing through the cool blues and greens of the thickly treed area. The IFF app flashed green once more, this time confirming Thad's identity.

Tiny IR signatures scurried ahead of the lieutenant, an advance guard of birds and small land creatures that had somehow made their way up onto the platform. Boone widened his search from that center point and, after several long minutes without spotting any other signatures, reported in.

{LT. Nothing in your immediate vicinity.}

{Nothing?} Thad sounded annoyed.

Boone widened his search, ignoring the clusters of hot spots crowded inside nearby buildings. *{Nearest movement's deeper in. Looks like a cluster of civilians heading for the tiki huts by the saltwater pool.}*

Thad gave a two-click. Boone moved on.

His next stop was the cluster of ships and concession stands directly below his perch. He caught a quick glimpse of Gabe as the agent ducked around the corner of a building, his form briefly lit by IFF green.

Boone had just begun widening his search around Gabe when the agent's odd actions registered. Puzzled, Boone centered on Gabe as the man backtracked a few steps, bent, and snatched something from the ground.

Boone zoomed in on the item in Gabe's hand. It looked like a shapeless glob of raw ActiveFiber material, the kind used by the entertainment carnies that roamed the sky park's sidewalks to create impromptu sculptures for visitors.

Now, I wonder what he plans to do with that…

* * *

Gabe had tracked down his share of suspects during his career as a special agent, but by and large, they'd been in urban areas. When Thad began divvying up the sky park, Gabe quickly offered to cover the town square, leaving the dense, jungle-like sectors to the two operators with more experience in that environment.

The fleeting glimpse of a figure disappearing behind one of the concession stands confirmed Gabe was not alone, but there were signs that suggested more than one person lurked in the area.

See one, think two.

The old adage wound through his mind, the thought spurring him to consider ways he might stack the deck in his favor. Which led to the shapeless form he held in his hands.

There were any number of ways he could put the abandoned clump of ActiveFiber to use. ActiveFiber's superlattice architecture was easily tunable, its 'carrier wave' receptive to any neural wire interface and capable of carrying out any number of basic commands.

His mind burned through several options, finally landing on the simplest: he would lay traps between buildings at several points of egress. There was enough ActiveFiber to extrude long ropes of high-tensile strength wire, thin enough to be missed by even augmented vision.

The soft scrape that sounded up ahead goaded him into action.

He worked swiftly, stringing the strands between buildings at knee level. Each time he set a trap, he marked its position carefully on his overlay. When the time came to run the gauntlet, Gabe was determined he'd be the only one to get through it unscathed.

Then there was the final piece of ActiveFiber he'd retained, the one he'd fashioned into a garrote…

31: CAMOUFLAGE

LAZY RIVER

The second of the sky park's two lazy rivers boasted a ribbon of water that doubled back upon itself in several places. By the time Asha reached it, the late afternoon sun was nearing the platform's horizon, casting the densely treed area in a pseudo-twilight.

Thick, leafy branches from trees and brush partially obscured her view, casting long shadows across the water's ceramacrete banks. The water gurgled softly, the current drawing empty boats along. They slid by on an endless loop, their seats devoid of passengers.

Asha crouched beside a cluster of bushes and did a careful visual sweep of her surroundings before digging her fingers into the soft loam at the base of one of the plants. Her hand came back up, filled with dirt, dried leaves, and moss. Reaching around for the small water pod still attached to her belt from earlier in the day, she carefully squeezed a small amount into the mix, creating a mud pack. This was quickly applied to arms and face.

That done, she rose and eased her way forward through the

brush. She heard a splash in the distance and moved silently toward it, darting from cover to cover. The dense foliage provided layers of concealment, which was both boon and hindrance. She divided her attention between the area ahead and the ground beneath her feet, careful placement rendering her steps silent.

Asha heard a noise just ahead, the rustling soft enough that it could have been caused by a bird or a rodent. Somehow or another, small creatures always seemed to find their way onto places like this.

She moved laterally with respect to the sound, her feet automatically seeking a path that would allow her to close at an oblique angle while offering the best cover. Whoever, or whatever, it was seemed intent upon moving toward the water.

There was a splash several meters ahead and to her left. It could have been made by one of the boats floating silently by as the water slapped gently against its sides. It could have been made by a small animal.

Or a big one, she thought. *The large, sentient kind.*

Asha went with her gut. She crept closer, positioning herself behind a bush that would provide her with a clear view of the boats as they drifted past. Then she stilled, melting into the shadows, and waited for whoever or whatever had made the sound to float closer.

Her eye on the reticle of her P-SCAR, she stroked her thumb down the rifle's biometric scanner to arm it. She tracked each small, covered boat as it neared, finger resting on the frame just above the trigger.

She had little warning. An awareness brushed at the back of her neck, causing the fine hairs to rise. She threw herself forward at the same time Boone's voice sounded inside her head.

{Asha! Down!}

* * *

Boone had fallen into a rhythm, cycling through the sky park and zeroing in on each team member, one after the other. He'd pause to scan the immediate area for unseen threats before moving on to the next.

His scope had just landed on Davila as the PFC slipped inside Bungee Two on the platform's far left-hand side. As with Ramirez, the building's IR scan revealed nothing. Boone moved on.

His next location was the lazy river—Asha's territory. He watched as the medic smeared mud across her exposed flesh to better camouflage herself, noticed the instant she tensed, sensing something up ahead. He lifted the rifle's scope a fraction, seeking whatever it was that had alerted her.

There was a flash of movement as a body slipped into the water behind one of the empty boats. The river hit the man mid-thigh. He sank quickly to shoulder level, his weapon held above the waterline, hidden just below the boat's gunwale.

Boone started to warn her but then his scope tracked back to the medic, and he realized she was already aware of the man's presence. She'd repositioned herself behind a bush, her gaze fixed on the floating vessel behind which he hid, her P-SCAR tracking the boat as it drifted slowly toward her.

A notification flashed on Boone's HUD, the scout app spotting movement directly behind Asha. Boone jerked his scope to the left in the direction of the new threat and realized the man was braced to fire. He sent a single round into the man's shoulder, the bullet's impact this close-in virtually instantaneous. A supersonic crack rent the air, and the man went down.

32: SUSPECT

CLOCK TOWER

Boone kept the downed man centered in his scope and his finger on the trigger as Asha rolled to her feet, weapon trained on the downed man. The medic approached cautiously. The man stirred, then froze when she stopped in front of him.

{Sitrep!} Thad's voice cracked across the combat net.

{One enforcer tagged, another got away,} she responded

{You take any hits?} The lieutenant's tone was sharp.

{Only casualty's his shoulder. A through and through.}

Thad whistled. *{Remind me to never piss you off.}* Then he added. *{Of course, I guess you could always just patch me back up…}*

Asha snorted at that. *{Afraid I can't take credit. It's not my handiwork.}*

{Thought I heard a crack from the Kingsolver,} Gabe replied.

Asha sent a mental nod. *{Bastard nearly got the drop on me. Nice shooting, Archangel.}*

Asha's praise faded into the background as the spotter drone alerted him to movement behind her. Quickly enlarging the feed on his overlay, Boone saw a hot spot moving at a fast clip through the foliage. The figure was racing for the water ride's border.

{Asha, your other tango just fled the river,} he reported, though the barrel of his rifle remained on the current threat lying on the ground before her.

{Asha?} Thad's voice was insistent.

{Hang on. I just told this bastard to cuff himself, or I'd have the corporal shoot him in the other arm.}

A beat later, and she added, *{Okay, he's giftwrapped for security. Dropping him off at the ride's entrance and then going after the one that got away.}*

That settled, Boone panned the scope to the next location. The situation at Bungee Two was the same as the one at Bungee One. Like Ramirez, Davila would have to clear the building the old-fashioned way, without his help.

Boone had just begun his sweep across the open pools when an alert popped up on his overlay. This one was from the surveillance drone he'd sent after the woman he'd encountered on the roof.

{LT? I just got a warning from the drone I sent after that maintenance worker,} he called out.

{What kind of warning?} Thad asked.

{She just breached the virtual perimeter I'd set.}

{Is she trying to leave the platform?} Asha asked.

{Possibly? It's unclear. Looks like she's in a maintenance room near the main entrance. It can't be too far from their loading dock. She's rummaging around inside a locker, and … }

His voice faded as he maneuvered the drone to better see what was inside. The small spherical object she pulled out was familiar. He tensed when she began punching in a command string to the control panel embedded in its side.

{Sir, it's a dazzler! I think she's got a—}

Boone swore when his transmission cut off abruptly and the combat net winked out. He tried reconnecting, but his wire sent back the message, 'signal lost.'

He rolled to his feet and paced the roof as he considered how he should proceed. He wasn't of any use as overwatch if he couldn't report on what he saw, and he was damn sure the jamming device that had just come online originated from the dazzler core he'd seen in her hands.

Folding the tripod, he secured it to his tac vest, packed up his sniper rifle and scope, and slung it over his shoulder. Crossing over to the door, he tried it and found it locked. This was no surprise. Had their positions been reversed, there was no way in hell he'd have left his opponent with the means to easily get back down to street level.

Davila's LockPik was still in his pocket; he pulled it out and tried it, but after a few seconds, it flashed red. It did no good to wish the PFC had swiped a crowbar instead. Davila would never have done anything that stupid anyway.

Crowbars were brutes. Once they broke a lock, the thing stayed broken. A LockPik was more civilized. It didn't break a lock; it merely worried at the problem until it came across a workable cypher. Boone didn't have the time for the thing to keep trying various iterations until it hit upon the right combination. He needed to get down to street level, now.

Frustrated, Boone stepped to the ledge and peered down at the building's faux-brick surface. The tower was about the same height as the free climbing wall his DIs had forced recruits to scale in basic, but it lacked the soft sand pit at its base.

He grimaced; he'd hated free climbing back then and was pretty damn sure this wasn't going to be any more fun. Knowing there was no way out but to go through, he swung a leg over the ledge and began feeling for toeholds, resolutely refusing to look down at the sidewalk below.

Six meters later and minus a few layers of scraped skin, Boone was far enough down to feel confident he could survive the drop and remain functional. Unlike his last fall through the air, this time Boone landed correctly, rolling out of it with just one or two more aches and pains to add to his tally.

Slinging the rifle over his shoulder, he unholstered his CUSP.

Holding it at low ready, he set off at a fast trot for the maintenance worker's last known location. As he went, he strained his senses to their limits and kept his head on a swivel, fully aware that there were still six tangos at large.

He kept to the shadows that reached long fingers behind each building, now that Little Blue rode low on the horizon. He made best use of these to conceal his advance. Official planetary sunset was still a few hours away, but the platform's sunset was upon them now. The angle of the star and the sky park's altitude combined to make that possible. As far as Boone was concerned, this was a good thing. The night was always best for hunting.

From the sound of running feet and anxious voices, there were still a number of civilians who had not yet made it to safety. He wondered fleetingly if it had occurred to the gunrunners that hostages were an option. He sincerely hoped not, but realized the time was quickly running out.

33: REGROUP

SKY PARK GROUNDS

Gabe drew to a stop when Boone's words cut off midsentence. Based on what the corporal had said, it was no surprise when the combat net flickered out of existence immediately after. It wasn't hard to figure out what must have happened. Somewhere in that stash of stolen matériel had been a Dazzler's core. Worse, they'd figured out how to use it.

The error on his overlay tracked with Boone's last transmission, flashing the words 'network unavailable' at him. A swamper would have continued to show the network as busy.

This changed things. They'd lost the ability to coordinate takedowns. Any tactical advantage gained from Boone's position atop the clock tower was gone. Gabe knew the kid was smart enough to figure that out on his own; chances were, he was already headed down to join the battle on the ground.

Gabe sidled toward the edge of a building, his focus once more on the two people in his immediate vicinity. He and the enforcer had been playing a game of hide and seek for the past ten minutes.

The third individual was a bit cagier; Gabe had managed nothing more than a quick glimpse of the woman. He was sure she was one of the smugglers the enforcer was hunting.

Time to thin the herd a bit.

With the garrote dangling from one hand, Gabe stopped just short of the corner. He knelt and grasped one of the ActiveFiber lines he'd strung. This one was attached to a planter on the other side of the walkway. He pulled gently on the line, increasing pressure until the planter moved just enough to make a low, scraping noise.

Up ahead, he heard a soft, indistinct sound and knew the enforcer's attention had shifted toward the planter. There would never be a better time. Gabe rounded the corner in a smooth move, the garrote held between his gloved hands already clearing the enforcer's head.

The man must have heard the slight whistle of the cord as it passed through the air. Instinct had him throwing a hand up; the ActiveFiber caught it, the garrote tightening around both hand and neck.

The enforcer jammed his weapon down, and Gabe danced out of the way just in time to keep a round of flechettes from tearing into his leg. The tiny, vaned projectiles chattered against the ceramacrete, the sound cutting into the relative silence of the nearby area, defeating entirely Gabe's reason for mounting a silent attack in the first place. Annoyed, Gabe shoved the enforcer forward, brought his CUSP up and shot the man in the back.

If the sound of flechettes hitting ceramacrete hadn't scared her off, the whine of his weapon's discharge would have done the trick. The patter of retreating footsteps confirmed his suspicions. His second target had fled at the sound of the scuffle.

"Thanks a lot, pal," he told the insensate man.

With a sigh, Gabe reached into a pocket and extracted a ziptie, which he slapped right beside the rope burn he'd left on the man's neck. Dragging the enforcer into concealment behind a low wall, Gabe made note of the location and headed reluctantly for the rendezvous point. At the moment, a regroup was more important than chasing down the one that got away.

Two blocks from where he'd left his victim, Gabe heard a noise. Pivoting, he brought his weapon around, only to jerk it back down to the pavement when Asha materialized from the shadows.

"Jammer," she said in a low voice as she crossed over to his side.

Gabe nodded his agreement. Wordlessly he motioned in the direction of the clock tower. They set out into the waning afternoon light.

"You have any luck back there?" Her voice was pitched so that only he could hear.

"One down; one got away. You?"

Asha grimaced. "Same. I ziptied the guy Boone tagged and stashed him under some bushes at the entrance to the lazy river. The other one ghosted on me."

"Okay, so that's, what? Six down?"

Asha began listing them off. "We have the guy who was chasing Boone. Thad took out another two…"

"There's the one Boone ziplined into." Gabe smiled. "You hit that one out of the park, if I recall."

Her lips twitched at that before continuing her tally. "Then there's the lazy river guy, and yours—"

Gabe lifted his ActiveFiber cord. "Call him Garrote Guy."

That earned him some side-eye. "Fine. Garrote Guy makes six. Which means there are still two enforcers and three smugglers at large, plus the maintenance worker Boone spotted."

Gabe stared thoughtfully up at the clock tower. "Boone's a resourceful guy. He'll have figured out by now that the jammer kills his overwatch. I think it's a good bet he's gone after that woman."

Their rendezvous point was only a few dozen meters away. No one seemed to have arrived yet.

"Over here." Asha motioned to an abandoned kiosk. "We can monitor the area from inside without being seen."

He followed her, pushing past a rack of shirts. "Guess not all their buildings have ES fields," he commented as he looked around.

Asha rubbed the shirt's fabric between her fingers. "Doesn't make much sense to equip them all, I suppose; the ones like these are too small to hold many people, anyway." She shrugged and turned to face him. "There's something else."

Her tone had Gabe's gaze swinging sharply in her direction. Digging a hand into her pocket, she pulled out a small, oddly shaped device.

"I think the enforcers can still communicate, even with the jammer."

He frowned. "That's not possible. The jammer's built to block all frequencies."

Asha lifted a finger. "All *modern* frequencies. Certainly, all military ones. But what if they're using ancient tech? Something that's lower frequency, different bandwidths?"

His eyes narrowed thoughtfully as he studied the item she held. "It'd have less reach. That's why we abandoned those for comms. What is it?"

"Could be a bone conducting mouthpiece," she said. "I heard the guy subvocalizing before he was ziptied. I found it when I checked him over."

Gabe held out a hand, and Asha deposited it into his palm. He peered intently at it, the item jogging something loose in his brain. "I think you're right. I've read about these in a history book," he said slowly as memory surfaced. "They were called molar mics."

She shot him a quick, warning look. "It might still be on, so maybe it's best if we—"

"Say no more." He handed it back to her. She waved him off, so he pocketed it.

"What do you know about them?" she asked.

"I don't think they've been used for a hundred years or more. What I find interesting is what this implies."

Asha's eyes held a knowing look. "The enforcers knew the gun runners had a jammer."

He nodded. "That means there's a ringer inside the den of thieves. My credit's on the park employee who's their inside man."

Asha's lips quirked. "Or inside woman, if Boone's guess is correct."

"Agreed. What I can't quite figure is why Mastai would let things go this far if they knew about it in the first place."

The medic tilted her head. "Give them enough rope to hang themselves?"

Gabe frowned. "Maybe. Something still feels off, though—"

He bit off the rest of his words, his head snapping around when motion in his periphery caught his attention. He held up a hand and then pointed.

Asha followed his eyeline. Across the open center of the town square in the area that bordered the second waterway came a scraping sound and the flicker of a shadow.

{You go left. I'll go right,} Asha sent as they ghosted out of the kiosk. *{Stay low.}*

They split up, using as many objects for cover as they could find. A sandwich board sat between Gabe and his objective; he crept up on it from behind and peered cautiously around. The sight that met his eyes had him rising to his feet. Several meters away, Asha did the same.

Their sudden appearance had Thad dropping the man he'd been hauling, weapon snapping up. It snapped back down the moment recognition set in.

The man at his feet was clearly out for the count. From the way Thad looked, Gabe wondered how close the other man was to being the same. The man's shirt was covered with reddish streaks, and blood trickled sluggishly from a wound on his upper thigh.

"What the hell happened to you, man?" Gabe asked as he jogged over to him. "You look like you've been in a slaughterhouse."

Asha joined them and motioned to the injury. "You need help with that?"

"Naw," Thad waved her off. "I'm good. Most of this isn't even mine," he added with a feral grin.

Gabe exchanged a quick glance with Asha, silently indicating he'd cover them. The medic holstered her CUSP and bent to examine Thad's wound. He brushed her hand away, and the medic glared up at him.

"Stand down, LT, and let me do my damn job." She began prodding at the wound. "Tell me what happened."

He pointed to the thief. "That one shot at me while I was in the middle of exchanging words with one of the enforcers."

"Words?" Gabe's brow rose, though his eyes didn't deviate from the surveillance he'd set for himself.

Thad made a fist; it landed with a light *smack* in his flattened palm. "I might have added a bit of punctuation to them."

"Of course, you did." Asha's verbal eye roll was blatant in her tone.

Gabe's attention was drawn to the cries of voices in the distance. "You run across any civilian stragglers?"

"Yeah," Thad's voice was tight. "About that... There were a couple of them when I got here."

His voice turned gentle as he reached out and grasped Asha's arm. Her hand froze against his thigh, and she rocked back on her heels, looking up at him. "*Cher,* they were some of Tatiana's friends."

Asha shot to her feet. "Which way did they go?"

Thad lifted his chin in the direction the girls had headed. A dense forest of green rose in the air, just beyond them, the beginning of the lazy river area. The only thing that broke the cluster of lush tropical plants were a pair of small bridges that crossed the river in two spots, and a small cluster of freestanding displays littering the edge of the walkway.

"Plenty of places to get lost in there." Asha's grim assessment hung in the air between them.

"Go," Gabe told her. "We'll wrap things up here and follow."

With a quick nod, Asha jogged off into the dense overgrowth.

34: MISSING GIRLS

APPROACHING LAZY RIVER

The fight Petra had just witnessed was as vicious as it was silent. Other than the sound of the enforcer's flechettes striking the ceramacrete, there had been very little noise. Petra watched in sick fascination as the stranger slipped a garrote around the enforcer's neck and pulled it taut. The enforcer fought back, but the stranger held the upper hand.

Who is this guy? she wondered as she backed slowly away. Petra's mind raced as she fought to reconcile what she'd just seen with what she knew about the young man Ike had initially described. The man who'd nearly decapitated one of Mastai's top enforcers couldn't possibly have been the Marine Ike chased.

For starters, he was older and far more experienced. And the way he struck, swift and silent, was unlike anything Petra had ever seen before. Not that she minded the assist. Thanks to Mystery Guy, there was one less enforcer after them, now.

The guy wasn't dressed like her team, nor like the enforcers. But he wasn't dressed quite like a visitor, either. He had the shorts and deck shoes she'd seen people wearing throughout the park, but that was a synthsilk shirt he wore, she was certain of it. And neither the P-SCAR slung over his shoulder nor the garrote in his gloved hands qualified as 'everyday carry' for an afternoon of leisure.

Could this be a rival cartel? That made no sense, though. How could they possibly know about the weapons? The theft was too small to warrant the attention of a competing faction. Disciplinary action from Mastai, she could understand. But this made no sense.

Unless...

If the man Ike chased was an off-duty Marine like he'd described, then maybe these were his friends.

*Ike needs to get his eyes checked if he thinks **these** people are Marines,* came her next sardonic thought. The way that man moved wasn't regular military—at least, not any regular military Petra had ever heard of.

Her feet continued to carry her away from the town square. Up ahead, the sidewalk split. To the left, the path would take her to the saltwater pool. The path to the right led into the lazy river. She angled right. As she neared the river walk area, Petra slowed.

Her steps slowed even further as she considered the unexpected development presented by the jammer. It had taken her by surprise—but it was a nice surprise. She'd have to be sure to thank Jay for that, after this shit-show was over.

It had to be Jay. It was exactly the kind of thing he would have thought up. If that Marine of Ike's truly was just one in a contingent of off-duty military personnel, running around playing hero as she now suspected, this could throw a nice wrench into their playbook, make it impossible for them to coordinate an attack.

Her thoughts stumbled to a halt when the snap of a twig alerted her to the fact she was no longer alone. Her eyes darted about as the crunch of footsteps shuffling through undergrowth followed. They landed on a spinner filled with lanyards boasting the Searcy logo. It was flimsy cover at best, but the only immediate thing she had at hand. She tucked herself behind it, peering through the brightly colored cords, her hand wrapped tight around her pistol as the man emerged.

The enforcer was wounded, Petra could see that immediately. The man limped, arm held tight against his body, a burn mark at his shoulder indicating a through-and-through from the laser end of a P-SCAR. Though the wound had cauterized, she imagined it hurt like hell. A slash along his thigh showed where another hit had scored, grazing him enough to wound but not incapacitate.

Petra sent the mystery man who'd wounded him a mental salute. He'd just made her job a hell of a lot easier. Lifting her pistol, she centered on the man's head—and then hesitated.

It wasn't like she'd never killed before. She had, back when she was a kid, a platform rat just trying to survive. But that was different; it had been self-defense.

She bit down on her back teeth, willing herself to recall that this was kill or be killed. That this man would see months of carefully laid plans in utter ruin, success ripped from her hands. The wrath built once more, and she locked it in a cage of steely resolve.

Her finger tightened on the trigger. He moved slightly just as she took the shot, unknowingly correcting her aim. It burned through his brain stem, the man collapsing in an uncoordinated turn, one knee bending before the other as his body crumpled to the ground.

Petra left him lying there, straining to hear if anyone was near. Finally, she approached, slowly and cautiously, her grip on the weapon tight enough to make her knuckles whiten. She kicked at him, and when she got no response, decided to drill another shot into the back of his head for good measure.

Holstering her pistol, she pushed the body over, intending to search it for weapons. She heard something clatter to the sidewalk. Bending, she scooped the item up, examining it in the waning light.

It was a molar microphone, the kind the cartel kept around for when they knew a jammer would be used on a job. She clenched her fist around the thing, pushed to her feet and pocketed it. Sparing the enforcer one last considering look, she turned down the path that led toward the river ride. A few meters in, she stepped off the path, sinking down behind a row of bushes and allowed herself a few precious moments to think.

It hadn't escaped her notice that this was the second enforcer she'd seen in as many minutes. At least two of the three men in her small band were now missing. First Ike, then Bobby. Right before the jammer kicked in, Kele had pinged to warn her he was being stalked.

She had to assume the worst. That meant there must either be more enforcers than Jay had counted, or…

She paused as a thought hit her.

Could Jay be in league with them?

She scooted deeper into the underbrush as footsteps sounded once more, this time from the paved path outside the ride.

* * *

Chris Reid worked his way against the flow of people, pushing past as they surged toward the tiki hut he'd left behind to search for the two teens. The longer he went without seeing them, the more worried he became. He checked the connection again; his wire still flashed 'network unavailable.' He knew all too well what that meant. Somewhere, someone had turned on a jammer.

During his thirty-year naval career, he'd never known the use of such a device to portend anything good. His pace increased, concern beating at him, not only for the missing girls but also for his own family—and by extension, everyone else on the platform.

He hung a left down the path that led to the lazy river, peering ahead into the shaded brush, but saw nothing. He stopped, deciding the girls likely wouldn't have taken this route. Backtracking, he emerged onto the main sidewalk and continued down it, coming to an abrupt stop when he spied the corpse sprawled face-up, dead eyes staring sightlessly up at the sky.

At the sound of running footsteps, Chris ducked into the foliage that bordered the walk, hand scrabbling for anything he could find he might use for a weapon. He executed a fast one-eighty when the teens he'd been searching for rounded the corner on a zero/zero intercept with the dead man.

Holding out his hands to stop them from coming any closer, he called out, "We've been looking for you. Are you two okay?"

The frightened faces they turned toward him was answer enough. The taller of the two cast a frightened glance over her shoulder and pointed back the way they'd come.

"There was a fight. One of the guys who came with Tatiana's aunt—" she stopped, on the verge of hyperventilating.

"Which one?" Chris asked sharply. "The dark-skinned one or the older one?"

"The first one," the other girl said. "Lieutenant Severance."

Chris moved in the direction they'd come, but the girls stopped him with their next words. "He shot a man and he told us to run."

Chris turned back to them. "Shot a man?" he repeated.

The girls nodded. "A man pulled a gun on us and told us to shut up or he'd shut us up," the first one whispered. "And then the lieutenant snuck up behind him with a knife and—"

She was interrupted by a shriek from her friend. Chris wheeled toward the new threat, only to realize the girl had seen the corpse.

"That's him! The man who threatened us!"

Chris stepped to the side, blocking their view. "And Lieutenant Severance did this?"

The girls shook their heads. "No, he… he… someone else was there," she tried to explain, but her words came out in a frightened tangle. "He started shooting and they were fighting, and then that man got away." She pointed toward the dead man.

"So there were three men there," Chris clarified.

The second girl nodded. "The lieutenant was shot in the leg, but he told us he was a Marine, that he'd be fine, and to get inside."

Chris drew in a deep breath, hating the decision he knew he'd have to make. Part of him desperately wanted to render aid to the wounded operator, but he had a responsibility to get these girls to safety.

He nodded. "The lieutenant was right, and operators like him are tough birds. Let's get you two back to the tiki hut with all the others and let the lieutenant and his team round up the rest of these bad guys, what do you say?"

* * *

Petra listened to the exchange with avid interest, especially when the man dropped the word *operator*. She'd heard special forces soldiers called that before, knew they were the deadliest, most highly skilled warfighters the Geminate Navy had ever produced.

No wonder the shit hit the fan today, she thought with dawning understanding. *We've had the deck stacked against us since the moment we set foot on this stars-cursed platform.*

As the man ushered the teens past the enforcer Petra had killed, a new and different plan began to form. According to the man, one of the operators had a niece among those stashed inside the tiki hut that was their destination.

She slid out from under the bushes, brushed debris off, and looked down at her park employee clothing. An abandoned t-shirt store stood just beyond the lanyard spinner where she'd shot the enforcer. With a quick wardrobe change, she should be able to slip inside that hut, posing as a park visitor—and then grab herself a bit of insurance to negotiate her way off this platform safely…

35: UPPED ANTE

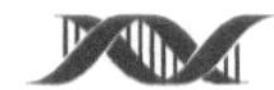

SKY PARK ENTRANCE

With the jammer online, Boone had lost his connection to the surveillance drone. He did have the woman's last location, though, and it was here that he headed.

He skidded to a stop just before the walkway widened into the broad, plaza-like entrance, surprised to discover the very person he sought, standing in plain sight. Confused, he ducked behind an oversized 'Welcome to Searcy Sky Park' sign. The projected holomap had a blinking red icon that said, 'you are here.'

He'd figured the woman would be hustling toward the dock, to load the remaining stolen munitions the team had yet to locate. But she hadn't. Instead, she stared up at the sky above the park for a long moment, before bending to set the toolbox down by her feet. Opening it, she rummaged around inside.

Right out in the open. Heedless of anyone who might come upon her.

Boone shook his head, puzzled by her actions. The woman's situational awareness and craftsmanship were surprisingly poor.

Granted, the Mastai enforcers and the gun runners themselves weren't exactly up to Navy standards. But this woman seemed to be lacking even their basic level of skills.

Something wasn't adding up. Her behavior didn't fit the other gun runners' M.O., at least, not what he'd observed of them thus far. From all reports, it didn't fit with the Mastai cartel, either.

But it sure as hell *did* fit a different group of people, he realized with sudden unease. An organization that had sprung into existence in the Sirius star system before Boone had been born.

When the woman stooped to pick up a toolbox, then turned to walk out into the center of the open plaza area, Boone's suspicions ratcheted higher.

Stars, no. Please tell me she's not with Secede Sirius…

What had begun as a group of misguided lunatics, a laughingstock political party that no one in the Alliance had ever bothered to take seriously, had in recent years turned into a clear threat. Word on the street was that a new leader had taken the reins. On the heels of that had come random attacks, all targeted against businesses whose parent companies were based outside the star system.

The attacks began as simple vandalism, property theft. And then they escalated. People were no longer safe; lives were lost. Secede Sirius took credit for them all.

If this mysterious sixth 'thief' was on a mission for that extremist group, Boone needed to get the word out—fast. He also needed to call in backup.

She closed the toolbox and rose, looking up with something approaching anticipation in her expression. Boone followed the woman's eyeline, half expecting to see a ship on a strafing run for the platform. But the sky was clear, the only thing visible through the ES field was the park's tether reaching up into the distance, to the counterweight that hung on its other end, in low planetary orbit.

He looked back down, his concern deepening to alarm when he caught the almost rapt look on the woman's face. He straightened from his crouch, body tensed to launch toward her.

He checked himself when another explosion rocked the sky park. The detonation was followed by an odd, singing sound. For a moment, it seemed to echo all around him. He spun in a fast circle as he sought its point of origin. And then he looked up.

Beyond the ES field that enclosed the platform, one of the four support cables that secured Searcy to its weighted tether had come loose and was falling toward the ocean below. Where the cable struck the ES field before slithering past came a sound unlike any he'd ever heard before. It was the eternal rasp of a fine blade, a high-pitched *zinnng* that stretched out in one long, ominous note. The sound was otherworldly, ethereal—and one Boone was unlikely to ever forget.

* * *

Asha came trotting back down the pathway—alone, and with a discouraged look on her face.

"No luck?" Gabe asked.

She shook her head.

Thad wrapped a hand around her upper arm and gave it a slight squeeze. "Don't worry. We'll find them, *cher.*"

His hand dropped as the unmistakable rumble of another explosion rocked the platform.

"Thad." Gabe's voice was laced with urgency, causing Thad to send him a sharp look. Gabe pointed upward.

Thad followed the agent's gaze—and blinked in disbelief as one of the platform's support cables came snaking down toward them…

36: TRACKING A TANGO

SKY PARK ENTRANCE

Boone's mind seized for one brief instant at the sight of the cable falling, and then the world snapped into crystal sharp focus. He had to stop her from detonating the other bombs he now suspected were connected to the remaining three cables.

Before he could act, she turned, racing for a door that wasn't listed on any map Searcy provided to its park visitors. If he were a betting man, Boone would wager that this was the loading dock's entrance.

With her back turned, he rose and slipped around the sign. There was no cover available anywhere. The open plaza was wide, built to accommodate the large number of visitors that poured in each day. If the woman decided to look over her shoulder, there'd be no hiding from her.

Twilight had fallen, which helped somewhat. The white dwarf star had dipped just below the platform's disc, casting a wash of vibrant color upon the noctilucent clouds that floated to either side of the sky park. They drew the untrained eye away from the shadowed disc… or so he hoped.

Hope is not a plan, jackass. Unfortunately, it was all he had.

He crept slowly forward as she fiddled with the door. Again, the woman's lack of training showed in her fixation with the lock, to the exclusion of all else. Boone heard her curse softly as her park ID failed to provide her entrance. He froze halfway there when she turned to cast a furtive glance over her shoulder. She bent and dipped her hand into the toolbox to retrieve a familiar cylinder.

A crowbar. Figures. Where was that when I needed it, back on that rooftop? he thought.

The crowbar worked its magic on the lock faster than Boone would have liked. He braced, readying himself to break into a sprint, so that he could catch the door before it sealed behind her—but she didn't open it. Instead, the woman grabbed her toolbox and jogged over to the turnstiles at the main entrance.

Not once did she look around. It was the only thing that kept Boone from being spotted. This baffled the hell out of him, but it was a break, and he'd take it.

She set the box beneath one of the turnstiles, nudging it further out of sight with the toe of her boot before pivoting and jogging back toward the door.

She palmed the door open and was through in a flash, Boone racing to catch it before it slid shut behind her. It turned out he needn't have bothered. The crowbar still clung to the lock, more evidence to support Boone's theory that, whoever she was, this woman certainly wasn't trained.

He detached the crowbar, thumbing it off and on to cycle and reset it, then ordered it to handshake with his ID token. After assuring himself that the unit would respond to his commands, and *only* his commands, he stepped back and let the door slide shut. He had a toolbox to investigate first before he followed her to the dock… but he had to make it fast.

Boone jogged over to the turnstile and knelt in front of it, carefully inspecting the toolbox for booby-traps before touching it. When he pressed the release that would trigger it open, nothing happened. The toolbox was locked.

Okay, then. We'll do this the hard way.

He pulled out the crowbar and set it against the lock. With a small flash of green and an audible click, the toolbox opened. He lifted the lid slowly, fingers running along the edges in search of internal traps that might have been set, but he found none.

Resting the lid against the turnstile, he peered inside. The platform was now too dark for anyone without augmented vision to see into the toolbox's interior. Fortunately, he had military-issued optics. His night vision outlined each item with a soft white phosphor, pulling every incident photon from the surrounding area so that he could see what lay within.

Boone spotted the core immediately. He had more than a passing familiarity with the spherical devices. He'd pulled his share of rotations in the armory aboard the *Callaghan,* and though his job had been to restock the handheld weapons his platoon used, it had been impossible to ignore his Navy counterpart working in the bay alongside him. While Boone stacked CUSP batteries and filled magazines from ship's stores, the ensign next door was busy swapping out battle drone cores.

This, he felt certain, came from the guts of just such a device. He drew it out to study it more carefully. Ordering his wire to handshake with the core did no good; the ping returned an 'access denied.' Frowning, he upwardly revised his opinion of the woman who was making her way to the loading dock. Setting the core aside for the moment, he returned his attention to the toolbox for a final assessment. What he found had his jaw tightening in anger.

There were no fewer than eight abandoned soft cases used for stabilizing explosive devices. They sat crumpled in the space beneath where the core had lain.

Other than that, the toolbox was empty… save for one lone, broken crawler.

So, this is how she set the explosive that just went off, he realized grimly.

Crawlers were machines that could be remotely controlled,

programmed to carry an explosive device and plant it safely wherever its wielder ordered it to go. The unit could also interface with the bomb and function as a remote detonator.

This particular unit was defective; one of its twelve centipede-like legs was bent at an odd angle, and when he tried to flex it, it broke off in his hands.

The thing must've errored out on her. Which meant…

He rummaged more carefully around in the toolbox, until he found what he was looking for: one final soft case, intact.

Knowing he'd already spent more time away from his target than he should have, Boone carefully lifted the soft case, palmed the dazzler's core, and headed back to the door that would lead him down to the loading bay.

37: EXIT STRATEGY

Tɪᴋɪ Hᴜᴛ

Oᴜᴛꜱɪᴅᴇ Sᴀʟᴛᴡᴀᴛᴇʀ ᴘᴏᴏʟ

The bomb went off while Petra's head was stuck inside the damn t-shirt. She staggered, her proprioception hampered by the soft material. Shoving her arms through its sleeves, she yanked hard on its hem and stumbled out onto the sidewalk once more. The ethereal singing sound of the cable striking the ES field dragged her attention upward and she gaped in horror at the sight it presented.

He wasn't supposed to set them where they'd do any harm! Livid that she'd been played and now more convinced than ever that Jay had never been a member of her small band of thieves, Petra raced to catch up to the man escorting the two teens.

*Whatever your end game is, Jay Henson, I am **not** dying for it! And if you're still alive when I get off this wreck, I'm coming for you…*

She spotted the three figures in the distance just as they came to a stop in front of the concession hut.

"Wait! Please," she called out, legitimate panic sounding in her voice. It caused the man to turn.

He nodded, but only after giving her a swift appraisal. That one look told Petra that taking the time to grab the t-shirt off the rack had been a wise move.

She came to a stop in front of him, breathless. Motioning to the hut, she asked, "Is there room for one more?"

The man stepped aside, wordlessly inviting her to precede him.

So far, so good. Now, to identify which brat belongs to those soldiers, grab her, and get the hell out of here.

There were several youngsters inside, but the girls arrowed toward the back where a woman stood alongside a small group of teenagers. Acutely conscious of the compact pistol resting in the small of her back, Petra took a more circuitous route, keeping her back to the wall. She took her time, sizing up the people in the small, confined space.

The girls huddled together, whispering, the two recent arrivals animated as they described their recent encounter. Petra sidled closer to see if she could identify which one in the group she should target.

* * *

"We need to shut this shit down, *now*." Thad indicated the remaining three cables. "There have to be access points for these somewhere. What do you want to bet they've been breached, too, and the same asshole who set off that last bomb has the others rigged?"

"Wait." Gabe snagged him by the arm as Thad turned away. "Even a place as old as this has to have a failsafe. Thrusters, small fusion drives, some sort of backup in case of catastrophic failure."

Thad paused, brows raised. "I hear you, hoss. But with a rust bucket this old, you want to entrust your life to the possibility they've been well maintained?"

Gabe remained firm. "One of us needs to head to the office; try to get plans for the platform, talk to someone in charge. With that thing being severed," he pointed skyward, "it changes things. We're not just cleaning out two small warring cartel factions. Something else is going on here. That's a terrorist threat."

Thad frowned. "You don't think this is a distraction, to buy them time to get away?"

Gabe shook his head. "We can't assume that, no." He inclined his head to the center of the platform. "Look, my NCIC badge got us inside once. I'll go; you try to secure those cables."

"Which one are you going to?" Asha asked Thad. She glanced at Gabe, and added, "If any of us sees Boone's Marine buddies, we can send them to the other two cable access points."

"Good thinking." Thad turned and pointed. "Straight up math says that's the cable that puts us at the most risk right now. I'll head there. Put Ramirez on that one," he pointed again, then pivoted and pointed a third time, "and Davila on the last one."

"Copy that," Asha said. Her expression hardened as her gaze swept the park. "We know which one's their leader; Boone's laundry room feed showed that clear enough." She looked back at Thad, determination flashing in her eyes. "I'll go after her and persuade her to give up intel on the remaining bombs."

38: INFILTRATION

Loading Dock

As Jayden entered the loading dock, her eyes landed on the shuttle Petra had commandeered. The vid recorder built into her wire's data partition captured the holographic logo emblazoned on its side, advertising one of the food and beverage companies that supplied Searcy with its concession material.

Since she'd been the one to arrange the rental, she'd purposely chosen a shuttle make and model that, after careful research, the legitimate food and beverage company had never owned. This would be yet another nail in Petra's coffin.

Satisfied she'd captured enough footage to document the shuttle, she spun, eyes seeking the transport she'd arranged for her escape. Tension flowed from her shoulders as she neared the sky park's maintenance shuttle.

In all, she reflected, *things hadn't turned out too terribly bad.*

Truth be told, adding military casualties into the mix could work in her favor. It would make the tragedy that much more newsworthy.

She frowned when she set her palm against the transport, and it didn't immediately open for her. She looked stupidly down at her hand, as if it were to blame. Then she shook herself with a wry little laugh at her whimsy. If she had learned anything in her checkered and storied career, it was that there was always more than one way inside a shuttle.

Her hand trailed along the side of the machine as she rounded the rear of the craft. She pressed her palm against its aft hatch, with no more luck than she'd had at the cockpit door. Frowning when it didn't respond, she continued her circuit, approaching the front from the shuttle's far side.

With the bulk of the large airframe now between her and anyone who might wander into the dock, Jayden felt a layer of tension flow from her. No one should be out now, considering the SI's evac order, but one could never be too careful.

Her eyes landed on the open charging port and the cable attached to it, and she smiled in relief, mentally chiding herself for not thinking of this sooner. This explained the locked doors. Safety precautions precluded entrance to the shuttle until the cable was disconnected.

She knelt beside the controls of the charging unit and got to work. Unfamiliar with how this specific model functioned, her hands fumbled around trying to find the release. She muttered a soft imprecation when it didn't immediately spring open.

"Damned ancient platform with its centuries old tech," she muttered, grabbing the unit with both hands and wiggling it side to side in an effort to free it from its clamps.

She stilled abruptly. *What was that sound?*

She sat quietly for a full minute, listening. When the sound wasn't repeated, she relaxed.

Probably this old hulk creaking, she decided. Losing a tether could shake things up a bit. With only three remaining cables, its center of mass would have shifted.

Returning to her task with renewed vigor, she yanked once more—and went flying backward when the thing finally came free.

She tossed the charger to one side and scrambled to her feet, sealing the shuttle's charging port. She was ready to get the hell off this rickety old platform.

In the end, it would all be worth it. The bombs were set to remote detonate; all that remained was for her to send the command codes. She'd wait until she was far enough away that the blasts wouldn't negatively impact her. And she'd be damn sure she got plenty of footage, too.

I deserve a medal for everything I've been through, she thought. *Infiltrating the cartel, behaving like the perfect little crewmember, sucking up to the arrogant and ambitious Petra Cooke.*

Looking at her overlay's chrono, she saw that the timer she'd set on the dazzler's core still had fifteen minutes left until it went dormant. Once the thing shut down, there would be chaos, the beautiful cacophony of panicked victims flooding the pubnet with their personal accounts of the tragic events at Searcy.

Their frightened pleas would hit the public net just as Jayden herself went live.

Damn, can I orchestrate a drama or what, she thought smugly, a smile teasing her lips as the shuttle's cockpit door finally opened for her. She slipped inside and began to power the unit up.

*　*　*

The moment Boone entered the loading dock, he heard a clanging coming from the far side of the bay. It sounded like his target was battling with a recalcitrant piece of equipment. He quickened his steps, needing to get on that shuttle before she departed.

Based on the sounds coming from its opposite side, he felt confident he could make it there in time. As he closed the distance, his eyes swept the stacks of boxes and equipment scattered against the dock's rear wall, seeking something, anything, that he could use to his advantage.

A coil of carbyne-jacketed nylon rope, lying carelessly on top of a pile of crates caught his eye. Adding the wire to his arsenal, Boone set off at a silent jog for the shuttle.

Coming to a stop beside one of its skids, he ducked his head to peer under it to confirm the woman's location on the other side. Based on the sounds she made, she appeared to be wrestling with the charging cable that was hooked into the shuttle's battery port.

He eased his way aft, crab-walking silently, one hand cradling the core while the other held his CUSP at low ready. His sniper rifle knocked quietly against his back at each step he took.

When he reached the rear of the craft, he placed a hand beside the palmpad that would open the transport's hatch and paused. Ducking his head once more, he kept his eyes locked on the woman's feet. They shifted back and forth, punctuated by grunts and quiet curses as she struggled with the recalcitrant cable. She staggered back with a sharp inhale as the cable came free, its end hitting the deck with a loud clang.

At the same time, Boone's hand slammed down on the hatch's palmpad. He slipped through as soon as the opening was wide enough to accommodate his frame, turning and palming the door shut as soon as he'd cleared it. He took a fast look around at the loading bay as it sealed with a soft hiss. Save for the two of them, it remained empty.

The woman had finished sealing the charging port. As she walked around the nose of the craft to get to the cockpit door, Boone did a quick recon of the interior. Other than a pair of cargo straps piled in a corner, it was empty. He added them to the coil of wire he'd procured and crawled into the passenger area, silently thankful for electrochromic windows that defaulted to opaque while the transport was at rest.

There were four rows of passenger seating between cargo and the cockpit. A quick assessment told him the best spot to hide was behind the first row. The high back of the row in front would completely obscure him from view. Through the cockpit windscreen, the top of the woman's head disappeared as she ducked beneath the air intake nacelle. It was time to move.

He slid into place, crouching just behind the pilot's side first bench as the woman opened the cockpit door. Boone slipped the carbyne-jacketed wire over his shoulder and set one of the cargo straps on the bench behind him within easy grasp.

Reaching under the bench, he carefully pushed the second strap until it overlapped the line where the partition between cockpit and cabin would rise. He'd been chewed out by Navy pilots for 'fouling the sensors' enough times to know how easy it was to do. The tip of a boot, a piece of poorly placed gear, or even the sleeve of a drakeskin suit could keep the partition from rising. The cargo strap would do the job just fine. The core he settled between his feet. CUSP in hand, he waited.

Given her lack of situational awareness up to this point, Boone was banking that the woman wouldn't check the shuttle's interior for intruders. He figured she'd be more focused on potential threats from the loading bay than any that might lurk inside.

He'd take her out if he had to, but it was a bit hard to get intel out of someone when they weren't conscious.

Just get in and fly the damn thing, he thought.

Fortune favored him. As he'd predicted, the woman's gaze remained fixed on the bay outside the shuttle as she slid into the cockpit. Not once did she glance behind her.

She operated the dock's ES field airlock system with a confidence that told Boone she'd done this a time or two. As she eased the transport out into Beryl's twilight sky, he shifted forward to catch a glimpse of the windscreen so he could get a feel for where she was headed. She banked and brought the shuttle to a hover. Curious he risked another look. The shuttle's holodisplay was up, the autopilot showing a racetrack pattern with the platform at its center.

He pulled back, mentally reviewing what he'd just seen, and came to a grim conclusion. At this distance, they were far enough away that the transport would be safe from any overpressure wave caused by another blast.

On the other hand… He looked down at the core. They were also far enough away that the core between his feet should no longer influence the platform. Thad and the rest of the team should have comms back by now.

39: UNJAMMED

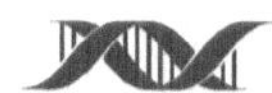

Sky Park Grounds

Thad was halfway to his destination when the combat net reestablished itself. He came to an abrupt halt as four icons populated on his overlay, each one designating the location of a team member.

{*Sitrep!*} he barked out, one eye on the sky park's map that displayed on his overlay, the other on his surroundings as he eased past a cluster of leafy vine-like undergrowth.

{*Bungee One clear,*} came Ramirez's voice. {*Ran into Agent Alvarez; he pointed me to cable three. On my way there now.*}

{*Bungee Two, clear, one tango trussed and ready for pickup,*} responded Davila. {*Need me at a cable, sir?*}

{*Affirmative. Get your ass over to the one by the infinity pool, port side.*}

Davila sent a fast two-click in response to Thad's command.

{*Found the guy you winged,*} Asha broke in.

Something in her tone caught Thad's attention. {*You bag and tag him?*} he asked.

{Nope. Someone else did. Permanently.} Asha's voice was hard. *{Even dead-checked him. Drilled him through the back of the head a second time, just to be certain.}*

{One of the smugglers?} Gabe asked.

Asha sent a mental nod. *{It must be. All the enforcers are accounted for. It tracks, especially if they've upped the ante with explosives. Based on Boone's surveillance feed, it must be one of the two missing women.}*

At her mention of the corporal, Thad's attention swung back to the icons showing over the combat net. The young Marine's ID was absent.

{Boone! Report.}

There was no response.

* * *

Petra had just determined which girl was related to the warriors who were indiscriminately taking out both her team and the enforcers when the jammer suddenly quit.

{Boss!} Delia's voice came across her wire a beat later.

{Where are you?} Petra demanded, opening the distance between herself and the gaggle of girls, now that she'd made positive identification.

{I loaded the goods onto the shuttle, like we discussed, and then came back out to find you and Kele when the net went down,} the woman replied. *{Boss... the tether. We need to get out of here.}* Delia's normally confident tone sounded strained.

{Yeah, I know. I'm working on a plan right now.}

Petra's gaze landed on the girls once more, but then moved on when she caught the man staring at her with an expression bordering on suspicion. She walked over to the entrance and looked out.

{Better make it quick, Boss. Hey, do you think the enforcers are responsible for the explosions?} Delia asked. *{Oh, and Jay needs to get his eyes checked. 'Only three enforcers,' my ass. This place is **lousy**

with them.}

{No, those bombs aren't Mastai.} Petra's voice turned harsh. *{Jay set them. And I don't think Jay's who he claims to be.}*

A shocked silence followed her declaration.

{Who is he, then? What's his angle? And how are we going to get out of this shitstorm?}

Petra smiled grimly. That was Delia, ever practical. Even the threat of imminent death didn't stop her sensible, pragmatic mind.

{As far as Jay goes, I don't know, and I don't care. I hope he goes down with the damn sky park. **You're** *going to get the goods up to the spaceport in orbit. We have clients waiting for us and deadlines to meet.}*

{What if I need to reach you? With the swamper in place, once I leave the platform…}

Petra's tongue probed the molar mic she'd stuck inside her mouth. *{Have you run across any of the enforcers by chance on your walkabout?}*

Delia's startled *{Yeah, actually,}* had her smiling.

{Where?}

{Well, there was this one guy lying beside a trash can, looked like he'd been banged up pretty good. He was obviously ziptied, or he would've gone after me, I'm sure,} Delia said. *{Got a real pissed expression on his face when he saw me, but he didn't move a muscle. Why?}*

{Apparently, our 'good buddy' Jay,} Petra leaned heavily into sarcasm, *{told them to expect a jammer.* **They** *came prepared. He's wearing a microphone that snaps around his back teeth. Go grab it.}*

{Copy,} Delia said. *{And… ewwww.}*

Ignoring that last, Petra swiveled to scan the people in the tiki hut, slowing when it came to the man who'd rounded up the girls. He wasn't looking her way, but some inner sense warned her to be wary of him.

After a few minutes, Delia returned. *{Got it, saliva and all. Good thing there's a lav nearby.}* Her voice turned businesslike. *{Headed for the shuttle now. You sure I shouldn't wait? What about those* *bombs?}*

Petra looked out through the hut's ES field and up into the sky. *{I hate to say this, but if Ike hadn't spotted that Marine, the enforcers would've gotten the drop on us. Whoever these people are, they've handled the enforcers just fine; I think they'll do the same with the bombs.}* She turned away from the view. *{I'm in with some of the park visitors. As far as they know, I'm one of them. I'll leave when they do, and rendezvous with you when this is over.}*

Her gaze settled on Tatiana. *{And if I need it, I have an insurance policy standing right in front of me...}*

4O: TABLES TURNED

Searcy Transport

With the shuttle flying a hold pattern around the sky park, Boone decided it was time to make his move. He shifted forward, but froze when he heard a muttered, "What in stars?"

He peered out. The woman in the pilot's seat was staring at the platform, confusion written on her face.

"That's not possible," she said. "I'm well out of range." Frowning, she began stabbing at the transport's comm boards.

Abruptly, Boone realized the source of her confusion. She was right; the transport *should* have been out of range of the jammer… had it been still on the platform and not resting at his feet.

He took that as his cue to move.

Rising from his crouch, he leveled the CUSP at her head and growled, "Freeze."

She did the opposite. Her head jerked around, her eyes colliding with his. Shock morphed into recognition and then anger as she realized who it was that held the weapon trained on her. As he'd predicted, she tried—and failed—to raise the partition.

"Where are they?" he demanded, his eyes drilling into hers as he sidestepped into the aisle, weapon locked on her face. *Damn, but she looks familiar. Where have I seen her before today?*

"Where are what?" She was one cool customer, he'd give her that. She'd recovered well from her initial surprise.

"The explosives you set on that platform. Where did you set them? And when are they scheduled to go off?"

Her eyes widened in mock innocence. "I have no idea what you're talking about. Like I told you on the roof, I'm a maintenance worker for the sky park."

"A woman, masquerading as a man, who just happens to abandon the platform in the middle of an emergency." He narrowed his eyes at her.

"I figured the best thing I could do was leave and bring back help. The rest is none of your business."

Boone's barked laugh held no humor. "Yeah, you see, I'm thinking it *is* my business." He shot a quick, pointed glance down at the pilot's holoscreen, where the aircraft heading was clearly marked. "Setting the transport's autopilot to circle the platform isn't going to bring Searcy any help."

A haughty look crossed her face. "The only responsible thing to do is to evaluate the situation first so that I can give the authorities as much helpful data as possible," she retorted smoothly.

"I'm curious. How are you going to explain away the dazzler core I found in your toolbox?"

Her expression didn't change, though her eyes blinked rapidly, an indication she was doing some fast thinking. She'd seemed confident in her conviction that she held all the cards, right up until he dipped a hand down and palmed the core. The CUSP's barrel never wavered as he showed it to her.

"Waiting for this to shut off? That's not happening any time soon." He cocked his head. "I suppose you'd need it to be off, so you can send the remote detonation codes to the bombs you planted."

Furious anger swept her face before it blanked. "I have no idea what you're talking about."

Boone cut her off. "You're going to give me the locations of each device you set."

Her lips slammed together, and she glared back at him in silence.

He shrugged. "No problem. My people will find them easily enough, after I turn you in to the authorities and shut the jammer off."

"Go right ahead."

Her tone held an edge of triumph to it that had Boone instantly wary. The only reason she'd respond in such a way was if she had some sort of a dead man's switch. Or if she were bluffing. Problem was, he couldn't afford to call her bluff. Nearly fifteen thousand lives hung in the balance.

He studied her as he tried to figure out how she'd set such a thing up. The only thing he could come up with was that the codes would automatically send if she lost consciousness, though the reasoning behind such an action escaped him.

Setting the core on the front row bench safely out of her reach, he moved forward until he could slip into the copilot's chair. His rifle banged softly against the side door as he settled into the cushion, but he ignored it, his attention focused on his target.

"All right, then. We'll do it this way. Hands out." CUSP still pointed at her, he dipped his shoulder, and the coil of cable slid down to fall into his palm. He let the loop he'd fashioned at its end hang free. It dangled in front of her.

"Hands," he instructed, extending the cable in her direction. "Through that loop. Now."

Her body stiffened, but she refused to move.

She's apprehensive. I can work with that.

He made a show of examining the weapon in his hand. He looked over at her.

"You know what this is?"

"Of course I do." Her words dripped disdain. "It's a CUSP. Law enforcement uses it."

He nodded. "So does the Geminate Navy. But *their* Compact Ultra-Short Pulsed weapon," he drew the words out, "doesn't just paralyze, or flash-bang or flash-blind. It also has a thermal ablation setting."

She stared at him blankly. He gave her a thin smile and let his eyes go flat and hard.

"Thermal ablation attacks your nerve endings. It isn't pleasant. In fact, it delivers searing pain. You won't be rendered unconscious. You'll just wish you had."

That was all it took; quickly, she shoved her wrists through the loop. He pulled on the cable, the wire tightening firmly about her wrists. Holstering the CUSP at the small of his back, he yanked on the cable, the action pulling her off balance. When she tumbled forward, he looped the cable around her torso, binding her arms securely to her sides. She began cursing, low and furious, when she realized he had her trussed beyond any hope that she could free herself.

"All right then. Let's have ourselves a little talk, you and me. Who are you with? Secede Sirius?"

When she still refused to reply, he shrugged. "Okay, then. We retreat until we're too far for your wire to send the remote codes to the detonators. You're still conscious, so no tripping a dead-man's switch. Easy fix."

Reaching across, he transferred the shuttle's controls to the co-pilot's station and turned the craft's nose toward Port Defiance. That done, he settled back, CUSP once more in his hand.

"Once we get outside detonation range, the jammer goes off, and I call in reinforcements."

A wild look crossed her eyes. She blurted out, "Not all of them are remote-code. Some are on timers. You leave the area, and I guarantee there's no way you'll be back quickly enough to save anyone on that platform."

He lunged for the holocontrols with his free hand, bringing the shuttle to a hover. Two thoughts crashed together simultaneously inside his head. First, there was confusion.

Terrorists don't overcomplicate things like this. What she's saying makes no sense.

The second thought, following fast on the heels of the first, was a hard anger.

"What the hell did anyone ever do to you, lady?" he snapped. "You would sentence thousands of innocents to death just to make a statement?"

"You don't know anything," she hurled back.

His thumb toyed with the weapon's dispersion settings, the movement drawing her eye. "Enlighten me."

She gave a bitter laugh, her head dropping back as she cast her gaze skyward. "Why did you have to show up, today of all days?" she said under her breath. "You've ruined everything."

"All a matter of perspective, I guess," he told her. "From where I sit, almost fifteen thousand people probably think it's a damned good thing I showed up."

She straightened in her seat, her expression blanking as she lapsed into silence

Boone felt frustration well. He had to get this woman to talk. At the very least, he had to neutralize her in such a way that it didn't trigger the detonation codes. His eyes landed briefly on the center console, and an idea began to form.

41: SAD FIVE BROS

SEARCY TRANSPORT

Boone kept the CUSP trained on the woman trussed in the pilot's seat while he reached over and opened the transport's center console.

"Look inside. Tell me what you see," he instructed.

The woman's eyes narrowed. "Do it yourself."

Boone lowered the CUSP, aiming it so that its beam would deliver a glancing blow. He fired.

She yelped and shrank away from him, her bound hands massaging her right thigh.

"The next one will be with my rifle, and not the CUSP."

"You… you wouldn't—" She glared at him, but he saw dawning belief in her eyes.

"Lady, you hold fifteen thousand lives in your hand. I'd shoot you in a heartbeat if it got me the intel I needed. Now, we can do this the hard way, with you bleeding all over the pilot's seat," he motioned to the console, "or you can pull out the first aid kit. Or don't. Depending on where I shoot you, it could take a while before you bleed out."

"This isn't cooperation; it's coercion," she snarled.

"You say potato," he said amiably.

She reached in and pulled out a first-aid kit. Based on its size, he was certain it would have exactly what he needed.

"Toss it to me, nice and easy," he told her.

She did as instructed. He snatched the kit from the air when it came sailing his way. Opening it, he rummaged around until he found its analgesic cylinder. He set the kit aside and dug into his pocket to retrieve the crowbar she'd left attached to the loading bay door.

He'd pretty much been a bust at any medic training he'd ever taken. But the technique the special operators back on Searcy had taught him today was one he'd consciously committed to memory. How ironic that, mere hours after learning about it, Boone would find himself needing to use it. He stared down at the narrow analgesic cylinder in his hand, more than a little nervous that he might make a misstep and fumble the process.

"What are you doing?" the woman asked.

He looked up. The wrath in her eyes had been replaced by a banked panic, though she worked hard to conceal it behind a mask of indifference. He thought about letting her stew, but then considered the psychological effect a trickle of information might have upon her.

"Just a little something I was taught by a Unit operator," he said noncommittally.

"Unit…?"

He smiled, but there was nothing at all friendly about it as he explained, "The Special Reconnaissance Unit. You know, the Geminate Navy's elite fighting force. They're the people on board that platform who are going to take you and the rest of the smugglers down." He let amusement seep through into his tone as he lifted the cylinder in his hand. "I just hope I remember how to do it properly. They only taught me this today…"

Leaving his words to hang between them, he dismissed her and focused once more on the cylinder he held in his hand.

He accessed the vid recording of Gabe's explanation that he'd stored in his wire's data partition.

"If you find yourself trapped and in need of a fast way to incapacitate the enemy, grab an analgesic med-bot cylinder out of any standard first aid kit." Gabe held up a hand, fingers spread as if holding an invisible canister between them. Then he motioned to Boone's shorts. *"You'll also need that thing you have in your pocket. Not the drones; the LockPik."*

"A crowbar would work just as well, ami," Thad said.

"True," Gabe agreed.

"The nano package inside the cylinder contains medical analgesic bots, programmed to block certain neurotransmitters in the central nervous system that send pain messages to the brain. With a simple bit of reprogramming, the bots can be retasked to send an entirely different message."

Thad leaned in, tapping his forehead. *"Store this acronym in your memory banks, hoss: SAD FIVE BROS."*

"Shouldn't that be 'five sad bros?'" Boone's voice asked.

One side of Thad's mouth kicked up at that. *"You'd think so, wouldn't you? But if you tried that, you'd never get it to work."*

Asha stepped in. *"Thad's right; it's SAD FIVE BROS,"* she said. *"The first step is to connect the LockPik or a crowbar to the top of the cylinder. Once it handshakes with the device, navigate through the following in the med-bots' menu—"*

Gabe supplied the list, the words softly spoken. *"First, you select '***S**ystem.' Next, '**A**dvanced.' Then '**D**eveloper options.' That's your 'SAD.' Then you'll need to trigger dev options **five times.**"* He stressed that last.

Asha took over the explanation. *"A new menu will pop up on your overlay. "Select 'B...R...O.' '**B**ackdoor', then '**R**eserve access,' and then '**O**verride.'"*

Gabe supplied the final step. *"That brings you to the final S in SAD FIVE BROS. Once the override menu pops up, it'll ask you to input the command phrase. That phrase is '**S**ilent Shield.'"*

Asha held up a cautionary hand. *"You need to know… this will alter the medical analgesic bots significantly."*

Boone paused the recording, chewing thoughtfully on the inside of his cheek. It was a complicated tangle of steps, but sure enough, the fifth time he pushed his military ID through to the developer options link on the menu, an entirely new set of choices emerged.

When he input Silent Shield, a question floated onto his overlay: 'Rewrite bot programming? Yes/No.'

He selected yes, and then waited. When the cylinder's dev menu flashed 'Operation Complete' at him, he knew he now held in his hand a way to get the information he needed from the woman seated across from him.

"But what does knocking someone out have to do with interrogation?" he'd asked, more confused than ever—not that he didn't appreciate the inside information.

Thad had grinned. *"Caught that, did you?"*

One corner of Asha's mouth curled in a wry smile. *"If you administer a half dose, you get a bot programmed to alter just enough neurotransmitters to change the subject's brain circuitry to be exceedingly trusting. That mental state is what was used in the previous century as a sort of 'truth serum' during interrogation. It was surprisingly effective, though experienced operators have been known to spoof it."*

She'd gone on to explain that the altered nanomachines also limited the subject's mental resources, impairing willpower.

Boone was banking on the combination of the two—trust and loss of self-control—to get him the information he needed. He was no interrogator, but he'd been taught basic tactical questioning, as had every Marine. Now all he had to do was implement what he'd learned.

Tossing the canister at her, he said, "Inject yourself."

"Oh, *hell* no."

He unslung the Kingsolver and aimed it at her thigh. "I'll begin with your left knee. You don't need it to talk."

Hate burned in her eyes. "What did you do to it? How do I know this won't kill me anyway?"

He shrugged. "You don't. Honestly, there's a good chance I didn't remember it correctly anyway," he lied.

She barked an incredulous laugh. "Go ahead, shoot me then. I won't do it."

He brought the scope to his eye and moved his finger to the trigger. It was enough.

"Okay, fine." Her hand shook as she pressed the med-bot cylinder to her forearm and pushed the injector button.

Boone powered the rifle down and set it aside, exchanging it for the CUSP. He watched her intently, wondering how long it would be before the neurotransmitter would take effect. That was one thing Asha had neglected to mention.

Thirty seconds passed. A minute, then two. Suddenly, she relaxed back into her seat and blinked sleepily at him. He took that as the signal to begin.

Half an hour later, Boone had heard enough. The woman was compliant, agreeably vacating the pilot's seat for the passenger section, where he used the strapping cables to secure her to the bench. Grabbing the core on his way back to the cockpit, he slipped into the pilot's seat and banked the shuttle into a tight turn that would bring the craft back on a sky park heading. Once the course was set, he turned the controls over to the ship's SI and lifted the core to examine it.

A drunken voice behind him complained, "You're going to ruin everything, you know?" Then the woman giggled.

He shot her an annoyed look from over his shoulder. "Do you have anything else to tell me about what you've been up to at Searcy? Anything else we should expect out of Mastai?"

"Nnnnope." Jayden said, popping the 'p' as she listed to one side and leered at him.

He tried one last time. "What about the explosive devices you set? Other than the remote detonation codes, is there anything else I need to know about them?"

The woman held her index finger up, but since her wrists were bound together and her arms lashed to her sides down to her elbows, she couldn't do much more than make an abortive attempt at the gesture.

"Nope. You dragged it all out of me. And I didn't mind telling you, either." Her brow creased in befuddlement. "I wasn't supposed to tell you all of that. Especially not about those last three."

She frowned, then straightened in sloppy indignation.

"You know, I was in the middle of setting those last four explosives when that bitch interrupted me? Things were going so well, too, until you showed up."

He glanced over at her and saw she'd leaned forward, straining against the cables that confined her.

"How can one Marine do so much damage, huh? And a guy stupid enough to turn a canoe paddle and a cable into a zip line, too." She threw her head back and cackled. "They were talking about it on the sky park's employee channel. Wish I'd seen it."

Boone had heard enough out of her. He reached for the analgesic cylinder he'd reprogrammed. "Didn't realize I was that entertaining," he said in a dry voice. "Okay, then. Nap time for you."

She nodded solemnly and even presented her neck to him so that he could inject her with the second half of the dose. It didn't take long; she slumped back in her seat and emitted a soft snore.

After one last, swift check of their heading, Boone turned his attention to the jammer. Synching with the unit once more, he ordered it off.

Instantly, the combat net snapped back into existence.

42: REPORTING IN

SEARCY TRANSPORT

It was immediately apparent that the team on the platform had been in contact with one another for some time. The conversation he joined was an active one and Boone knew better than to interrupt its flow. He waited for the rapid-fire exchange to subside before inserting himself into the conversation.

Before he had a chance to jump in and apprise them to his presence, Thad barked, *{Boone. Sitrep!}*

Boone repressed a smile. He should have known the Unit operator would have his eye on everything at once.

{I followed that hunch, sir.}

{The woman on the roof? Was she their sixth man?}

*{Yes. Well, sort of. She's the person **they** think of as their sixth man, except she's not really. She's not who they think she is. She's also the one responsible for bringing Mastai in on this whole situation,}* he told them.

{Well, hell,} Asha muttered. *{What's her angle?}*

Boone didn't immediately answer her question. *{I inserted into *her transport before it took off,}* he continued. *{I have her in custody now, as well as the dazzler core she was using to jam signals in the sky park.}*

Thad's avatar nodded. *{Thought something like that must have happened when our combat net came back.}*

{She's the one who set the bombs. There are a few more scattered around the park like the first one that went off. According to her, they're all programmed so that she can detonate them remotely. If what she told me under the influence of these med-bots can be believed,} he cautioned.

Boone pushed a map across the net, dropping pins on the location for each bomb. *{I've transmitted the disarm codes, but…}*

{But it might be wise to approach them as if they're still armed. Agreed,} said Gabe. *{What about that second explosion that went off?}*

Boone grimaced. *{They're all rigged, sir. She seated each bomb inside a crawler and then sent it up the cable far enough so that it can't be easily reached.}*

{We figured the other cables were rigged. I'm at one of the access hatches, Ramirez is at another. Davila's headed to the fourth one,} Thad replied. *{Did they have remote codes, too?}*

{They do,} Boone said slowly, *{but I didn't get a confirmation burst back from one of them.}*

{Which one?} Thad demanded. He chuckled dryly when Boone highlighted it on the map. *{Figures. That's the one in front of me. Just my luck, I guess.}*

{Have you reported this yet?} Asha interjected. *{You're outside the sky park; you might be far enough away to catch a node not impacted by the swamper.}*

Boone smacked the side of his head. His first instinct had been to contact Thad and the team. Plus, he'd completely forgotten the swamper. He tried to access the pubnet and got the same 'system busy' signal that had plagued them on board the platform.

{No joy on the pubnet, but I know where the swamper is. It's tangled in a mess of wiring on that clock tower's roof. Davila's good

with comms; he should be able to disengage that thing without doing harm to the platform's main node.}

Over the net, Boone saw Davila give him a thumbs-up. {Can do, sir, if you want me to head that way instead.}

Thad sent the PFC a curt mental nod. {Okay, since Boone received confirmation pings from the other two cables, we'll assume they've gone dormant. Davila, head to that clock tower and get that thing offline.}

{Sir…} Boone broke in again. {About the last remaining bomb, the one that's not responding to its shutdown code. I have an idea.}

He spared a look down at the Kingsolver in his hands.

{Shoot,} Thad ordered, causing Boone to cough a startled laugh.

{Actually, sir… that's exactly what I was going to suggest. I have eyes on the crawler. I can target its legs. Shatter them, and drop the thing into the ocean.}

There was silence on the other end.

{You ever done anything like that before, hoss?} Thad's voice was neutral, but Boone could hear the skepticism lurking just beneath the surface.

Boone took his time to consider the question before replying. {I've taken down grizzlies from horseback at three hundred meters,} he said.

Thad's avatar took on a skeptical cast. {That's a far cry from shooting a crawler holding a bomb, attached to a floating platform's cable, twenty-five kilometers in the air.}

Boone shrugged. {Its cross-section isn't that much different than a grizzly's head at this distance. Like I said, I'm comfortable with the Kingsolver, and it's comparable to the shots I've taken from horseback with the same weapon. Plus, it's not like I can hurt the cable itself.}

Gabe spoke up. {He's right about that. Hard to hurt self-healing carbyne fibers. What do you have loaded in there, son?}

{It's .308.}

There was a pause on the other end.

{You got any idea how hard that shot would be for a **Unit** sniper, much less a Marine lance corporal?}

Boone tried not to let the lieutenant's lack of faith in him rankle. Thad didn't know his history with his dad's Kingsolver, nor his proficiency scores, nor how many tens of thousands of rounds he'd shot with this very weapon.

{If I can do it} he said evenly, *{it'll save someone from having to crawl up there and manually defuse it.}*

{C'mon, Thad. Let him try.} Gabe said. *{What's the harm? Or are you that eager to climb that cable?}*

Thad made a strangled noise that almost sounded like a laugh. *{You make that shot, hoss, and I'll owe you a beer.}*

{I'm in, too,} Gabe added. *{And there might even be—}*

{Hold.} Thad cut in, the word brittle and hard, and devoid of its previous humor. The entire combat net went still, waiting for his next words.

{We have a situation.}

43: HOSTAGE

Chris Reid continued to keep a covert eye on the concession stand's newest arrival. The woman's behavior struck him as off somehow. It wasn't any one thing he could put his finger on. The woman was skittish, but that could be explained away as nerves. Stars knew the bomb that took out the support cable was enough to rattle the most seasoned soldier.

She was dressed in one of the t-shirts the sky park sold, which also worked in her favor. Asha Thacker had reported the smugglers were dressed as park employees. The dead man lying on the walkway a dozen meters away confirmed that.

Perhaps it was the way the woman stayed along the periphery. She kept her back to the wall, as if instinctively trying to keep someone from sneaking up behind her. That alone wasn't a crime, and he wasn't even certain she did it consciously.

The way she kept stealing looks over at the girls, though, was concerning. They'd gathered around his wife and were now busy relating the incident to her in hushed tones. The stranger's expression conveyed an almost studied neutrality, but she'd drifted close enough so that she could overhear what was being said.

The woman struck Chris as a powder keg just waiting to ignite. *Or a gun runner with a dragnet tightening around her.*

He moved through the crowd, headed in her general direction.

When the jammer cut out, the woman's head lifted. She turned to the tiki hut's entrance, her body language telegraphing that someone had contacted her. She relaxed and nodded, her gaze cutting over to the girls once more.

That did it. Instinct had him interposing himself between the woman and the girls. As he moved, the woman straightened, her eyes cutting over to meet his. Before he could reach her, she bolted. She ran straight for Amy and the girls, seized Tatiana by the arm, and pulled her aside.

Chris didn't need to hear the gasps to know the woman had pulled a weapon.

* * *

A priority ping cut into the combat net, drawing Asha to a stop. Minimizing the team's chatter, she accepted the incoming call.

{We have a situation.} Chris Reid's voice was grim.

{What kind of situation?} she asked.

{The hostage kind.} Reid paused. *{One of the smugglers has your niece.}*

Asha drew in a sharp breath. *{Where are you?}*

{Concession hut, just outside the saltwater pool.}

She changed direction. *{I'm on my way. Keep her there. If she tries to leave, stall her,}* she told him, breaking into a jog.

{I'll do my best. And Specialist… Without any way to contact the authorities, Posse Comitatus doesn't apply,} he reminded her. *{You and your teammates are citizens who have the right to defend yourselves in a life-or-death situation. But if you feel you need an authority to justify your actions, you have mine.}*

Asha sent him a nod. *{Thank you, sir. I appreciate that. I'd like to bring my friends in on this conversation, now, if you don't mind.}*

{Of course.}

It didn't take long to bring Thad and Gabe up to speed on the situation.

44: FIGHT OR FLIGHT

Transport Outside Sky Park

Thad pushed a quick, *{Archangel, mission's a go; report back when complete,}* and then the combat net lapsed into silence.

Boone wondered briefly what had developed on the platform but figured he was in no position to do anything about it, so dismissed it from his mind. Besides, he'd pretty much cut his own marching orders; now, he needed to prove he was up to the task.

He unwound from the pilot's seat and strode aft to check on his prisoner. The woman's pulse was slow and steady, indicating she was still out. Asha hadn't said how much time the knockout dose would last, so Boone figured he'd better get moving.

After checking her restraints, he backtracked to the cockpit and pulled up the shuttle's emergency procedures in case of catastrophic failure. As expected, the transport's first line of defense was for the SI to take over, piloting the vessel to below three thousand meters, which was the point where atmosphere outside the craft became sufficient to prevent the occupants inside from experiencing hypoxia.

That wasn't of much help to Boone. He needed a way to keep breathing while exposed to the nearly nonexistent atmosphere outside that cockpit door. He kept poking around until he found backup canisters of supplemental nitrox. These had a fine layer of dust covering them. Boone wasn't surprised; he couldn't recall a single incident in recent years where the canisters had been used.

They were, however, exactly what *he* needed to safely open the cockpit door—and take those shots the lieutenant was so doubtful he could make.

There was one more thing Boone wanted to arrange, to ensure his aim was as steady as he could make it. He hunted around in the aft hold for another strap used to secure cargo, but he'd used the only two the shuttle had to secure his captive.

Checking her pulse one last time and finding it remained slow and steady, Boone decided to risk it. He removed one of the two cargo straps securing the woman to the passenger bench, retreated to the pilot's seat, and raised the partition, sealing off the cabin.

The cargo strap was made from a stripped-down version of ActiveFiber that would accept only a handful of commands. He elongated the band until it spanned across the cockpit's hatch at shoulder level. With no way to mount a tripod, this would serve to steady the rifle's barrel.

Unslinging the Kingsolver, he positioned the nitrox canister's cannulas and affixed the unit to his tactical vest. Then he double-checked the seal between cockpit and passenger area one last time, to ensure there would be no loss of cabin pressure.

With a deep breath and a muttered, "guess I'm as ready as I'll ever be," he overrode the lock on the cockpit door and slid it open. Air escaped in a rush, and a sheet of biofilm fluttered past—an old invoice, long forgotten. The transport's drives ratcheted in volume, jumping from a low drone to a dull roar.

The shuttle's sensor feed was less sensitive than the ones the military used, but it had been sufficient to spot the crawler. Taking temporary control from the SI, he nudged the craft higher until it was slightly above the bomb, and then locked it down, placing the

SI autopilot into a hover.

He brought the Kingsolver to rest against the strap and peered through the scope. Slowly, he traced the cable until he found what he was looking for. Stroking the biometric handle, he released a scout. The drone flew from the transport, immediately gathering telemetry: wind speed, distance to target, angle of shot.

He dropped a targeting mark on the crawler's top set of legs, and then its next, and its next. He'd begin at each end and work inward. After dropping marks on all of them, he sighted in on the rear set of legs, using the scout drone's telemetry. He waited, timing the shot against the light buffeting of the craft, learning its rhythm.

Ordinarily, there wouldn't *be* a rhythm. Chop, what pilots called air turbulence, wasn't usually something one could predict. But this turbulence was caused by the heat signature of the sky park's platform. And so, it had a rhythm of sorts.

He rode with it for several beats, getting a feel for it as the crawler bounced up and down in his reticle. He waited, cognizant not only of the beat of the wind, but also the beat of his own heart. When everything synced, on the next downbeat, he shifted his finger from the trigger guard to the trigger and, on an exhale, took the shot.

The crawler's rear legs exploded in a shower of tiny fragments. Through his scope, Boone saw the crawler rock and then settle. He moved to the top, rode the wave, waited for sync, and pulled the trigger again.

The crawler had begun to sway; these next shots would be trickier but not impossible. He lined up on the center pair of legs, his finger stroking the trigger.

And then the shuttle rocked violently.

Boone gripped the strap to steady himself as wake turbulence from a rapidly departing ship buffeted the transport.

{LT! Shuttle just departed the platform and is headed for orbit. Vessel is accelerating and will soon be out of range.}

{You planning on shooting her down, Corporal?} Thad asked dryly. *{The Kingsolver's badass, but it ain't **that** badass.}*

That hadn't been what Boone had meant. Belatedly, he

explained.

{Sorry, sir. The Kingsolver's able to spike her, if you'd like. Then we can track it.

{Do it.}

Boone had already made the switch from his main barrel to the narrow barrel that ran above it, the one that was able to tag a subject with a spike from the Navy's database. Once tagged, anyone with the app and that spike's unique code would be able to track the shuttle anywhere in Alliance space.

Peering through the scope, Boone moved the Kingsolver's barrel up and to the right, waiting for the scout drone to work the math and provide a firing solution. His reticle flashed red, and he pulled the trigger. Light erupted; through the scope, he saw an icon appear with a small 'positive ident' tag that indicated the spike had affixed itself to the shuttle's port-side aft panel.

{Done.} Boone dropped the spike's code onto the combat net.

{Good job. Has that bomb been dealt with yet?}

Boone's attention returned to the cable and the crawler, which the wake turbulence had set to swaying.

{Negative. Wake turbulence interfered with my final shot. Waiting for it to settle.}

Even as he sent the thought, he could see that the turbulence was dying down. It, too, had a rhythm. Pushing every other thought from his mind, Boone settled behind his scope once more and began the targeting dance…

45: POSSE COMITATUS

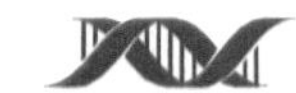

TIKI HUT

SALTWATER POOL

Chris Reid stood between the people crammed inside the concession stand and the woman holding a pistol against Tatiana's temple. His back was to his wife, his son, and the rest of the evacuees. The ES field that hemmed them in glowed faintly around the edges of the hut, backlighting their captors in an eerie and vaguely threatening glow.

Chris knew his body wouldn't provide much protection against the threat, but it was all he had to offer, and he'd be damned if he would stand by while some cartel thief threatened innocents.

"You need to keep a cool head," he advised the woman holding the gun on them. "Theft of military munitions is something you can walk away from after serving some time. Hell, kidnapping, too. But you're going to want to think long and hard before you use that thing."

He tilted his head to indicate the pistol in her hand. She was a little more than two meters away. He'd tried to maneuver himself closer, find a way to get inside her guard and disarm her, but the woman was nervous, not stupid.

She'd hit him with a hard look and then ordered him to step back. He retreated, but not by much.

"You wound or kill any innocents and the Alliance court system will *not* let you walk. You know this." He kept his voice low and even. He let the weight of his words carry the implied threat.

She glared back at him. "What are you, a lawyer?"

He gave an easy shrug and smiled, playing into her assumption with his non-answer. His attention ratcheted up a notch when her eyes darted to one side, and she brought her free hand up to her ear.

He hadn't noticed her wearing an earpiece, but her mouth was working as if there was something foreign and uncomfortable in it. He'd heard of such devices, ancient bone transmitting technology that operated on underpowered, narrowband frequencies too low for the jammer to block.

As a former boat driver, Chris knew a Dazzler's core targeted only the civilian and military comm frequencies currently in use. The fact this woman had such a device was proof that someone had come prepared to circumvent the jammer once it was turned on.

* * *

{I'm on my way to the tiki hut,} Asha said, projecting steel into her voice. *{Going to recon.}*

Thad sent her a headshake. *{Can't let you do that, cher.}*

{My niece is in there, Thad.}

"I know. That's exactly why you shouldn't be the one to go," a low voice called out behind her.

Asha spun to find Thad closing on her position. She tilted her chin in the direction of the cables that flew above their heads.

"I thought you were needed elsewhere."

Thad crossed his arms and sent her a flat stare. "Boone's got it handled. Gabe's on his way, too."

Asha licked her lips. By the look on Thad's face, it was going to take some convincing before he'd see things her way.

An incoming ping from Chris Reid had her holding up her hand. She brought Thad in on the conversation.

{I have an idea,} the Navy man said. *{You wouldn't by chance happen to have come across a device that looks like an earpiece or a microphone, would you?}*

Asha and Thad exchanged a surprised look.

{Actually, yes. One fell out of the mouth of an enforcer we took captive. Agent Alvarez called it a molar mic,} she told him.

{Why, Colonel?} Thad asked.

{Because the woman holding Tatiana hostage has one. She's using it to communicate with someone, I think. Maybe you can use it to talk to her.}

"Worth a try," Thad murmured. "Especially since Gabe's en route with the damn thing in his pocket."

{Thanks for the heads up,} she told Reid. *{We'll do that.}*

* * *

By the expression on her face, the person on the other end wasn't giving her news she wanted to hear. Suddenly, she spoke, and Chris realized why.

"Tell *Aunt Asha* that I have her damn niece," she snarled. "And if she wants to see her alive, you'll all back the hell off and give me safe passage to the loading dock."

Chris kept his face impassive, but inwardly, he smiled. Based on her words, Asha's team had figured out a way to communicate with her.

Mentally, he composed what he was about to say with the same care he would approach a war game on the Navy ship he'd once commanded. While she was distracted, he used that opportunity to take another step toward her.

"You've swamped the pubnet," he said, pushing his words to Asha at the same time so that she could hear. "No signal can get through. But even if they could call for reinforcements…they wouldn't. It's illegal. Posse Comitatus."

The woman's expression morphed from irritation at his interruption to confusion—exactly as Chris had hoped. Very few civilians were familiar with Posse Comitatus. He was banking that she didn't know about it either.

"The military has no jurisdiction inside Geminate space," he explained. "Besides, there's no Naval officer around to *authorize* such a takedown," he carefully emphasized the key words he wanted them to hear. "Even if there were, they'd be crazy to try to take on an armed cartel agent, holding this many people hostage."

Her glare heated. She advanced on him, her pistol swinging away from Tatiana to center on his chest. He now had an opportunity to disarm her, but he'd have to do it carefully, and he'd have to do it fast. There were too many civilians around who could get hurt.

Come on, he thought, *just a little bit closer…*

"Look," he added, "with the pubnet down, there's no way anyone could inform the authorities about this anyway. Besides, *you're* the one with the weapon—"

On those last words, he moved. He grabbed the hand holding the gun, forcing it down. Something shifted in her eyes and she went wild, fighting like a woman possessed. Chris recalled too late that, though he kept himself fit, he was a man who'd been driving a desk for the past two decades. Perhaps this hadn't been the smartest move after all.

He heard three fast pops, felt something impact his torso. He took a step back, surprise suffusing him. That same surprise seemed to cross the cartel woman's face, as if her finger had involuntarily tightened on the trigger without her conscious knowledge of it.

He took another step when he heard his wife scream his name. He turned toward it, some vague sense of urgency telling him he needed to go to her, while the analytical part of his brain registered that he'd been shot.

For some reason, his legs weren't working right. He fell, eyes widening in horror as his eldest son rushed toward the woman, rage written across his face.

"Chase, no!" he shouted, but the words got stuck in his throat as something warm and wet clogged it, and the words came out more of a garbled whisper.

He felt hands on his face, so warm, and looked up through blurred vision to see Amy, his wife, kneeling over him, a sharp, panicked expression on her face. She jerked her head up at the sound of their son's voice.

"You shot my dad! I'm gonna *kill* you!"

The hard slap of a fist against flesh sounded as Chase's voice cut off and another one took its place. "Kid, you just volunteered to be my next hostage."

Just before he lost consciousness, he heard the cartel woman who'd shot him order the ES field off.

And then his vision tunneled into one narrow, dark hole…

46: MAN DOWN

Gabe grabbed Asha's arm before she could launch herself down the pathway toward the tiki hut.

"Wait up." When she pulled against his hold, he gave her a slight shake. "*Listen* to me. We have a man down—"

"And a kidnapper holding my niece hostage," she interrupted.

"—*so*, when we go in, Thad and I will go after her," Gabe said, and then talked over her incipient protests. "You're on Reid. You're the only one here who has a hope in hell of saving his life."

"That's a low blow. You all have triage training, and the tiki hut won't have anything but a standard med kit. You're both capable of stabilizing him as well as I am," she countered.

Thad nodded toward two security men in park uniforms running their way. They carried a stretcher between them, loaded with paraphernalia. "Looks like your argument just flew out the window, *cher*."

"I ordered them to pack up and follow before I took off," Gabe explained, turning back to Asha.

Reluctantly, she nodded. "Copy. I'm on Reid."

After the security team handed over the medical supplies, Gabe and Thad helped Asha carry them to the tiki hut. As they neared the building, Asha tried repeatedly to raise Colonel Reid, but there continued to be no answer.

They came to a stop well before they reached the hut. *{Full recon before we approach,}* Thad ordered.

They split up, clearing the surrounding area.

{Nothing. No evidence anyone's nearby,} Gabe sent as they reconvened at the rear of the hut.

{She's got to be long gone by now,} Asha said.

Thad inclined his head. *{True, but I still want eyes on before we go in.}*

Asha shook her head. *{Wish I'd thought to grab a canister of surveillance drones when I kitted up.}* She pointed at the back entrance and then up to the roof. *{I'm lightest, least likely to be heard. I'll go up, peer inside.}*

{Don't forget the basics. Stay frosty, cher.}

Asha spared Thad a mildly peeved look. *{Yes, my niece is involved, but this isn't my first rodeo.}*

{It'll be your first that involves family. That changes things. Remember the OODA Loop: Observe, Orient, Decide, Act.}

Not bothering with an answer, she marched over to the hut and began stacking nearby boxes until they were tall enough to gain roof access. From there, she eased her way down the hut's sloping front until she came even with the glowing blue light of the ES field lining its edge. Sliding forward until her head just crested the roof's threshold allowed her to take a quick, careful peek at the tableau inside. She pulled back and ordered her optics to display what the brief glimpse had recorded, then sagged in relief when she caught sight of Tatiana.

{Target's gone,} she reported. *{I'm going to drop down, get them to turn off the ES field.}*

Her comment was met with two-clicks.

She grabbed two fistfuls of faux palm leaves in her hands, piked herself into a forward roll over the edge, and dropped lightly to the ground below.

The movement caught the attention of several park visitors. Frightened faces looked back at her, and she abruptly realized they were staring at her P-SCAR, slung tightly across her chest. Lifting her hands, palms open, she smiled encouragingly and took slow, deliberate steps forward. Stopping just outside the ES field, she motioned for them to let her in.

There were several headshakes, and no one ventured near the hut's controls. Quashing her frustration, Asha peered around those in front, trying to find her niece. She didn't see her, but she did see Amy, the colonel's wife. Pointing frantically at the woman whose tear-stained face remained downturned, hands cradling her husband's head, Asha mimed that she was here to render assistance.

One of the teens near the front turned to the woman and said something Asha couldn't hear. When Amy looked up, her eyes widened in recognition. She shouted something to the people by the ES controls, beckoning wildly for Asha to come in.

The moment they dropped, dozens of voices assailed her, all demanding to know what was going on.

"Medic! Coming through," she shouted in a voice that would have made her Drill Sergeant proud. Shoving her way to where Amy crouched, she knelt beside the fallen man.

Amy Reid's eyes met hers, the other woman's desperate. "Please… do something."

47: RECALLED

TRANSPORT OUTSIDE SKY PARK

Once he and Gabe hauled the medical gear into the hut and handed it over to Asha, Thad pulled Davila off swamper duty long enough to use the private's P-SCAR as a poor man's scope. It wasn't as good as having Boone on overwatch, but the PFC was able to use infrared to identify hot spots. Most weren't moving; there were two that were.

"The one by the town center's most likely park security," Gabe said thoughtfully. "Those men who delivered the gear to us."

Thad scraped a hand down the stubble that had begun to form on the side of his jaw. "Agreed, but we can't afford to assume." He shot a look at the agent. "You good with the town square again, while I track the other one?"

Gabe nodded. "Makes sense. You've already cleared that lazy river area once. You know it better than I do."

That settled, the two men separated. Thad had just reached the border where the lazy river began when Boone called in over the net.

{*Target down,*} he reported. {*I'm going to take down the others,*} *too, just to be safe.}*

The corporal's voice was calm and easy. Unruffled, as if he were taking practice shots at the range, not hanging twenty-five kilometers above the planet's surface, out an open cockpit door, and firing on a platform's tether.

Boone had asked his prisoner about each device's yield. Thad was as surprised as the corporal had been to learn the woman neither knew nor cared. *What kind of fucked up person does that?*

Thad stifled the urge to pepper him with questions. *How many shots did it take to unseat the crawler? Did you have any trouble taking the shots? Any indication of failsafes?*

Thad forced his mind back on his own objective, the woman who, even now, was stealing through the dense undergrowth with a teen held at gunpoint.

{Negative,} he told the young Marine. Quickly, he filled him in on the hostage situation. *{Need you back inside, Marine, you copy?}*

{Yessir. On my way.}

* * *

The chop around the platform had kicked up since he'd taken down the crawler with the defective bomb. He peered through his scope's optics and saw exactly what he expected—the second crawler he'd intended to target was bouncing around inside the viewfinder like a kid on a sugar high.

Guess it's a good thing I've been recalled, then.

Disengaging the shuttle's autopilot, he flipped the craft into a loop that would bring it even with the platform's lower level. Sealing the cockpit's outer door, he dropped the partition that separated him from the cabin, allowing the cockpit to repressurize.

As he neared his destination, a warning popped up, alerting him that the sky park dock's ES field was still up and that the landing would be aborted. Overriding the transport's safety protocols, he forced the small vessel to land on the narrow lip that jutted out beyond the ES field. It was a tight fit, but by slewing the craft sideways, he managed to set it down. The transport's magnetic locks secured the shuttle in place.

A quick scan of the dock's exterior revealed a maintenance door just to the left of its ES field generator. Boone grabbed the nitrox cylinder and reclaimed the strap he'd used as a sling for his rifle's barrel.

He stopped to add the strap to the restraints securing his prisoner, and then moved aft to the cramped cargo area. Sealing the partition that separated cabin from cargo hold, he donned the cannulas once more and cycled the shuttle's rear hatch.

Boone wasn't sure how much air was left in the nitrox canister, so he wasted no time. Pulling Davila's LockPik from his pocket, he slapped it onto the door's keypad and silently urged the small unit to hurry up and work its magic.

A few seconds later, he heard a click and a hiss as the maintenance door opened and its atmosphere evacuated. Boone stepped inside.

The door slid shut behind him, and his optics cycled to night vision when the area didn't automatically illuminate. He was in a tunnel. Boone broke into a trot, rounding a corner and then coming to a stop when the short dogleg terminated at the main docking area.

Closing the tunnel's inner door behind him, Boone shut off the nitrox canister and dragged in a lungful of fresh air as he looked around. Built into the near wall were a series of lockers. He headed over to look inside. The first contained an atmospheric suit with a CO_2 scrubber that looked like it had seen better days. He pulled it out and studied it carefully. The seals looked cracked, the material brittle where it had been folded.

"Damn thing looks like it's been stored in here longer than I've been alive," he said under his breath. He knew beggars couldn't be choosers, but he'd look long and hard for something else before he'd trust his life to that thing.

He moved on to the next locker. This one looked promising. Sitting at the base of the locker was an ES field disruptor. Unlike the atmospheric suit, the disruptor looked well-maintained. Boone stared at it for a long moment, debating the wisdom of using the disruptor to breach the airlock's ES field versus trying to find a way into the sky park's system and cycling the airlock using a computer override.

He was familiar enough with disruptors; they were commonly used by his platoon to breach abandoned mining platforms where smugglers had holed up. But they took time. It wasn't an easy feat, either. ES fields looked transparent to the naked eye, but they were anything but that. The two-layer quantum stasis field was a topological construct, generated from a toroidal field-inside-a-field, with dark matter axions comprising the inner ring that was then encased in an electromagnetic field.

The quantum stasis was strengthened through thousands of invisible threads spun from 2-D graphene. Each time an ES field was turned on, the filaments cascaded from the field's frame, directed along a precise path governed by the axion-EM field.

Breaching one took time, and that was in short supply. The disruption field created a dampening wave function, countering the field effect at a quantum level. In theory, it perfectly canceled out the wave function of the field it was breaching.

In theory.

Since ES fields were a product of quantum field theory, the mathematical description of the field's quantum state at any given point in time was more of a probability distribution than a precise measurement. The distribution contained all possible measurements of the field at a given point.

In addition, there was another little problem; introducing a temporary field that exactly cancelled out the existing quantum stasis field would destroy the one currently in use. That would permanently disable the loading bay's airlock, leaving it open to the nearly nonexistent atmosphere outside and rendering the bay unusable. Leaving that as a last resort, he shut the locker and moved over to master control, a small booth in the rear of the bay, offset to one side. Jogging over to it, he powered up the unit. Shockingly, no access code was required. With a mental shrug, Boone flipped off the outer ES field and, using the connection his wire maintained with the shuttle's Synthetic Intelligence system, ordered it to power up the drives and remotely pilot the ship into the bay.

48: BAIT AND SWITCH

The shuttle settled onto the loading dock's rails with a soft thump. Boone hopped inside the back of the transport and made his way through the cabin to the cockpit to power down the shuttle. He'd just taken a seat in the pilot's chair when something smashed into him from behind.

What the —? He jerked around to see his prisoner, once more awake, eyes blazing in anger. She'd managed to move from her seat and had come at him with both fists. He realized it had been a while since he'd checked on her.

"Bastard," she hissed. "You've ruined everything."

Boone biolocked the rifle and set it carefully aside. He grabbed the modified analgesic cylinder from his pocket and approached her again.

"Time for another dose," he told her.

She backed away, falling into her seat, and brought her knees to her chest. Boone mistakenly assumed she was shrinking back from him in reaction. He was wrong.

Her legs exploded outward in a vicious kick, her aim perfect. Her foot made contact with his hand and the cylinder went flying.

"If I can't have what I want then *you* can't have what you want," she hissed viciously. "What you and your friends are doing is illegal. Posse Comitatus."

He bent to retrieve the analgesic cylinder, brushing aside his irritation.

"Lady," he ground out, turning to face her, "in case you hadn't noticed, I'm off duty. Just a civilian trying to stay alive."

"By drugging me? That's assault!" Her expression turned smug. "I've heard of that drug, you used on me. It's not reliable. And I still have the codes. Up here." She tapped her forehead awkwardly with her bound hands.

He didn't answer her taunt, just slammed the cylinder against her neck and pressed. He frowned down at the thing when she remained upright and noticed that her kick must have dislodged the crowbar. Apparently, that allowed the medical bots inside to revert to their manufacturer's programming.

"I also have access to the public net now," she said triumphantly. "You can't stop me."

With a growl, Boone whipped the CUSP from the small of his back, thumbed it to its highest setting, and shot her, point blank.

"And stay down," he muttered.

He pushed past her, dropping to the deck just outside the shuttle. He stopped when an alert popped up on his overlay. Its contents had him wishing he'd shot the woman with something that was a little more permanent.

The lone bomb that had not accepted its disarm code—a bomb that *should* have been lying in the bottom of the Pelican Ocean— had just armed itself. Its proximity warning was flashing, telling Boone he was in the blast radius, and had thirty minutes to get clear.

Boone would have sworn the woman was giving him honest intel under the influence of the neurotransmitter med-bots, but her words just now made him uneasy. Had she accidentally swapped one of the bombs and not realized it, or had she truly given him misinformation?

Not that it matters, he thought grimly, staring at the proximity warning flashing at him. This warning was clear proof that the bomb Boone had shot down *wasn't* the one that had refused its disarming code. That particular one was still attached. And it had just begun a thirty-minute countdown sequence.

{Uh, guys? I think we have a problem…}

When Gabe responded, Boone swiftly brought him up to speed. As he did so, he cast his gaze around the dock, hoping that a solution might jump out at him. And then, one did. His eyes landed on a box labeled 'atmospheric suits' with the logo for the ride, the Sudden Death, emblazoned on its sides.

{Can you take the shuttle back out and target the correct one?} Gabe's question cut in on his thoughts.

Boone dragged his attention back to the conversation as he crossed over to the box and looked inside. He shook his head. *{Honestly, that's no longer a sure bet. Winds have kicked up. I think it's faster if I do it the hard way.}*

By Gabe's response, Boone could tell the agent expected the worst. *{**What** 'hard way'?}*

Lifting one of the suits from the box, Boone went for levity when he answered. *{So… remember what Lieutenant Severance said about no more aerial stunts? Afraid I might have to ask you to belay his order…}*

{Stars gone nova, what has your pet corporal done now, Gabe?} Asha's voice sounded amused, but there was an underlying strain to her tone that told Boone the medic was in the middle of something. Whatever that was, he suspected it wasn't good.

He held back the reply he wanted to give at her snarked 'pet' reference, opting instead for a simple, *{There's an atmospheric suit here. It's got the logo of that Sudden Death ride on its sleeve. I can use that. I'm sure that access hatch will have tethers, too. This platform wouldn't pass code without things like that in place. Their safety margins are much greater than the kind I'm used to working with in the Marines.}*

{You've done this kind of thing before, Corporal?} Gabe asked.

Boone barked a harsh laugh. *{Not even close.}*

There was a pause. When he returned, Gabe's voice was calm and smooth. *{All right, son. Give me details. Which bomb, how high up, and what's your plan to get to it?}*

Boone took a deep breath. *{It's attached to the cable by the starboard infinity pool. I'm sure the access hatch will have climbing ascenders; that's S.O.P. for this kind of thing. The grips will lock into place. I'll be perfectly safe.}*

{Or at least as safe as anyone can be with your ass hanging from a cable, twenty-five kilometers above the Pelican Ocean,} Asha cut in, her words dry.

{Or that.} Boone admitted.

{You be sure to tether yourself good to that cable, son. Don't make me deliver the news to your platoon leader that I lost one of his men to a fall from an amusement park ride.}

Gabe's threat brought a grin to Boone's face. It was all too easy to envision his platoon sergeant busting his ass posthumously for getting himself killed.

{Copy that.}

A quick glance over at the transport he'd just brought inside had him changing the subject. *{What do you want me to do with the woman? She got a bit unruly, and I had to CUSP her. She's sleeping it off but could come to at any time.}*

{Park security's riding herd on the prisoners for us. I'll send someone down there to take her off your hands.} Gabe said.

{Okay, then. Guess I'll head out.} With a last look back at the shuttle that held his unconscious prisoner, Boone lifted the suit he held in his hands.

At least these are in better shape than that one in the locker…

49: RIVER DANCE

LAZY RIVER

Water slapped the sides of the boat with a soft gurgling sound as its prow moved silently along. Thad bent forward, his P-SCAR raised and his eyes intent on the heat map his augmented vision provided. Both ahead and behind, trees dipped their leaves toward the river's edge, starlight sifting through their upper branches. High above, Beryl's orbital space station gleamed softly in the white dwarf's light.

He'd tracked the woman to a two-story structure up ahead. It encased a water slide park-goers could use to join those swimmers floating along the inner canal. The building was little more than façade, a fanciful art piece used to conceal the slide as it arched over the outer canal where boats passed by on an endless loop.

{Hey, ami, you still got that molar mic on you?} Thad sent to Gabe.

{I do. You need it?} the other man replied.

Thad reached out a hand to the lazy river's ceramacrete bank, pulling the boat to a stop alongside it. Stepping out and into the underbrush, he released the boat, sending it floating along its way.

{I'm thinking about engaging our kidnapper in a little psyops. Mess with her head a bit. You know, maybe throw a little of that NCIC magic at her. You in?}

There was a mystified silence from Gabe's end. *{NCIC—? I'm not sure I want to know what it is you think I do for a living...}*

{C'mon, hoss. Don't tell me you don't profile people when you investigate a crime.}

{Thad, she's not going to give herself up, if that's what you're asking.} Gabe's tone was dust-dry, as droll as Thad had ever heard it.

{Just get inside her mind a little, rattle her a bit. That's all I'm asking. Distract her while I sneak up on her.}

{Would it help to have a direct line to her hostage?} Asha interjected. *{Turns out she took Reid's eldest son. His wife says the kid's got a good head on his shoulders, though he's understandably upset. He thinks she killed his dad.}*

Thad considered that offer as he slipped from tree to tree, the dark shadow of a castle, complete with crenellated towers looming tall as he neared.

{Your call, cher. You're with the mother. How're you reading the situation?} He altered his heading, circling around the structure, looking for a way in that didn't involve a water entry.

{Earlier, I would have been fifty-fifty, but now that Reid's stabilized, well... she is, too. If that makes any sense. I say yeah, let her connect you two.}

Thad sent her a mental nod and continued his recon. He spied a door inset into the far wall. Upon closer inspection, he saw that it was a lift. He dismissed that as a possibility; the minute he called for the car, she'd hear it moving.

A ping sounded over his wire, and he accepted it. Asha gave him a quick introduction to Chase Reid, and then backed out of the connection.

{How you holding up, hoss?} he asked the teen.

{Better, now that Specialist Thacker told me my dad's going to

live,} the boy replied. *{Do you want me to talk to her, try to distract her?}*

{Nope, got that covered already. What I need you to do is remain compliant. Don't do anything to spook her,} he ordered, *{or alert her to the fact we're having ourselves a little chat.}*

Chase sent a mental nod. *{I can do that.}*

{Good. Now, I want you to be very careful to not react to what I'm about to tell you, okay?} At Chase's nod, Thad continued. *{I'm right outside this building. What I need to know from you is if you think she's aware of that. Has she said anything to suggest she knows I'm closing in on her?}*

The boy hummed. *{Well, yeah, but nothing specific.}*

{Which direction is she looking right now?} he asked.

There was a pause. *{Uhm, she's looking down at the water, and out the open hole where the boats pass through.}*

Thad crouched down beside the base of the building. *{Which direction? Where they enter or where they leave?}*

{Where they enter.}

He nodded. *Good.* He could work with that. He looked over at the massive weeping willow that had been strategically planted along the banks, right where its branches rained leaves down upon the entrance. It had one main branch strong enough to hold Thad that extended out over the water.

{Uhm, now she's getting agitated. Looks like she's talking to someone…}

Thad ghosted over to the base of the tree, his P-SCAR centered on the building as he went. He rounded the trunk and stopped when it concealed him from view.

{Listen up, Chase. I'm setting up a coordinate system. Boats entering is north. As you face that direction, to your left is west, to your right is east. Boats leaving, that's south.}

Thad spit out the words, rapid-fire as he began to climb. If Gabe was already doing his NCIC thing, then Thad was on the clock.

{Okay, kid, you're going to give me a running commentary, starting now. I need to know which direction she's facing at all times.

Go.}

Chase sounded off. *{North, now east. No, north. A little east again...}*

With Gabe as his distraction and Chase as his inside man, Thad stretched out prone along the branch, inching his way carefully forward, doing his best to test its strength as he went, and doing a significant amount of praying that it would hold.

50: TICKING TIME BOMB

SKY PARK GROUNDS

Boone's feet pounded the pavement as he raced through the emptied park, the sound of his boots slapping against ceramacrete loud against the humming backdrop of the platform. His destination was another half kilometer away, but he could see the infinity pool in the distance. Its surface was glasslike, gleaming under the light reflecting off the spaceport that hung overhead.

To its left, behind a long, narrow tiki hut filled with park visitors was a small maintenance shed. Thrusting through the shed's roof was an access tunnel that stretched up to meet the sky park's ES field.

That was his destination.

He ground to a halt just in front of the door, and it popped open for him, programmed to accept his ID token, courtesy of the advance work Gabe had done with the office staff. Sending the special agent a mental thank you, Boone stepped inside.

The shed smelled of sweat and grease, and boasted a small workbench that was surprisingly tidy. Beside the bench, hung on pegs along the far wall, were cables, tethers, wire clippers, and other assorted tools. What he didn't see were the ascenders he'd been banking on finding. Without them, climbing that cable would be a virtually impossible task.

Willing himself to stop and approach the problem with calm and logic, Boone methodically began searching through the shed, working his way from left to right. The fourth drawer he opened had what he sought.

Unslinging the sniper rifle and setting it aside, he stripped out of his tactical vest and unfolded the atmo suit. He'd had the suit perform a systems' check before he left the dock and had even brought a spare along with him, just in case.

On a deep breath, he slipped into the suit, trying not to consider the differences between one of civilian make and the kind his platoon used while on missions in the black.

Sealing the suit, he had it sync with his wire and perform one last systems' check. When everything came back green, he grabbed the tether and a pair of ascenders and approached the tunnel.

"Whose brilliant idea was this anyway, Brady?" he muttered to himself under his breath. "How many times has Ramirez told you never to volunteer for anything?"

Gritting his teeth, he headed up. At the hatch, he pulled his hood over his head, confirmed a positive seal, took a few breaths of stale suit air, and then triggered the hatch open.

A carbyne ring was welded to the hatch's frame; it was to this that he affixed one end of the tether. The other, he connected to his suit. Refusing to look down, he clamped the ascenders around the cable and began to climb.

* * *

A slight breeze from the platform's air circulation stirred the branches that cascaded over Thad, concealing him from the woman inside. Gabe had informed him moments ago that the woman's name was Petra.

From the heat map on Thad's overlay, whatever the NCIC agent was saying had wound the woman up good and tight. She kept her hand wrapped around Chase's bicep, but her movements were jerky and tension-filled, the barrel of her pistol swinging from 'north' to 'east' to 'north' again in spasmodic, erratic motions.

{Ease up on her a bit there, hoss,} he sent to Gabe. On another channel, Chase continued the litany, chanting, *{East, now south. East, north, east…}*

Thad pulled the rock he'd pocketed, wound his arm, and let the thing fly. As expected, when the thing connected with the side of the building, she whirled to face it.

Thad had his P-SCAR up to his eye before she'd completed her turn. *{Lean back and look away,}* he sent to Chase…just before he pulled the trigger.

The first two shots hit center mass, and then the barrel of Thad's rifle lifted, the third shot piercing Petra Cooke through the throat. As she fell to the ground, Thad called out to Chase, *{Get back!}*. He dropped from the tree and raced forward, his weapon sighted in on her slumped form.

He slipped through the opening and closed quickly, kicking her pistol away from her reach. With a quick look over at the kid, he asked, "You okay, hoss?"

Chase nodded, but even through the ghostly phosphor of Thad's night vision, the kid looked pale. He was gulping air and swallowing convulsively.

"Deep breaths," Thad advised, his attention back on the woman he'd shot. "Put your hands on your knees and bend down. Deep breaths. You're okay. Your dad's okay. It's all over."

51: LEFT SWINGING

SEARCY SUPPORT CABLE THREE

The climb to reach the bomb took a precious ten minutes. Once there, Boone tried yet again to override the device, but it refused to accept the command string. Afraid to mess with it too much longer, he pulled a plasma cutter from the tactical vest he'd donned over the suit and, one by one, severed the crawler's limbs.

He drew in a deep breath when the last leg snapped and the thing tumbled free, sparking once where it hit the platform's ES field on its way down to the ocean below. He sucked in another lungful of air before pocketing the cutter and easing the ascenders back down the way he'd come.

He paused when the connection he'd had with the transport, which he'd forgotten to dissolve, notified him that the vessel was being powered up. Concerned that the thieves had made their way to it, he overrode the startup sequence, shutting the system down once more.

He reached out to Gabe. *{Are you sending someone out in one of the transports? The shuttle I just docked has powered up.}*

{No,} said Gabe. *{The only person we sent down there was a security team member to round up your prisoner. Hang on; let me check in with them.}*

Gabe came back online, voice tight. *{They haven't made it there yet. You think it's the maintenance worker you captured?}*

Boone sighed. *{It's possible. I underestimated her once before,}* he admitted. *{She took a pulsed CUSP blast, full-strength. I suppose it's possible she's recovered.}*

{I'll send Davila down to check it out. You said you were alerted?}

{Yessir. I'd forgotten to release the override codes when I left the shuttle, and I got a notification on my wire.}

{Davila's on his way,} Gabe told him. *{He'll be on the lookout for your hostile. What's your status?}*

{Bomb's on its way down to the ocean. The right one, this time. On my way back down now,} he said.

{You tethered to that cable, son?} Gabe's voice was sharp.

{Sir, yes, sir. This soldier does not have a death wish, sir.}

As he spoke, he released the bottom ascender and pushed it down by another half meter. Mentally re-engaging its clamp, he eased himself down while releasing the top ascender and sliding it down to meet the first one.

{Copy that. Keep us apprised.} With that, the connection closed.

Minutes later, the high-pitched whine of a shuttle hit his ears. He twisted to try to locate the sound's origin and was dismayed to see a familiar sight. Apparently, Davila hadn't made it to the dock in time.

Boone expected Jayden to head for the coast, but the woman flipped the shuttle and headed back for the platform instead. More precisely, she angled the transport up, toward the tether. Boone's heart sped up when he realized that it was on a heading that would bring it perilously near him. And it was closing fast.

He attempted to raise her on the guard frequency all ships were legally required to monitor. When nothing happened, he shot off a warning broadband across the pubnet.

{Vessel approaching sky park: Break off, break off, break off.

You're getting dangerously close to the support cables!} He repeated the warning, dismayed to see the vessel angling carefully so that is drives wash were pointed directly at him.

{Sitrep!} the command sounded over his wire just as he looked up to see the woman crouched inside an open hatch, weapon raised.

Damn fool! Boone clung to the cable as it whipped back and forth in a frenzy. His hands gripped the ascenders until his knuckles were white, his legs wrapped around the cable as his body was flung back and forth, helpless victim to the crazy resonance the wash from the engines had induced.

{Corporal! Sitrep!} The words snapped at him over the combat net, but his focus was entirely on the shuttle as it hovered a scant and perilous thirty meters away.

He heard the whine of the weapon's discharge and realized he was being shot at. Oddly, that made him laugh.

Good luck with that, he thought. The crazy woman didn't realize the engine wash was by far the more deadly of the two. It was clear, even from this distance, that she lacked the training to know the weapon tucked securely in the pocket of her shoulder would do him no harm. Forget thermal bloom rendering the weapon useless at this distance; the wild swinging of the cable made targeting him next to impossible.

Abruptly, he realized he'd yet to respond to Gabe's command. *{Searcy transport, lone shooter,}* he reported, the words staccato in their brevity. *{Engine wash. Can't hold on much longer.}*

He heard Thad swear. *{You'd better hold on, hoss. We're on our way.}*

But Boone knew they'd be too late. He had to act now if he wanted to survive this.

His assailant disappeared into the shuttle, apparently coming to the realization that killing him by laser-fire was a nonstarter. Then the shuttle began to move. The first pass nearly ripped him from the cable. He wouldn't survive another.

Her pass had been so close, he felt like he could practically brush his hand against the engine's nacelles. The thought gave him an idea. It was batshit crazy, but it just might work.

He waited until she was at her furthest distance, turning for her next pass. Releasing one of the ascenders, Boone reached a hand down, unclipped his tether, and coiled it, just like he'd done countless times back on the ranch. Holding the coil in the same manner he'd use when roping a calf, he braced himself as best he could, clinging to the cable with one hand and both feet, and then waited for the next close pass.

He'd only get one chance at this, and timing would be critical. Even then, he knew there was a better than fifty percent chance this stunt would take him down, too.

The shuttle began its run. Boone's muscles strained, pouring every ounce of strength he had into his grip on the ascender as the cable began swinging wildly once more. He waited until the shuttle's air intake was within throwing distance, then swung the tether with all his might. It flew true, in a long looping arc, directly toward the nacelle's air intake, but Boone didn't wait around to see. With both hands now gripping the ascender, Boone sent the app that controlled it a mental command—and suddenly he was in freefall, the ascender plummeting half a kilometer toward the platform below him.

Above his head, he heard a horrible grinding noise as the tether fouled the shuttle's drive. The cable he was connected to shuddered as the tether snapped tight, and Boone prayed that the ring that secured it wouldn't hold.

The numbers ticked down on his app and he knew he'd have to engage the ascender's grip once more if he wanted to avoid splattering himself against the maintenance hatch below.

He ordered the app to begin braking in short pulses and quickly felt heat begin to build up through his gloves. With a sudden snap, the tether gave way, and out of the corner of Boone's eye he saw the shuttle fall away.

He wasn't slowing enough. Worse, a warning telltale began to flash, signaling the ascender in use was overheating. Boone braced as best he could and freed one hand, the other blindly grasping for the second ascender clipped to his suit.

Affixing it to the cable while the carbyne line whizzed past at an alarming rate was like trying to thread a needle while racing along on horseback. On his third try, it snapped into place. He began engaging it mere seconds before the first ascender went into shutdown.

The plunge took thirteen seconds before he started to slow. It was the longest thirteen seconds of his life. He braved a look down and saw to his relief that the hatch was open, with both Thad and Ramirez braced to catch him.

He was still falling at a good clip, though the ascenders had done a fair job of slowing him. He winced in anticipation as the last few meters flew past—and then he was in, snagged by the combined strength of his platoon mate and the Unit operator.

All three went tumbling to the floor of the maintenance tunnel, the impact rattling Boone's bones.

Beside him, Thad rolled to his feet with a groan and with hand signals, ordered Ramirez to seal the hatch. Boone decided he'd just hang around on the floor for another few seconds.

"Well, hoss, I'd say you've just about used up your quota of damn fool stunts for the day," the operator drawled.

Boone cracked open one eye. He waved a hand in half-hearted acknowledgement to Thad's statement. "Sir, yes, sir," he managed.

A dark-skinned hand came into view. Boone grasped it, and Thad drew him to his feet.

"The shuttle?"

"Being escorted back to Port Defiance," Thad said. "And a Novastrike filled with Marines just docked. You can stand down now. Reinforcements have arrived."

52: AFTERMATH

SKY PARK GROUNDS

Early the next morning, Boone received a summons, inviting him to the Port Defiance branch of the National Security Agency. Mystified and a little unnerved, he complied. He arrived to find Thad and Asha waiting for him outside. Shortly thereafter, Ramirez and Davila showed up.

"Are we in trouble or something?" Davila asked, nervously looking about.

Thad dipped his chin and looked at the private from beneath lowered brows. "You got something to be nervous about, hoss?"

When Davila's eyes widened, Asha dug her elbow into the operator's side. "Lay off, LT. You're scaring the crap out of him."

Ramirez took a wide step to his left and shot Davila some side-eye. "Dude. Not literally, I hope."

Ignoring the antics of his platoon mates, Boone turned questioning eyes on Thad. "Why *were* we called here?"

The operator hooked a thumb over his shoulder. "Duncan Cutter invited Gabe to question the suspects. We," his finger helicoptered around, indicating their small group, "get to watch.

Duncan Cutter? Ramirez mouthed to Boone. *Director of the NSA?*

Boone lifted a shoulder in a half shrug.

Asha looked at Thad. "Who arranged this?" she asked.

Thad crossed his arms. "Chris Reid. Cutter dropped in to check on him at the hospital." His lips twitched. "Apparently, he and Lane double-teamed him. Cutter gave in, after the colonel cited Gabe's familiarity with the case."

Asha nodded. "Nice of him to do that. Of course, Chris has a vested interest in the case, considering they held his son hostage and nearly killed him." She headed for the steps, calling out over her shoulder, "Well, come on. We don't want to miss the good parts."

* * *

The woman seated across the table from Gabriel Alvarez looked defeated. As Boone, Thad, and the rest watched from an adjacent room, the NCIC agent pushed a plas sheet forward and tapped a finger to call her attention to it.

"That's the woman who flew the shuttle I spiked?" Boone asked quietly as they stood around the holoprojection that showed the interrogation being conducted next door.

"Yep. Name's Delia," Thad said in an undertone as Gabe began questioning the woman. "The Navy tracked her all the way to the orbital station. They were waiting for her when she docked."

"Lone surviving member of the smuggling operation," Asha murmured. "Talk about bad career choices."

They lapsed into silence when Gabe's voice filtered in from the other room once more. "So, you didn't know your boss had ordered the person you knew as Jay Henson to plant bombs on the platform?"

Delia shook her head wearily. "No. Like I said, when Petra finally told me about it, she was livid. Jay was only supposed to set charges to scare people into thinking there was an attack. No one was supposed to get hurt, and we sure as hell weren't out to kill anyone. That would have brought too much heat and attention down on us."

Gabe nodded. "That's what I figured. Did you know Jay Henson was Jayden Harte?"

"The newsnet anchor?" Delia looked startled, and then a thoughtful expression crossed her face. "I honestly didn't, but now that you say it, yeah, I can see the resemblance."

"And you didn't suspect her, when she joined Mastai six months ago?"

The woman shrugged. "A lot of folks in the cartel don't like to talk about their histories, where they came from, that kind of thing. We don't press. All that matters is they do their jobs, and they do them well."

"And Jay—Jayden—was one of those people. So, you really didn't know anything about her?"

She shook her head. "Only that Jay had a reputation for being a hard worker, and responsible. Those two qualities can move you up pretty quickly in the ranks."

Gabe shot her a speculative look and then asked a final question. "Whose idea was it to place those charges?"

The woman looked embarrassed. "Petra said it was Jay's," she admitted. "But she'd been led to believe they were harmless."

Thad pushed away from the holo. "A frickin' *news* anchor," he said with disgust.

Asha shook her head. "Hard to believe she'd go to all that trouble. Staging an internecine war between Mastai and the smugglers, then faking a Secede Sirius attack? All for ratings to boost a flagging career."

Boone lifted his hands, and then let them drop to his sides. "That's what she told me, yes."

They'd held an informal after-action report among themselves while waiting for law enforcement to debrief them. Unfortunately, the confession Boone had extracted from Jayden was inadmissible as evidence since it had been done under the influence of the med-bots.

Thad hooked a hand around the back of his neck and looked up at the ceiling. "I looked her up last night. Something about her name…" His voice trailed off. He tilted his head, his eyes seeking Asha's. "Did you know she was a war correspondent? A reporter, embedded with the Navy during the Zosher incident in the Sargon Straits."

The medic's brow creased. "Wow, that was decades ago, but…" Her gaze grew distant. "Now that you mention it, she was everywhere on the newsnets back then. I even saw her dressed in SDU baselayers, reporting live alongside Marine fireteams."

Thad grunted. "It'd explain how she was aware of Posse Comitatus, too. Never known a civilian to have the first clue about such things, and the news usually gets stuff like that wrong, too."

Ramirez's head had been bouncing back and forth between the two like a spectator at a tennis match. "Dude, I don't remember any of that…" he said to Boone under his breath.

Asha shot the young Marine an amused look. "That's because you're just a pup."

Thad ignored the exchange, his gaze riveted to the holo once more. Boone turned to look.

Delia's interview had drawn to a close. An NSA agent had arrived to escort her from the room. In the hallway just beyond the agent stood Jayden Harte, flanked by two more agents.

Boone studied her as she entered. She had a confidence bordering on arrogance, and her carriage held an almost regal bearing, despite being dressed in orange coveralls with her wrists bound in front of her by mag-cuff bracelets. The woman looked nothing at all like the maintenance worker she'd imitated the day earlier.

"That was some acting job she pulled yesterday," Boone said, his amazement at the transformation drawing him closer to the projection.

"Un-frickin-believable," Thad repeated. "And all for ratings."

They observed as Gabe questioned Jayden thoroughly. It slowly became clear to them all that the woman held no remorse for her actions. By the end, even Gabe was having a difficult time remaining impassive.

When the session came to an end, they trooped out of the Agency's viewing room and were guided by a service SI to a nearby break room to await Gabe's return. On the newsnet holo playing in the corner was splashed the headline, 'Former Geminate Nebula News Reporter Jayden Harte Held for Questioning on Sky Park Attack.' The sub-header read, 'news anchor accused of inciting skirmish to reinvigorate waning career.'

Boone glanced away as live images from the sky park filled the screen. With an annoyed growl, Thad grabbed the controls and turned off the newsnet feed. Asha moved over to a credenza where carafes of coffee sat behind small stasis fields. She poured Thad a cup, then offered one to Boone.

He wordlessly waved away the offer, too restless to take a seat. For the first time in more than twenty-four hours, his mind wandered back to the decision he'd have to make upon his return to Ouray base.

He was startled to feel a hand come down on his shoulder. He spun, shrugging the hand off, only to freeze when he realized what he'd just done… and who the hand belonged to.

Asha's knowing look met his. "It's normal to be a bit punchy after what you've been through. I won't tell you to relax; you'll unwind at your own pace soon enough."

Her gaze shifted from him back to where Thad and Gabe were discussing the results of the questioning. A long moment passed, and then her voice sounded quietly beside him.

"You couldn't find two better role models to pattern your career after," she murmured. "Stars know, Thad and I have pulled each other's asses out of a sling more times than we can count."

Her words made Boone realize how intently he'd been studying the two men. It was obvious that she'd noticed.

"I've seen you watching them," Asha said. "Let me guess; newly promoted lance corporal, trying to decide exactly what direction you want your military career to take?" She inclined her head once more to the two men. "Either one of those would be a fine role model to pattern your life after. Though they pursued two completely different paths."

"What's it like, being with the Unit?"

Asha's expression took on a contemplative cast. She looked down and her hand came to rest on the weapon holstered at her waist. After a beat, she looked back up at him.

"I've only just been tabbed, mind you. But I've been deployed in places where operators were inserted. I've seen them work, and I am honored to call several of them friend." She looked off into the distance, seeing something only she could see. "In some ways, it's a study of extremes and contrasts. You see great sacrifice. You see the worst of humanity, but you also see the best as well. I do know this: I'll never regret my decision to join the Unit. The missions they run and the actions they take under cover of night and out in the deepest black are what keep billions of people safe back home."

Something in Boone shifted. Her words drew him, had him responding to a calling deep within, a purpose he'd not truly known existed before today.

She looked back at him, the ghost of a smile playing about her face. "There's a famous pre-Diaspora saying. I don't recall its exact wording, but it goes something like this: 'the worlds can rest easy at night, secure in the knowledge that rough warriors stand ready to fight, prepared to visit a fierce reckoning upon any who would do them harm.'"

Boone had heard something similar, though the words seemed to vary with the telling and the one who delivered the lines.

"The life is not for everyone," she admitted. "But I can't think of a single thing I'd rather do."

She pushed away as Thad and Gabe neared. Flashing him a quick smile, she added, "I guess you've had enough lecturing out of me for one day.

"Thanks." Boone dipped his chin. "I appreciate it. And I think… I think I know what I'll be doing, once I get back to Ouray, and we've wrapped up this whole mess with the platform."

Asha straightened as Thad came to a stop in front of them.

"Marching orders, LT?" the medic asked.

Thad slapped a hand on Boone's shoulder and then looked over at Asha. "C'mon, let's get the hell out of here. Seems I owe someone lunch. Maybe even a beer tonight, at the Thirsty Whale."

He shot Boone a long, searching look. "And someday, just maybe, there might be a recommendation coming your way, when the time is right. That is, if the Q-course interests you?"

His question had Boone's spine snapping straight. "Sir! I..."

Boone's words tumbled to a halt, his gaze straying to meet Asha's. The medic gave a slight nod, understanding clear in her eyes.

Boone turned back to Thad.

"Thank you, sir," he said quietly. "Yes. Yes, I'd like that very much."

I hope you enjoyed Boone's story. He ends up playing an integral role in the Biogenesis War trilogy.

If you don't mind, please take a minute to leave a short review on Amazon. Not only would it make this writer a very happy person, but your review also makes a real difference. It's an effective way you can help to keep this series going. The more reviews, the easier it is for new readers to find these tales!

Keep turning the page for a special preview of the first book in the Biogenesis War trilogy, *The Chiral Agent*.

WANT UPDATES?

Connecting with you as a reader is one of the most rewarding things about writing. I'm active on Facebook at LL Richman's Spacetime Speakeasy. There, you'll receive the latest news about new books, giveaways, get some behind the scenes intel on the science used in the books, plus some really bad dad jokes.

Use the QR code below to get to the Speakeasy, or the following link will take you there: bit.ly/SpacetimeSpeakeasy.

I hope you enjoyed Boone's story. Keep turning the page for a special preview of the first book in the Biogenesis War main trilogy, **The Chiral Agent**, available in ebook on Amazon, or in print from any book retailer.

PREVIEW:
THE CHIRAL AGENT

DEADLY DISCOVERY

Advanced Isolation Lab
deGrasse Research Torus
Vermilion, Luyten's Star
Geminate Alliance

THE SPECIMEN CASE was unique. Tucked away in deGrasse's Advanced Isolation Lab, it was disguised as a large gray shipping crate, purposely mislabeled as cleaning supplies. One look inside instantly dispelled that fiction.

It contained no solvents, no soaps. Yet neither was it a standard specimen case. There were no compartments designed to isolate biological samples, laid out in neat, sterile rows.

Instead, opening this case was like falling into a looking-glass microcosm teeming with native life. Segmented into four terrarium-like vivariums, each biosphere was host to its own species: insect, arachnid, rodent, reptile.

The specimen case was unique in another significant way. The biospheres within were engineered from unique molecular building blocks found on Vermilion, the sole habitable planet orbiting Luyten's Star. The life found here was unlike anything else humankind had discovered in all their centuries-long exploration of the universe.

For all but a select few in the Geminate Alliance, it didn't exist.

When the first reports made their way to Alliance headquarters in Procyon, the decision was made to place Luyten's Star under interdiction. The discovery was deemed too dangerous, too easily weaponized. Until Geminate scientists could fully decode what they'd found, all information pertaining to the discovery had been classified, reports redacted.

The Navy's premiere research station was secretly relocated to Luyten's Star, and placed in orbit above Vermilion. DeGrasse was staffed by a small team of civilian researchers under contract to the Alliance. These were recruited by the Navy's Advanced Research Agency, and sworn to secrecy about their work.

The decision to interdict Luyten's Star had been made in the hope that news of the discovery could be contained, the sensitive information hidden from the prying eyes of Alliance enemies.

They failed.

AWAKENED

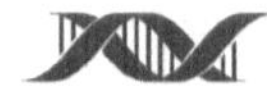

LOCATION: UNKNOWN

"HOLY—! SARGE...IT's alive!"

The exclamation pierced through the fog that cocooned Micah's mind. Distantly, it registered that he was lying on his back, somewhere cool and dark. With effort, Micah pushed against the mental fog that clung to him like a sticky web. His limbs felt leaden, his eyes refused to open.

A second voice joined the first.

"Of course it's alive," the sergeant responded. "It's biomatter. Living tissues and shit."

The sergeant's gruff tone reminded Micah of his drill instructor back at OCS—the kind of person who didn't suffer fools or idiot officer candidates.

The sergeant wasn't done. "Just do what the eggheads in research ordered and burn it." He barked the order, his voice growing louder as he neared Micah's location. "Or do I need to shove my boot up your ass to get you to do your job?"

"But I have neural activity on scan," the first man protested. "That's a *person* in there, Sarge, not biomatter. Already sent a ping to let Doc Janus know." Agitation was replaced by urgency as his voice drew near. "Hey, grab the emergency kit by the door, willya? I've got to get him out of there."

Micah heard the sergeant sigh. "Dammit, corpsman. Why'd you have to go and run a scan?" His tone was a mixture of annoyed and tired. "Couldn't you have just done as Janus ordered? Now *I* gotta do as he ordered."

Those words stirred a vague sense of unease in Micah. It turned to alarm when he heard the sound of a firearm being unholstered. He fought to throw off the haze that clouded his mind, to reach out, call a warning.

"Sarge? What…wait— " The corpsman's words cut off at the sound of a directed energy weapon being discharged. Micah's gut clenched; he knew what that meant.

"Sorry about that," the sergeant muttered. Footfalls closed the distance as he stopped in front of the dead corpsman. "You were a good kid, too."

There was a grunt, followed by a soft scraping noise, and annoyance returned to the sergeant's voice.

"Well, hell. Now I have two bodies to dispose of. You damn well better be good for the credits, Janus," the man muttered, "or I might have to pay your pogue ass a visit, too."

Janus. Micah forced his mind to latch onto the name. Not that he was in any position to share—

In a moment of clarity, he recalled the evanescent wave nanocircuitry wired into his neural net. It was something every Alliance citizen received when they came of age.

Micah's wire had been upgraded when he joined the Geminate Navy. The implant was military-grade and encrypted, allowing him to connect to any secured network. He reached mentally for it, cursing his drug-induced fog. His thoughts were clumsy, his implant a slippery and elusive thing.

A thundering scrape of metal above his head interrupted his attempt to connect with the dormant unit. His brain nudged at him, the sound vaguely familiar. Something landed with a dull thump overhead.

The corpsman's body.

A spike of adrenaline cleared his thoughts, and he realized what his subconscious mind had been trying to tell him. He knew now where he was being held: inside an incinerator.

His limbs twitched as he strained to overthrow his paralysis. He had to get out before the thing fired up.

Easy there. You'll be fine.

The thought startled him, seeming to come from nowhere, but he'd run out of time to analyze.

With a deafening roar, the incinerator fired up. All around him, the inferno raged, heat building in the darkness until he knew no more.

* * *

"Shit. He's not dead."

Micah jolted back to awareness as the words brought memory flooding back. He was still supine, still in complete darkness. He was as surprised to find himself alive as the voice sounded.

From what he could tell, his situation hadn't changed, although he seemed to have a clearer head this time around. He had no idea how long he'd been out, but he remained unable to move, to speak, or even to open his eyes.

The voice sounded again. It was the sergeant from before.

"Now what do we do? Janus said we need to scuttle all the evidence before fifteen hundred hours."

His query was met with a curt response.

"Then kill him again, soldier. And this time, check your work."

The new voice was female, her words chilling. They galvanized Micah; he fought for mobility, to no avail.

The sound of soft footsteps heralded her departure, followed by the sergeant's softly muttered, "Damned Akkadian. I didn't sign up for this shit."

The man began to move toward Micah's location, but was

brought up short when a resounding clang sounded in the distance. The noise elicited a string of curses from the man, the words fading with distance as he ran to investigate.

In the next instant, Micah felt a slight breeze caress his skin. Within seconds, his mind was much more alert than it had been mere minutes before, when he'd clawed his way to consciousness. His arm bumped against a smooth surface and he froze, arrested by the knowledge that he could now move.

This was a significant improvement.

He turned his attention to his surroundings, to finding a way out of his confinement. The cushion of chill air around his face suggested close quarters. He reached a cautious hand up and met resistance, ten centimeters above him. The cold leaching from it into his palm suggested some type of metal.

He pressed his other hand beside the first, then slid both apart, using the movement to measure the space that held him. Another twenty centimeters and both hands stopped, having found the sides of his prison.

It suddenly registered that *he* was cold.

Where the hell am I? he thought.

There was the briefest of pauses, and then an answer sounded inside his head.

Base Morgue. Level -10. deGrasse Torus. Luyten's Star.

The words jolted him. These weren't his thoughts. He knew this with certainty, but *how* he knew escaped him, since they hadn't come across his wire. After almost two decades living with the unit embedded in his skull, he'd become used to feeling the presence of the neural implant. It was always there in the back of his mind, like subliminal white noise.

Until now. Its silence was glaring, and yet a voice was unmistakably there.

Deal with it later, Case, he told himself. *Survival first.*

He ran his hands blindly along the seam of his prison walls, seeking a way out. His fingers stilled momentarily as it came to him that his wire wasn't his only nonfunctioning implant. His optical augments weren't working properly, either.

He should have been able to scan the area on all EM bands, the coolness of the metal above him registering in muted blues and purples. Instead, he was enveloped in an unrelenting blackness.

Now would be a good time to leave.

With this newly transmitted thought came movement. The darkness split above his head, broken by a shaft of light. His eyes slitted shut in response to the sudden brightness. The light played down his torso as the platform on which he lay slid out of the wall—a wall of identical drawers, each the exact dimension of the space that confined him.

And then it hit him. He wasn't just in the base's morgue, as the voice had indicated. He was on a freaking *slab* in the morgue. In one of its self-contained storage units, each of which could be individually incinerated.

Which explains why I'm still alive, he realized. *Somehow my unit must have malfunctioned.*

He turned his head, eyes darting about the room. He was alone, the sergeant nowhere to be seen. Expelling a breath, Micah sat up. The chill air hit his naked flesh as he assessed his condition.

Get dressed.

The mental words were punctuated by the sound of a locker opening against the far wall. Micah gripped the side of the platform, the sharpness of its metal edge grounding him as he considered what to do.

Shaking his head, he hopped down from the cold, steel surface. As he strode toward the locker that sat invitingly open, thanks to his mysterious benefactor, he reviewed what he could recall of deGrasse. He knew the morgue was on the military side of the torus. He'd been here once before, to….

His mind hit a blank wall.

Frustrated, he grabbed the boots that sat atop a folded flight suit, dropping them to the deck beside his bare feet. He reached for the clothing but then froze, fingers wrapped around the fabric, when he saw the weapons the suit had hidden. A pulsed energy sidearm lay beside a sheathed tanto knife. The first was a civilized, non-lethal weapon; the second was a brute force instrument.

He knew the tanto's carbyne-edged blade would have twice the tensile strength of graphene and, though he'd never had occasion to test it, could likely cut into bulkhead. One glance at the maker's hallmark stamped into the handle also told him the knife would be perfectly balanced. It wasn't the kind of weapon one wielded against one's fellow soldiers. Micah's eyes narrowed thoughtfully as he contemplated the unlikely duo.

An unspoken mental nudge spurred him back into movement. Shrugging into the suit, he grabbed the sidearm, clipping it and its spare batteries onto his belt. He left the tanto for now, as he shoved his feet into the boots, tucking his pant legs into the tops and sealing them.

He stood—then froze, attention arrested by his reflection in a nearby mirror. The flight suit was standard issue. Unremarkable, except for its missing rank and nametag. But his face….

It looked wrong, somehow. He raised a hand, running it through short-cropped hair in confusion, stiffening as realization came to him.

Micah was left-handed, and yet he'd reached with his right. His hair, which stubbornly grew in one direction, now fell to the wrong side. He leaned closer, noting other subtle irregularities in the face that had stared back at him for the past thirty-five years.

What the—?

They're coming. Leave now if you want to live.

The words were followed by a panel sliding open in a nearby bulkhead. Across the room, Micah heard the pounding of feet in the passageway leading to the morgue. The sergeant was returning, and he wasn't alone.

Leave. **Now**.

There was a sense of urgency to the words that propelled him forward. He spun, lunged for the tanto blade. Palming it, he slammed the locker door closed and turned to face the yawning blackness.

"Who the hell are you?" he demanded, slipping though the panel. It slid shut behind him, darkness enveloping him once more.

An image appeared in his head, a mental construct of a lab he knew he'd never seen and yet somehow recognized. Abruptly, he realized the feeling of familiarity wasn't coming from him. It emanated from the same place as the foreign thoughts that he now understood were being pushed to him from…someone else.

Your destination. Hurry.

"Who *are* you?" he repeated as he followed the mental nudge that urged him forward.

There was a pause. The response, when it came, had him reaching for the bulkhead to support himself, his mind spinning in confusion.

I am you.

The completed trilogy is available in e-book format on Amazon or in Kindle Unlimited, and the print book can be ordered from any book seller.

WHAT'S REAL...
AND WHAT'S FICTION?

When Kirkus recently reviewed *The Chiral Agent,* one phrase leapt out at me. They said that my "technology and bizarre extrapolations show a high level of narrative imagination...."

That was quite a compliment, but truthfully, I was a bit surprised by it. I don't think my extrapolations are all that terribly imaginative.

And then it hit me, in a *duh,* smack-the-forehead kind of way. Part of my writing process involves research. A *lot* of research. Don't get me wrong; I enjoy it. I wouldn't do it otherwise. But a significant chunk of that content comes from scholarly papers submitted for peer review, so they might not be all that easy to find.

Here in this section, I've curated a partial list of current research that influenced this book. I've also included links, so that you can read more about them if you're so inclined. Hopefully the links will remain active for years to come. If you stumble across a bad one, please feel free to email me at richmanscifi@gmail.com and I'll try to fix it.

Do I extrapolate from these starting points? You bet I do. After all, this story takes place three hundred years in the future. And that brings me to a confession I need to make: I think the science that I envision in these books is much more likely to be realized in the *near* future than it is in a distant one.

I don't think futurists can predict too far ahead with any degree of accuracy. We can throw a dart at a target with some precision ten to twenty years out. If we're lucky, we might remain somewhere on the dart board at fifty years, but we're well outside the ring. A hundred years out? Better make sure you stay well clear of the person slinging that dart!

History is filled with examples of this. In 1830, Irish professor and scientific lecturer Dr. Dionysius Lardner stated, "Rail travel at high speed is not possible because passengers, unable to breathe, would die of asphyxia."

Compare that to Lockheed's SR-71. As of this writing, it remains the fastest human-piloted airframe in history, despite having been retired in 1999. With a top speed of Mach 3.3, the SR-71 Blackbird, which was designed in secrecy in the 1950's, could outfly a missile.

Conversely, rail speed in 1830 when Lardner penned that comment was a whopping—wait for it—thirty miles per hour.

Mach 3.3 is 2500 mph. Divide by thirty and you get… Yeah, the SR-71 moves more than 83 *times* as fast as the locomotive Lardner predicted might asphyxiate a human. Whoops, big miss.

How about this one? In 1883, Lord Kelvin himself said that x-rays would prove to be a hoax.

Then there's the Boeing engineer who remarked after the first flight of the 247, "there will never be a bigger plane built." Anyone ever heard of the 247? It could carry ten passengers. *Ten.*

The fundamental flaw in each of these cases is that they failed to take into account something known as the Chicago Pile moment. A moment like that is where a landmark breakthrough occurs, like it did in 1942 under the bleachers at Stagg Field in Chicago when Enrico Fermi successfully conducted the first human-made, self-sustaining nuclear reaction.

Which, by the way, Einstein himself famously said in 1932 would never happen!

With that rather long-winded caveat, I present to you the current research that is being done, right here, right now. They're the foundation for what I call the WAGs—the wild-assed guesses—that proliferate throughout my books.

Stealth Technology

Did you wonder how Boone and his fellow Marines could traverse the Atliekas without being detected? In the first chapter of this book, 'Pirate Nest,' I mention a 'meringue' of aerogels and metal foams that are used to disperse and absorb all EM signatures, effectively masking them from detection.

In the main trilogy, I mention that ship's hulls are surfaced with MXene membranes. This fictional 2D material, spun into a 3D coating, functions as a sieve to harvest hydrogen from the interstellar medium as the ship transits through it. It's also an integral part of the tunable stealth shielding that covers Shadow Recon ships, used to insert Unit operators behind enemy lines.

Wait, did I say *fiction?*

We're living in a time when incredible strides in materials science are being made, where 2D materials such as graphene are playing increasingly larger roles.

Recently, another 2D material was engineered. Let me introduce you to the material known as MXene. That's pronounced Maxine, in case you were wondering. (I was, so I looked it up.)

MXene is only ten years old. It's the 'new graphene,' the cool new kid on the block. And when I say cool, I mean *really* cool.

It can be used in all sorts of applications[1], from desalinization (it can trap the energy of sunlight to purify water through evaporation, with an energy efficiency that's off the charts) to chemical sniffers (its 'nose' is the most sensitive ever reported). They also function as high-permeability hydrogen-selective membranes[2] for hydrogen production and carbon dioxide capture.

What? That's... not science fiction. It's science fact.

Both these 2D materials have also been spun into aerogels, porous, ultralight materials with extremely low density. Scientists call these 'meringues.' They've discovered MXene exhibits an interesting property when it's formed into an aerogel. When combined with nanocellulose[3], it turns into a high-performance electromagnetic interference shield[4].

EM shielding is common today. Electronics components are everywhere throughout our homes, our cars, the places we frequent. Most require shielding so they won't impact neighboring components or block signal transmission. But that same technology can be used for something known as *multi-spectral camouflage.*

In a word… stealth.

Boone and his fellow Marines manage to avoid detection in the pirate's den by wearing drakeskin suits. These suits make them invisible to detection across all EM bands. Although this is a familiar and well-used trope within science fiction, real scientists have been making great strides toward realizing this.

Ever heard of *metamaterials?* Metamaterials are engineered structures[5], created to interact with the electromagnetic spectrum in precise ways. The link in the previous sentence will take you to *Nature* magazine's curated list of articles on that topic. But I have a few specific examples to share with you as well:

A Canadian camouflage company, Hyperstealth Technology, has patented a material[6] that bends light around an object, causing it to become invisible to the naked eye. They're not the only organization trying to crack this code[7]. Plenty of groups are working on ways to spoof the EM spectrum. Problem is, they may succeed at one wavelength, but fail at others. Still, it's a start.

One final thought before we leave the topic of stealth: Most of what I've shared with you thus far focuses on EM shielding. That makes sense. To remain stealthy, our heroes need to have a way to block emissions along the full electromagnetic spectrum as they fly through the black, from infrared to ultraviolet and everything in between.

But that's not the only thing they need to worry about. When they're in an atmosphere, as they were on the pirate's platform, they had to worry about sound as well. Sound waves are mechanical waves, not electromagnetic ones. They require a medium through which they can propagate.

Studies are currently underway on graphene-based aerogel meringues[8] that researchers predict we'll see in use by 2023. To give you a feel for the material's sound-blocking effectiveness, if an aircraft's nacelles were coated in this meringue, it would reduce the deep-throated roar of a jet taking off to the whirr of a hairdryer.

The audio chaff the Marines deploy could very well have its basis right here.

Brain-Machine Interfaces (aka 'the Wire')

How do I envision the wire working? To describe it, I need to first talk a bit about how the brain works. I'm no neuroscientist, so this is an oversimplification, but here are some of the basics:

The way our central and peripheral nervous system works is through messaging. Messages travel between individual neurons in the brain, relayed through dendrites and axons. Dendrites bring information into the cell, axons draw them out. For communication to occur between neurons, an electrical impulse has to travel down that axon until it reaches a synaptic terminal.

(Please don't mistake axons for axions; those are hypothetical elementary particles some scientists believe might be a component in dark matter—if they exist.)

The spikes are brief, one-millisecond changes in the electrical potential across the cell membrane. During this brief spike, electrical current flows in the space surrounding the cell. And *that* can be detected! Of course, you'd need a very sensitive electrode to do that.

Enter the Defense Advanced Research Projects Agency (DARPA). They're funding a project to develop a tech that will not only detect the signals, but to translate them, and then *transmit* them… all without invasive surgery.

The program is known as N3, Next-Generation Nonsurgical Neurotechnology. Rice University's Robinson Lab is part of that initiative, and they've developed MOANA, a brain-machine interface that uses a combination of optics and magnetism[9] to make this happen.

They're not alone. There are plenty of companies out there who are making quiet advances in this field. Battelle is one of them. They've already developed NeuroLife (not to be confused with Elon Musk's infamous Neuralink). NeuroLife is a neural bypass technology[10] that has enabled a quadriplegic to move his hands using only his thoughts. Now, Battelle has been funded by DARPA to develop an injectable, bi-directional Brain Computer Interface.

SAD 5 BROS, Truth Serum, and Medical Nano

Truth serum is a fascinating subject. It falls under the squishy realm of neuroscience. We still know surprisingly little about the mind and the brain, though recent studies suggest we're on the cusp of some major discoveries. Notice my use of both the words 'brain' and 'mind.' These aren't interchangeable. The first represents the hardware; the second represents the software.

The truth drug Boone uses in this book doesn't yet exist, but neuroscientists today believe it might soon. I researched the history of such drugs, and found out some fascinating things:

We've known for centuries that certain chemicals affect the human body. Yes, you read that right: centuries. Ether was first synthesized in 1540. Nitrous oxide, laughing gas, was discovered in 1772. In both cases, the effects were treated as nothing more than parlor tricks and would continue to be viewed in that light for nearly four hundred years.

The first time a chemical compound was used to alter a person's mental state for a specific purpose was in 1844 when a dentist used ether[11] to anesthetize a patient while extracting a tooth.

The use of medical compounds as truth serums is almost exactly a hundred years old, as of this writing. The drugs used interact with the mind by inducing a desire to please. This was eventually found to be unreliable when investigators realized the drugs often 'lead the witness.' In an effort to please the interrogator and give him the answer he sought, a person under the influence of such drugs might admit to something they'd not actually done.

We've come a long way since the 1920's. Back then, the study of medicines that altered the consciousness used the black box approach of trial and error. Neurotransmitters weren't discovered to exist until 1921, and it wasn't until the 1940s-1950s that specific ones were identified. It took another forty years[12] before functional magnetic resonance imaging (fMRI) would give us a glimpse into the inner workings of the brain by mapping neural activity.

As you can see, neuroscience is truly in its infancy, and there's a lot of room to grow.

Will we ever crack the truth serum code? Some neuroscientists believe we might. A 2014 article suggests the most likely candidate would be a neurotransmitter drug that would generate a feeling of trust[13] in the subject. It would encourage truth telling, rather than saying whatever makes the questioner happy.

Thus, Sad 5 Bros was born.

As for the medical analgesic nano in the canister Boone altered, yes, it exists today! Granted, it's not in bot form, nor can it alter pain-signaling from a neurotransmitter—at least, not yet.

Today's nanoanalgesics[14] provide targeted medicine that delivers lower and more effective doses directly where needed, reducing toxicity to other organs.

Nanomedicine is an exciting and rapidly accelerating field, with new medicines being introduced every year. I discussed it briefly in the forward to The Chiral Protocol.

We're using nanoparticles to fight cancer in a big way[15], both in chemotherapy and in radiation therapy. They can increase the photoelectric effect, which in turn makes that relativistic beam of electron particles a much more efficient killer[16] when turned on malignant cells.

We even have chiral nanoparticles. These chiral supraparticles[17] encase cancer-fighting drugs, providing protection to their cargo while delivering it directly to the source.

There are tons of other nanomedical therapies being developed right now. Some of them include novel new ways medics can triage on the battlefield. These encase material that promotes bone and skin regrowth in clay nanoparticles[18] that are made to break down slowly over time.

The research we're seeing in nanomedicine is truly

extraordinary. I think you'll find the future for this particular industry is very bright, indeed.

What does all this mean? As I said earlier, I believe the science of the Biogenesis universe is far closer to being realized than the three hundred years the stories envision. It's an exciting time to be alive, isn't it?

L.L. Richman
Leawood, 2021

LINKS:

---

[1] https://www.nanowerk.com/mxene.php

[2] https://www.nature.com/articles/s41467-017-02529-6

[3] https://onlinelibrary.wiley.com/doi/10.1002/advs.202000979

[4] https://www.sciencedaily.com/releases/2020/07/200702113703.htm

[5] https://www.nature.com/subjects/metamaterials#:~:text=Definition,than%20the%20wavelength%20of%20interest.

[6] https://www.dezeen.com/2019/11/07/hyperstealth-biotechnology-quantum-stealth-invisibility-cloak/

[7] https://interestingengineering.com/invisibility-cloaks-are-no-longer-just-science-fiction

[8] https://scitechdaily.com/meringue-like-graphene-based-aerogel-material-could-make-aircraft-as-quiet-as-a-hairdryer/

[9] https://magneticsmag.com/magnetism-plays-key-roles-in-darpa-research-to-develop-brain-machine-interface-without-surgery/

[10] https://www.battelle.org/government-offerings/health/medical-devices/neurotechnology/neurolife-neural-bypass-technology

[11] https://www.ncbi.nlm.nih.gov/pmc/articles/PMC4920664/

[12] https://www.theguardian.com/science/blog/2013/jun/25/neuro

science-media-neuromania
[13] https://www.businessinsider.com/is-there-such-a-thing-as-truth-serum-2014-10
[14] https://pubmed.ncbi.nlm.nih.gov/33883067/
[15] https://www.ncbi.nlm.nih.gov/pmc/articles/PMC6745263/
[16] https://www.nature.com/articles/s41598-020-72268-0
[17] https://pubmed.ncbi.nlm.nih.gov/31686433/
[18] https://link.springer.com/article/10.1007/s10924-019-01586-w

NO ONE SAID
THERE'D BE MATH

In addition to research, these books have a fair amount of math in them. It's a good thing, too, because believe it or not, I have readers who check me on my calculations.

In this book, it begins in the very first scene: "Nine Geminate Navy Marines shot silently through the black, catapulted from a destroyer's missile tubes…"

For a lot of folks, this might be skim-over material. But at least one physicist worked the problem, and then questioned me on it.

Is that number believable? Let's take a look.

Boone and his buddies experienced 100 gs for two seconds. That time interval is based on the catapults used on U.S. aircraft carriers[19]. But how many gs can the human body withstand?

The highest acceleration recorded was experienced by USAF Captain Eli Beeding in 1958, on the Daisy Sled. According to the National Academy of Sciences, he "was exposed to 2,139 g per second to a peak of 40.4 g for a duration of .040 second. … The dynamic response to the impact was a peak measured on the sternum of 82.6 g, at 3,826 g per second."

Pretty amazing stuff for 1958, considering they didn't have access to any of the cool tech the Geminate Marines have. If you'd like to read more about the infamous 'G-Machine,' check out this article in Air and Space Magazine[20], and if you'd like to read more about Captain Beeding, check out his Wikipedia article[21].

How fast do spaceships travel? Within the Biogenesis Universe, I've built in limitations, given the damage the Scharnhorst drives do to the Interstellar Medium. This means that ships within a star system are limited to the use of fusion drives and are constrained by the speed of light. That doesn't mean they can't go fast, though!

It's all relative, really. Ships accelerating at a constant one gravity will achieve speeds on the order of millions of kilometers an hour by the time they've traveled a few AUs.

In Boone's case, his ship began ten AUs away, at the capital planet of Ceriba. If the destroyer constantly accelerated to the halfway point before flipping to decelerate, and did so at one *g*, the ship would reach *ten million* kilometers per hour.

Our pirates are hiding out 75,000 kilometers inside the Procyon belt. On an astronomical scale, that's nothing. The Geminate destroyer that patrols the system is used to traveling such distances in an eye-blink, so to approach such a location stealthily will require some finesse.

To determine how easily those nine Marines might navigate the fictional Atliekas asteroid belt, I took a close look at our own. Sol's belt lies between Mars and Jupiter, and we've amassed quite a bit of information on it, thanks to missions like NASA's New Horizons. That data is readily available, so that's what I used for the Atliekas.

You probably already know that these regions of space *aren't* the densely packed minefields that Hollywood has made them out to be. According to Alan Stern, New Horizons' principal investigator, Sol's belt is so spread out that the chance of running into an asteroid is vanishingly small, much lower than one in a billion[22].

"If you want to come close enough to an asteroid to make detailed studies of it, you have to aim for one," he said. And if you were to gather up every rock in Sol's asteroid belt into one planetary mass, that planet would be *two thousand times smaller*[23] than Earth!

We also know a surprising amount about asteroid belts that orbit other stars, and that knowledge is growing. For example, Epsilon Eridani has three belts: two rocky ones and an outer icy ring. The inner belt is nearly identical to the one in our own system, whereas the outer belt is twenty times denser than its inner twin.

We only recently discovered evidence that asteroid belts exist in *binary* systems. It wasn't until 2017 that astronomers discovered rocky debris orbiting the white dwarf system, SDSS 1557, nearly sixteen hundred light-years away!

So… about that math.

It takes between three and six years for our own asteroid belt to complete one rotation around the sun. That translates roughly to a speed of eighteen kilometers per second, or 64,800 kph.

Wait. It only took Boone and the team a little over an hour to get to the pirate's den. That 100-*g* boost isn't going to be nearly enough. What gives?

As was stated in chapter one, the Marines on the *Callaghan* were *already* traveling at a fast clip. They left those missile tubes at a velocity that added 7,000 kph to the destroyer's *existing speed*. (If you want to run the numbers, I had the destroyer at 65,000 kph, decelerating to match the orbital speed of the asteroid belt.)

But there's one more thing to consider: you see, the pirate base *does not remain still.* It's in motion, in an orbit that exactly matches the velocity of the asteroid belt.

In the time it takes the Marines to reach the base, it's moved nearly *33,000 kilometers* spinward. The good news is that at such a small distance relative to the star system itself, we can ignore curvature and just assume the movement was in a straight line.

By the time Boone reaches the pirate platform, I've given enough information so that if you really wanted to work the problem, you could do so. It's just a matter of plugging in numbers and dusting off that equation you learned in high school that you swore you'd never use in real life: the Pythagorean Theorem.

We end up with a diagram that looks like this:

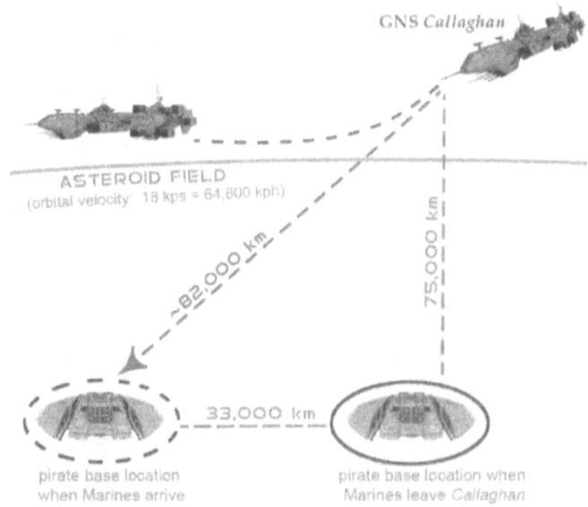

The *Callaghan* had to eject Boone and his companions at an angle of twenty-three degrees with respect to where the pirate den was located when they first left the ship. They also had to travel along the hypotenuse, which added nearly 6,000 kilometers to their trip.

Whew!

That's one example out of many that crop up within the pages of these books. Writing hard science fiction, even science fiction adventure stories, is certainly a different beast from other genres!

---

[19] https://science.howstuffworks.com/aircraft-carrier3.htm

[20] https://www.airspacemag.com/history-of-flight/the-g-machine-16799374

[21] https://en.wikipedia.org/wiki/Eli_Beeding

[22] https://www.space.com/16105-asteroid-belt.html

[23] https://www.sciencedirect.com/topics/earth-and-planetary-sciences/asteroid-belts

TERMINOLOGY

ActiveFiber – a tunable material with catalytic properties, comprised of a nanoparticle superlattice that 'listened' on a carrier wave for instructions on how to reshape itself. Most spacefaring ships and space stations layered their bulkheads with an ActiveFiber coating, which could be used to reconfigure the interior structure. The fiber is infused with nanobots, which can absorb a contaminant, break it down into its constituent parts, and reuse the material.

Calabi-Yau Gate – This method of folding space bends the compactified branes stacked within the Bulk of hyperspace, allowing for instantaneous travel in normal spacetime, from one location to another, regardless of distance.

Colloid Nano – Colloids are extremely tiny insoluble particles that are so light, they remain suspended in air. When grafted onto nano, colloid nano clouds can be released.

Thanks to brownian motion, the force of the particles in the air around them is greater than the force of gravity attempting to pull them down, therefore they float and are susceptible to the activity of air currents.

Navy reconnaissance uses it in concert with a magnetic field to launch colloid audio chaff, a sound attenuating field that can encase a soldier.

Crowbars and LockPiks – Both are lock-picking programs, although LockPiks are covert, where Crowbars are overt.

A Crowbar is a brute-force version that borrows click-assembly techniques used in chemistry to rapidly alter the properties of existing nanolocks. Pre-loaded common codes, or 'bricks', give the

Crowbar a jump-start, pushing a cascade failure into the lock that cracks it wide open. In the process, it renders the lock useless.

In contrast, a LockPik is a slower and more subtle app that works to subvert a lock while maintaining its program integrity so that it can be reset back to original specs after the LockPik's use

DBCs – A digital-to-biological converter capable of printing complex, synthetic biological material from detailed molecular diagrams transmitted to it.

DUET Wires (aka "the wire") – DUET stands for Direct Uplink Evanescent Telecom. Much to the dismay of the corporation that invented the tech, that name never took hold. Commonly known simply as 'the wire,' a DUET implant is embedded within every human when they come of age, and is included as a part of the educational system of most sovereign star nations.

Receiving a wire must wait until the brain has reached certain development criteria, as its integration evolves after the initial implant.

Evanescent (E-V) Nanocircuitry – E-V nanocircuitry is the foundation upon which the DUET system was launched. The core communication unit embedded in the brain makes use of the optical phenomenon of evanescent modes with imaginary wave numbers and a poynting vector of zero to achieve the mathematical equivalent of quantum tunneling for the instantaneous transmission of information.

Helios – Fast-action spacecraft, considered the workhorses of the Alliance Navy, and capable of carrying an entire squad of fully-kitted Marines. A small percentage of Helios are modified as a Direct-Action Penetrator stealth vessel.

All DAP Helios vessels are assigned to the Geminate Alliance's

Special Reconnaissance Unit, often referred to as SRU or simply, The Unit.

The teams that fly the DAPs are known as Shadow Recon. They deploy on classified missions, inserting elite special operations teams into destinations where conventional warfare is inadvisable.

Scharnhorst Drive – The Scharnhorst is an interstellar drive that generates a Casimir bubble. This allows the drive to harness the Scharnhorst effect, a phenomenon in which light travels faster than c. The drive allows a ship inside its bubble to travel at triple the speed of light.

SmartCarbyne Nanofloss – Carbyne, a chain of single carbon atoms, has twice the tensile strength of graphene. A lattice of ultrafine carbyne filaments, when implanted, will reinforce bone, muscle, and sinew.

Some branches of the Geminate Navy receive a variant of carbyne nanofloss, which functions as an endoskeleton implant.

SmartCarbyne is a unique variant, capable of altering its state. It was originally created to protect military pilots during high-g maneuvers. Its ability to turn 'on' and 'off' made it ideal for protecting the soft tissues of vital organs.

A SmartCarbyne lattice is controlled by an implanted accelerometer. When disengaged, the atoms are in a disorganized, soft state. When experiencing acceleration greater than what the human body can withstand, the lattice automatically hardens, protecting the pilot.

Spike – Special operations electronic breadcrumb trail, only useful at short range. Each spike has a unique geometric signature. That signature is contained in the Alliance military database. An app registers the negative space created by each spike on whatever surface it resides. Once a person or item has been spiked, the search app keeps track of the void that particular spike makes, pinpointing its location while it remains in range.

TENGs and PENGs– Triboelectric nanogenerator batteries are power-harvesting batteries that capture the electric current generated through contact of two materials, converting movement to stored energy. PENGs are piezoelectric nanogenerators that charge using ambient sound in the atmosphere around them.

Ziptie – The Ziptie is a nano breach application used as a restraint. Once placed onto exposed flesh, the app immediately unpacks itself, blocking an individual's wire from transmitting a call for help, and rendering body augmentation inert. A military version can take control of a soldier's SmartCarbyne endoskeleton, rendering the victim temporarily immobile.

WEAPONRY & ARMOR

Banshees – Fighter-bomber drones, usually under the command of a flight crew's co-pilot. Each Banshee mounts a five-centimeter laser and is capable of strafing runs. In addition, each carries a pair of missiles, their yields varying by Banshee model type.

CUSP – Compact Ultra-Short Pulse pistol uses a pulsed, laser-induced plasma to either paralyze, flash-bang, flash-blind, or deliver searing pain, depending on the weapon's setting.

Dazzlers – Decoy ECM (electronic countermeasures) drones, usually under the command of a flight crew's co-pilot. Each drone emits ECM and can jam signals, robbing enemy ships of their ability to coordinate their attack.

Drakeskin armor – A carbyne-reinforced synthsilk skinsuit used by special operations forces when infiltrating hostile territory. The suit has a nanoweave embedded into the topmost layer of fabric that is tunable to the environment, providing visible-spectrum stealth. The fabric is made of metamaterials, which use transformation optics to shield the wearer from view by controlling electromagnetic radiation and guiding incident waves around the wearer.

Houghlin Kingsolver Sniper Weapons System – the HK includes a sniper rifle, scope, and tripod, and is used mainly by Special Reconnaissance Unit operators. Its double barrel allows it to shoot projectiles as well as to spike a target with a tracker.

P-SCAR – Pulsed Special Combat Assault Rifle.

RAU-19 – Railgun mounted on DAP Helios attack craft.

ALSO BY LL RICHMAN

You can always find the most up to date listing of book titles on LL Richman's website, www.llrichman.com.

THE BIOGENESIS WAR SERIES
The Chiral Agent
The Chiral Protocol
Chiral Justice

THE BIOGENESIS WAR FILES: THE EARLY YEARS
Operation Cobalt
Ambush in the Sargon Straits
The Chiral Conspiracy
Sudden Death

THE VISION RISING SERIES
Vision Rising
Vision's Gambit
Vision's Pawn

THE BATTLEFIELD DIPLOMACY SERIES
Battlefield Diplomacy
Lost Colony
Insurrection

THE ENFIELD GENESIS SERIES
Alpha Centauri
Proxima Centauri
Tau Ceti
Epsilon Eridani
Sirius

THE SOL DISSOLUTION SERIES
Venusian Uprising

Assault on Sedna
The Hyperion War
The Fall of Terra

ABOUT THE AUTHOR

L.L. Richman has a diverse career background, having spent more than a decade working in radiation physics, and twice that as a director of film and video. An avid pilot and photographer, Richman can often be found flying a Piper Cherokee or photographing Deep Sky Objects (DSOs) late at night.

WANT UPDATES?

Join the VIP Reader's Group. You'll get news of upcoming books, behind-the-scenes glimpses of life with a physicist, and views from the cockpit. And cats, because the feline overlords insist.

Go to llrichman.com and sign up.